THE Mix-Up

A STEAMY ROMANTIC COMEDY

By

Melanie Munton

The Mix-Up

Southern Hearts Club Book Three

Copyright © 2021 Melanie Munton

All rights reserved

Cover Design by L.J. Anderson at Mayhem Cover Creations

www.mayhemcovercreations.com

Print Edition

This is a work of fiction and any similarities to persons, living or dead, or places, actual events or locales is purely coincidental. The characters and names are products of the author's imagination and used fictitiously.

Table of Contents

Chapter One – The Duchess and the Boss 8

Chapter Two – The Meet, Greet, and Retreat 22

Chapter Three – The Bathtub Fortress of Pot Solitude 28

Chapter Four – The Competitive Edge 37

Chapter Five – The Not-So-Evil Twin.. 48

Chapter Six – The Business Lunch Face-Off................................ 55

Chapter Seven – The Nail and Bail.. 60

Chapter eight – The Snakeskin Infraction 69

Chapter Nine – The Shelf Life of Love 80

Chapter Ten – The Jazz Club Scuffle Shuffle.............................. 92

Chapter Eleven – The Stamp of Denial....................................... 99

Chapter Twelve – The Helicopter and the Harpy 109

Chapter Thirteen – The Spiral Into Madness 117

Chapter Fourteen – The Wine-ing and Pine-ing 125

Chapter Fifteen – The One Night Proposal............................... 136

Chapter Sixteen – The Viewing Room Vacuum........................ 146

Chapter Seventeen – The Oral High Club................................. 154

Chapter Eighteen – The Kiss of Death...................................... 163

Chapter Nineteen – The Therapy Hour Sloshing....................... 171

Chapter Twenty – The Night Before Christmas Puns................. 181

Chapter Twenty-One – The Flight From Hell............................ 196

Chapter Twenty-Two – The Best Shopping Partner Ever........... 203

Chapter Twenty-Three – The Jaded Non-Believer 211

Chapter Twenty-Four – The Romantic Ice Skating Montage 217

Chapter Twenty-Five – The Surrendering 222

Chapter Twenty-Six – The Middle-Aged Hooker 228

Chapter Twenty-Seven – The Ball Dropping............................. 234

Chapter Twenty-Eight – The Reckoning 241

Chapter Twenty-Nine – The Naked Ambush............................. 246

Chapter Thirty – The Secret Poet.. 254

Chapter Thirty-One – The Reckoning.. 265

Chapter Thirty-Two – The Tub for Two.................................... 279

Epilogue – The Birth of Baby Boss Man 286

Also by Melanie Munton 290

Sneak Peek of The Divorce Attorney... 292

Acknowledgments... 301

About the Author 304

Also by Melanie Munton

Southern Hearts Club:
The Divorce Attorney
The Six Month Lease

Brooklyn Brothers:
Lace & Lies
Scars & Sins
Booze & Bullets

Sultry Nights:
Salsa (Sultry Nights 1)
Tango (Sultry Nights 2)
Rumba (Sultry Nights 3)
Samba (Sultry Nights 4)
Mambo (Sultry Nights 5)

Standalone romance:
King of the Court
The Unforgettable Kind

Slow Seductions series:
Casual Affair (Slow Seductions #1)

Sweet Attraction (Slow Seductions #2)

Cruz Brothers series:
Playing for Kinley (Cruz Brothers #1)
The Art of Sage (Cruz Brothers #2)
Always Mickie (Cruz Brothers #3)

Timid Souls novellas:
Stubborn Hearts
Unexpected Love

Possession and Politics Trilogy:
Part One
Part Two
Part Three

1

The Duchess and the Boss

"WOULD YOU RATHER...date a man who has the back hair of a wooly mammoth, an incurable gambling addiction, or a disturbingly large collection of Precious Moments figurines?" the husky female voice in my earbud asks.

"So, my only choices are three of your ex-boyfriends?" a different, higher pitched female voice quips.

I choke on my mouthful of coffee. Instead of spewing it all over my computer screen, I manage to contain the spit take to an unladylike dribble down my chin.

"Hey, the only one I actually dated was the gambling addict, thank you very much."

"Wasn't he the carnie?"

I muffle my laughter with my hand, but an indelicate snort still escapes.

An indignant huff comes from the first woman. *"No, he was working in his food truck at the carnival. He wasn't a carnival employee."*

"Which is why you didn't realize he was only five feet tall." The second woman turns her mouth away from the microphone

to cackle. *"He had to stand on a footstool just to see over the food truck window."*

"The only reason I went on three dates with him was because he was hilarious. I swear, he could have done stand-up comedy."

"It probably wouldn't have made a difference if he was standing up or not."

A *ba-da-cha* sound effect comes over the airwaves, making me grin as I type up a quick email on my keyboard.

"Hysterical," the first woman mutters.

"No, what's hysterical is your track record. A five-foot-tall, gambling addicted carnie? You can't make that shit up."

"He wasn't a carnie!"

I randomly stumbled across this podcast a couple of months ago and have since become obsessed. Real Talk Romance is a refreshing show that offers a no-bullshit approach to love and relationships, hosted by a twenty-something woman named Kennedy Rhodes. Nicknamed The Love Cynic, Kennedy is based out of Savannah, which is not too far from my home base of Charleston. Her hilariously blunt and unapologetic opinions on the existence of true love and the realities of modern romance called out to me from the get-go. She often brings her best friend on the show, who's far less cynical than her but a riot in her own right. And when they start riffing on listeners who call in or on their own real-life stories, Kennedy slays me.

A cynic after my own heart.

Her personality actually reminds me of my cadre of girlfriends that I've been tight with since college—my former roommate Sloane Williams, Harper St. Clair, and her ex-stepsister, Quinn Prescott. Hell, I listen to Kennedy's podcast so often I consider her part of our makeshift family.

Few people can get away with listening to a podcast while hard at work at the office, but The Colson Group is not your average marketing and advertising firm. It's a pretty informal working environment, which is right in my never-take-life-too-seriously wheelhouse. My boss is pragmatic in his approach to his business operations, as well as to his employees. Basically, Mr. Colson doesn't care what we do or what we wear while at work, so long as we aren't complete slackasses and the finished product is up to his absurdly high standards. The only time we're required to adopt business attire is when we have client meetings. Other than that, short of ratty sweatpants and the grungy T-shirt we slept in, we have free reign over our own dress code. Hence why I'm currently sitting in my desk cubicle in dark skinny jeans, peep-toe heeled ankle boots, and a scarlet chiffon blouse that I forced myself to tuck in.

My one, tiny concession to professionalism.

My boss understands that he's more likely to get the highest level of productivity from his team if we're happy and comfortable. I respect him for that.

But that's where the respect ends.

Because for whatever ungodly reason, the man constantly sees to it that I'm neither happy nor comfortable when I'm within these walls.

Ryder Colson is a thirty-one-year-old genius entrepreneur. He's worth millions. He founded this company while he was still in college and built it from the ground up. He's respected among the wealthy and elite all over the Lowcountry region. He has a sterling reputation for being a generous philanthropist and an all-around stand-up guy.

He's also a world-class d-bag.

Mostly just to me.

Probably because I use more than half my brain power and rise to his overachieving expectations without hesitation or complaint. He doesn't appreciate being questioned or challenged—I excel at both. The fact that I don't just lie down and roll over like a good little minion whenever he assigns me a new project has raised his hackles ever since I started working for him ten months ago. I actually speak up and throw out my opinion even when he doesn't ask for it, which he rarely does. But I'm one of the best employees he's got.

And he damn well knows it.

Although he acts like he'll burst into flames if he ever admits it out loud.

If I didn't work so hard, he probably would have fired my insubordinate ass a long time ago out of spite. And if I wasn't so foolishly in love with my job, I would have quit after the first torturous week in his insufferable presence. Toward me, he's nothing but a condescending, swaggering, egotistical jerkweed who's a wee bit too big for his britches.

But if I can take a cue from Kennedy and get a little real here...I was the one who started our feud. Sort of. Looking back, I can admit I was the first to ring my bitch bell and declare war. True, he was quick to bang his dickwad gong in retaliation, but it was me who threw the first punch.

You would have, too, though.

You see, Ryder and I may have—*inward cringe*—slept together. Once.

It was before I started working at The Colson Group. Before I ever even knew who the man was. It was pure coincidence, or a perverse twist of fate, that we happened to bump into each other at a random bar one night. Flirtation ensued, we went back to his place, had sex, I snuck out the next morning while he was still asleep—because I'm respectful and classy like that—and we never saw each other again.

Until my first day of work two weeks later.

He called me into his office to welcome me to the firm. Since his HR Director does all of the hiring, he never interviewed me. I froze in the middle of his corner office, like Hermione Granger had just waved her wand and cast the "*Petrificus totalus!*" spell on me.

But *him?*

Oh, that bastard had the nerve to look right through me.

Like he'd never seen me before in his life. Like I hadn't been writhing nakedly beneath him, squirming on the end of his dick like a worm on a hook, just two weeks prior.

I was so outraged that I fantasized about plucking his too-long eyelashes out with a pair of tweezers.

One. By. One.

Sure, I was tipsy that night and parts of the evening are a blur. But I wasn't so far gone to not remember the face of the man I slept with. To not remember the actual sex. He, on the other hand, must have bedded so many women in his time that he's unable to pick my face out of the lineup. Or he masked how wasted he really was that night—extraordinarily well—and he honestly doesn't remember me.

And even if he did remember me, Ryder has a firmly established, strict rule of never dating employees or clients. It's a well-known fact in our company that Ryder Colson never mixes business with pleasure. No exceptions.

Not that I'm interested in any inter-office philandering. Frankly, I don't give two rats' behinds whether or not Ryder Colson remembers doing the naked bump and grind with me ten months ago. In the beginning, yes, my ego did take a serious blow and plunged to the bottom of the ocean, like a submarine after getting hit by an enemy missile.

But I'm over it.

And after that first day in his office, *enemy* is exactly what my one-night-stand-turned-boss became.

It's a daily battle to remind myself that it doesn't matter— that *he* never mattered. I'm a big girl who buys her panties from the big girls section of the store. After all, that wasn't the first time I've ever had casual sex and it won't be the last.

But here's the part that really chaps my ass. Just straight-up irks the bejesus out of me. Ready for it?

That infuriating man gave me the best sex of my life.

I'm pretty sure anyway.

Again, parts of the night are a tad fuzzy. But overall, it was good for me and I thought for him, too.

I guess the former Duchess of Charleston is just that forgettable.

Yes, I named my vagina. She's made enough decisions in my life and given me some of the best nights ever that she deserves a name. But for reasons soon to be revealed, I had to remove the title of duchess from her nameplate. The down south missus is now and will forever be known as the Countess of Charleston.

And my boss doesn't remember spearing her with his royal scepter, the son of a bitch.

So, you try working for a man who treats some of the best pleasure you've ever known as inconsequential as a hangnail and see if you don't constantly sport Resting Bitch Face around him.

A thin manila folder is dropped on top of my French fade manicure, halting my progress in the email I'm furiously typing. My fingers pause as I suck in a much-needed breath. Because only one person in this entire office would have the steel-plated balls to do such a thing. And unfortunately, he's the one who signs my frigging paycheck.

I hear a muffled male voice and know he's probably telling me to "turn off the squabbling, men-bashing drivel" and pay attention. That's exactly what he called Kennedy's show one day when he swiped up one of my earbuds before I could stop him to find out what I'm always listening to.

I tap my Bluetooth earpiece, turning it off. But I don't look at him. Why? People not making eye contact when they speak to him is one of his biggest pet peeves.

Heh. Take that, prick.

"Gee, sorry, boss man. Didn't quite catch that."

He pauses for a moment, probably to grind his teeth together hard enough to give himself a migraine. "Spec sheet for prospective client," he grates in a low voice, referring to the folder still balanced on my hands as I resume typing. "Look over their queries and come up with an approximate quote, as well as a realistic timeline for each individual project."

My eyebrow notches up, though I keep my focus trained ahead. "I guess saying 'please' is too big of a time waster?"

"Yes. Since I know you're going to do it regardless, that one syllable would have been a waste of my time and breath."

I slowly nod at my computer screen. "Yep. Better save all that hot air for the next ass you have to blow smoke up."

"Better than kissing those asses."

I click my tongue against my teeth. "If I were you, I'd start puckering up because your personality is severely lacking in both charm and tact."

"From the horse's mouth, huh, duchess?"

Now, *now*, I look up at him.

Did I mention that Ryder Colson is a brutally beautiful man? Because *of course* he would be.

His hair color is somewhere between dark blond and light brown, complementing his golden skin tone. It's slightly longer on top and cut shorter at the sides. He always somehow manages to get that floppy part to sweep across his forehead at just the right angle to look suave. A small strand perpetually hangs over his left eyebrow, no matter how many times he shoves it back. His eyes are a soulful blue, his nose is long and straight, and day-old stubble claims permanent residency on his square jawline.

Worst of all, his bottom lip has this full, rounder thing going on that pisses off my neglected libido to the point that I want to dig my teeth into that flesh until I draw blood.

Easy, girl. Your momma didn't raise no psycho.

Despite the casual leniencies he affords his employees, Ryder never dons anything other than crisp, immaculately tailored suits. Hellaciously expensive ones that I'm pretty sure he has shipped in from London. As the owner and CEO, he frequently meets with clients, in and out of the office, so he always has to look professional. And flaming hot.

Damn him.

Hey, I'm human. He's sex on two legs. There's nothing criminal about noticing it.

And did you catch his name for me? *Duchess.*

I don't know where it came from. He just assigned it to me that first week. I could have reported him to HR a million times for the inappropriate moniker and slapped a lawsuit on him if I wanted. But I just let it ride for some bizarre reason. Probably because HR would have a field day with all the dirt he could shovel at them about me.

But now you see why I had to re-name the va-jay-jay.

I dagger him with a look that would eviscerate a lesser man. And as much as it galls me to admit, Ryder here could never be categorized as *lesser* in any aspect of his life. "You could have just emailed this to me, you know. No need for these precious heart-to-hearts of ours."

His navy eyes dance with something resembling amusement. "Now, what kind of person would that make me when I can clearly see how cutting me down at every opportunity brings you such joy?"

I narrow my eyes. "A prospect you're more than familiar with."

He smirks. "I don't cut you down, duchess. I vex you. There's a big difference."

"The end result is the same no matter what verb you use," I say through clenched teeth. "Clearly, your overall goal is to piss me off."

He shrugs, like the apathetic jerkoff he is. "You do your best work when you're exasperated. Part of my job as boss is to keep my employees motivated."

"You're confusing infuriation with motivation."

He slides his hands in his pockets, far too casually. "And yet I know you'll have that to me by the end of the day. Seems my methods are effective. If it ain't broke, don't fix it, right?"

My teeth clamp down on my tongue to silence the instinctual vitriol.

I'll do a swan dive into a river of boiling lava before I ever give him the satisfaction of being right.

I can't resist a challenge. He knows I'm going to bust my ass every day at work, no matter how acerbic our conversations get. Something about Ryder's demeanor toward me, his work ethic, and his general expectations of his employees have always lit a fire inside me, making me want to rise to the occasion. It's irrational—and just plain idiotic—how much I've wanted to impress him from day one. Ever since I found out that my boss has absolutely no memory of sleeping with me, I've been determined to prove myself.

So help me Mary Magdalene, I will *make* him remember me.

My nails dig into my palms as my hands fist on top of my keyboard. "If *you* don't want something broken, I suggest you clear out and let me get back to doing my job. Which, by the way, is making you look good." I wink. "Just in case you've never noticed."

Realistically, my mouthy ass *should* have been fired after my first three days at TCG. I talk to Ryder like I would any annoying asshat, yet it somehow works for us. Exchanging jabs, slicing with our words, pushing our patience to the tipping point—it's our rhythm. It's cohesive. It's comfortable.

It's confusing as hell.

Because the two of us actually make a good team.

The corner of his mouth tips up in his signature cocky grin. "Oh, believe me, duchess. I've noticed how good I look. But it's nice to know I'm not the only one."

My mouth tightens into a firm line. He looks proud of himself. "I'm forced to look at your smug mug almost every day. Trust me, whatever appeal you have toward other women has grown stale here."

He snickers. "Keep telling yourself that."

Deciding the conversation has spiraled far beyond nowhere, I turn back to my computer. Sometimes the best way to get rid of him is to ignore his bait.

It doesn't work.

He stays right where he is, hovering beside my desk. "Got plans tonight?"

My fingers pause again. In the ten months I've worked here, he's never once asked about my personal life. "If you're planning on dumping a huge workload on me and making me stay late, forget it. I'm busy."

Though it wouldn't be the first time I've had to cancel my plans because he's forced me to burn the midnight oil. Although he's never asked anything of me or anyone else that he isn't willing to do himself. Oftentimes, those late nights involve me working at my cubicle or in the conference room, while he remains camped out in his office.

But tonight is too important.

"Hot date?"

Surely, I'm imagining the clipped way those words come out.

"Harper and West are having a celebration party," I answer, intentionally not addressing his hot date comment. Let him think I'm bringing a date to the party. I'm not, but he doesn't have to know that.

Why do you think he'd care?

"Ah, yes," Ryder muses. "West extended me an invitation to that. Business seems to be going well for him."

I absolutely hate that he knows anything at all about my close-knit group of friends. But when Harper's boyfriend West was looking for investors for his helicopter charter business a couple of months ago, I threw Ryder's name out. He likes to make smart investments in local businesses, and he certainly has enough money. I thought there was potential for both of them to benefit from a business partnership. Even more maddening, Ryder and West get along like old schoolyard pals. Harper told me the two men have had drinks together several times and seem to have a lot in common.

I don't like it.

Don't like him infiltrating my life outside of this office. I need the boundaries we've drawn at work to stay in place all the time and everywhere.

I'm staring at my computer screen, but I might as well be looking at the Matrix for how little I'm comprehending what I'm seeing. "It is. He's getting more charters than he can handle. He's had to hire an assistant to help him with the scheduling and payments."

Ryder makes a noise of approval. "Glad to hear it. And Harper's cosmetics business?"

I can't stop myself from smiling.

I'm so stinking proud of that girl, it's dumb. After years of hiding away her talents and being too timid to take charge of her life and pursue her dreams, Harper finally quit the job she hated, threw her demented mother out of her life, and started her own company for real. The blond-haired, green-eyed, Barbie-lookalike is a chemistry nerd, and utilizes those skills to make her own beauty products from scratch.

"Doing better than she ever expected," I reluctantly answer him. "She's got a strong social media following already, and is looking into opening up a retail space." She's got so much inventory at this point, a third of it is currently stashed in my spare bedroom.

Tonight, we're all celebrating the success of their young companies, Charleston Charters and Harper West Products.

"So, you'll be there tonight, then?" Ryder asks, a curious lilt in his voice.

I warily raise my gaze to meet his, not liking the sound of that at all. "Yeah... Will *you* be?"

Bemusement creeps over his features. "I said West invited me."

Shit balls.

I never thought about West inviting him. It makes sense, of course, since Ryder's investment helped get Charleston Charters off the ground. Literally.

I'm completely at a loss for words. The only other time this has happened was the moment I walked into his office and realized that I've had my boss's dick inside me.

Thank sweet baby J, my desk phone starts ringing.

Ryder's eyes flick sharply to it, looking briefly annoyed. Then his expression transforms, reflecting his trademark arrogance. "Get those quotes to me by the end of the day, and I'll let you buy me a drink tonight."

My jaw hits the floor as he struts off to his office, all nonchalant.

We have never spent any time together outside of this office. Except for the sex he doesn't remember having, which I don't count. We've never blurred the lines between professional and personal, aside from the extremely *un*professional way we speak to each other during work hours.

Point is, we've never lifted the curtain of boss and employee.

Once I realized who he was that first day, I insisted on dropping that veil between us and *never* peeking under it again. If we interact at Harper and West's party tonight, that veil could very well be pulled back. Some of those lines might smear. And since I can vividly recall the unicorn sex with Ryder—the type of fantastical sex you think is just a myth, the kind you think you'll never see in person—I don't need him around me while *I'm* around tequila.

The Countess can't be trusted with a buzz.

She gets a little too flighty for her own slutty good.

By four o'clock that afternoon, I have the quotes ready, my inbox cleaned out for the weekend, and a strategy for the evening. The name of the game with Ryder tonight at the party will be avoidance, plain and simple. Just because he's my boss doesn't mean I'm required to acknowledge his existence outside of these walls.

Yeah, that'll work.

I knock on Ryder's office door with the same manila folder from earlier clutched in my hands, though it's much thicker and heavier now.

"Come in," he calls out from the other side.

I push open the door and stride toward his desk, keeping my attention focused on the documents in the folder as I quickly review them. "I've got all the information you *didn't* ask for. I only included two rounds of focus groups in the quote. We can obviously schedule more if their timeline for the research phase is flexible."

This is actually a big potential client. If we can land this account, TCG could see a crazy amount of growth in the next twelve months.

I glance up to find Ryder's contemplative gaze locked on me, his finger tapping against the surface of his desk. "I'll review everything and pass it along to them if I like what I see."

I just manage to resist rolling my eyes, so familiar am I with his routine of busting my balls. "Will I get points deducted for not showing my work, boss man?"

Bewilderingly, Ryder's gaze darkens with sensual intent for a split second. But that odd expression is abruptly wiped from my memory when a bark of masculine laughter comes from my left.

My head whips around in shock.

I didn't realize anyone else was in the room with us. Although how I could have missed the stud standing by the windows with his back to us is a mystery. The lightweight sweater he's wearing fits snugly over his broad shoulders. His dark jeans mold beautifully to his tight ass. And he's tall. I love tall.

Intrigued, I slant a questioning look at Ryder who's glaring at the man's back.

"It's about time someone had the stones to knock you down a peg, bro," Tight Ass says.

Wait...*bro?*

I'm frozen on the spot when the stranger turns around and reveals a face I've seen every single weekday for the last ten months.

It's Ryder...but it's *not.*

What the f—

"Hi." The man approaches me, sticking his hand out. "I'm Myles, Ryder's brother."

My eyes grow so wide, I'm surprised they don't fall out of my skull and plop onto the carpet at my feet. My heart stutters in my chest, over and over again, making it hard to draw in a breath.

Brother. Ryder has a brother.

And they're obviously identical twins.

How did I not know about this?

Myles suddenly jerks to a stop and squints at me. "Wait, don't I know you?" He looks to wrack his brain for a moment before his eyes clear with recognition. "You're *her*. You're *that* girl."

And that's when I know for sure.

I never slept with my boss ten months ago.

I slept with my boss's twin brother.

2

The Meet, Greet, and Retreat

"HOLD ON, YOU TWO KNOW EACH OTHER?" Ryder snaps from behind his desk.

I'm still stunned mute, so Myles takes the liberty of answering for me. "A little." A gleam enters his eyes. "We've only met once. It was a while back. Isn't that right...?"

Several beats of silence pass as I openly gape at him. I don't shake myself out of it until Myles lifts an expectant, if not amused, eyebrow.

"Gretchen," I supply robotically. I'm barely aware that I even have faculties, let alone that I have control over them.

Myles's mouth stretches wide. "Right. Gretchen. We got to know each other pretty well one night, didn't we? All night, if memory serves."

Ryder shoots to his feet, eyes wild. "*What?*"

My attention swings to him, some of the numbness fading as I take in his extreme reaction. My cheeks heat when his fiery blue gaze pierces straight through me. Why do I feel like a teenager whose parents just found an empty condom wrapper on her bedroom floor?

"You two *slept* together?" Ryder hisses accusingly at me, venom dripping from his words.

My mouth opens. Then closes. Nothing comes out.

I can hear Kennedy's voice in my head. *Sorry, folks, my audio seems to be malfunctioning.*

"It was what, like, seven or eight months ago?" Myles asks me.

"Ten," I find myself whispering. "Ten months. Just before I started working here."

Ryder's eyes dart to mine and hold. I can see the wheels behind them turning rapidly, trying to work out exactly what this all means.

I see the moment when it happens.

When he must realize that I slept with his twin brother before I ever started working at TCG and met him. When I was shell-shocked to come face-to-face with someone I *thought* was a one-night-stand. At my job.

"I never told you I had a brother," Ryder says slowly, working out the equation before him. "And he never mentioned he had a twin, did he?"

My chest rises and falls with my heavy breaths. "No."

Ryder's lips roll inward. I can feel Myles's inquisitive stare shift between us as he watches our interlude with rapt attention.

"So, this whole time," Ryder goes on, "did you think it was *me* you slept with?"

Okay, this is seriously the most horrifying moment of my life. And for a frame of reference, the first period I ever got was on a day that I chose to wear white shorts to school.

"I-I don't—" *I don't know what to say.*

I'm not used to feeling the sting of humiliation. Embarrassment doesn't often breach the fortress walls I've erected around myself. My self-possession is an impenetrable barrier that nothing too uncomfortable ever penetrates. Because I don't allow it to.

"You did," Ryder decides on his own. "But I didn't acknowledge that I'd ever met you before that first day in my office. Is that why you've always been so snippy with me?" Under his breath he mutters, "*Un-fucking-believable.*"

That manages to clear some of the fog in my brain. "I'm snippy with you because you're an overbearing, impatient perfectionist whose all-superior attitude grates on my last nerve."

Myles clutches his stomach as he dissolves into laughter.

Moving my gaze between the brothers, I study Myles closely, looking for any features or defining marks that would distinguish him from the man I've known for almost a year.

There isn't much.

At least, nothing I would have noticed while under the influence and in low lighting. His eyes are the same blue as Ryder's, same golden skin color, same jaw shape. Their hairline is even identical, though Myles's hair is longer and touches his ears. But it could have been just as short as Ryder's ten months ago.

In short, Myles is as much of a hot tottie as his brother.

Though much more charming, it would seem. When our gazes connect, his mouth sensuously curls up in the corners. It's a provocative grin if ever I've seen one.

This *man has seen me naked.* Myles, not Ryder.

"Sorry for the confusion, Gretchen," Myles croons smoothly. "I guess being under the influence that night isn't the best excuse."

When he makes a blatant perusal of my body, he doesn't even try to hide it. I'm confident in my own skin, but with Ryder in the room, glowering at his brother as he checks me out...I'm feeling pretty awkward.

I'm a five-foot-seven, twenty-five-year-old with generous C cups and a pear shape figure. Thanks to my father's Greek heritage, my skin is on the almond side, and my dark chestnut hair is thick, shoulder-length, and permanently wavy. I stopped straightening it years ago because it never stayed that way longer than thirty minutes. If there's one feature that I both love and hate about myself, it's my eyes. They're a unique, bright silver color that attract strangers' stares like moths to a bug zapper. Their spooky astonishment tends to get both annoying and creepy. Because of this, feeling gawked at isn't anything new for me.

But when Myles's blue eyes droop in an appreciative way, I instantly feel uneasy. Which doesn't make sense. I should be relieved that it was never my boss I slept with that night but his equally attractive twin brother instead. I should be flattered that Myles is sober now and still remembers me. I *should* be reacting in kind and taking him up on the obvious invitation in his eyes.

Just a teensy problem with that: he looks exactly like my boss.

How can I ever look at Myles without seeing Ryder? Is that even possible?

"If I'd been smart enough to get your number that night, believe me, I would have called," Myles murmurs, pitching his voice lower. "And you ran out on me the next morning before I could ask for it."

In my peripheral vision, I notice Ryder's gaze fly to me and bore right through my skull. But I can't bring myself to look at him. I'm too busy getting lost in my complete bafflement as the puzzle of the last ten months breaks apart and piece-by-piece, begins to reassemble itself to form an entirely different image.

That man gave you the best nooky of your life. Him. *Not the one behind the desk. Not the one you work for.*

Allow me to introduce my alter ego, the old hag.

Beyoncé has Sasha Fierce. Jennifer Lawrence has Gail. I have the old hag.

Don't worry, I'm not going to go all Sally Fields' *Cybil* on anyone's ass. I don't have a split personality. I've just always identified with the female geriatrics of the world. Aunt B. Ethel Mertz. The granny from *Beverly Hillbillies*. All the *Golden Girls*. Strangely, I feel a kinship with the eighty-year-old woman digging for caramels at the bottom of her purse. The kickass grandma Svengali who's been around the block a time or two and keeps a forty-year-old dial-up vibrator stashed beneath her pantyhose. *That's* my kind of spirit guide. My conscience has always sounded like a grouchy old lady looking for her six cats anyway. I think somewhere down the line, my brain just created an amalgam of my fantasy grandma guru. And thus, the old hag was born.

Gotta admit, it's fun to constantly disappoint a cranky old curmudgeon.

And the old hag can't begin to process what's happening inside this office. Not without a full bottle of gin and a bendy straw.

Myles chuckles. "And hell, if I'd known you've been working for my brother this entire time, I would have—"

"This is inappropriate to discuss at work," Ryder interrupts curtly. "I expect my employees to maintain professionalism at all times, Myles. If you have personal matters to discuss with Ms. Castellanos, do it outside of this building."

How did he manage to say any of that with a straight face? The line of communication between the two of us is the very definition of inappropriate. Why is he suddenly acting all stiff and calling me "Ms. Castellanos" in front of his brother?

Ryder shoots me the briefest of side glances, some kind of warning flashing in his eyes, before reverting his attention back to Myles.

As for Myles, he looks completely nonplussed by his brother's terse words. "No wonder you sounded so miserable when you first walked in here." He tips his head at Ryder. "Dealing with this little ray of sunshine every day wouldn't put a smile on my face either."

Ryder frowns. His gaze slides back to mine as he studies my reaction to that statement.

I don't give him anything. Besides, my thoughts are too chaotic for any emotion other than abject mortification to show on my face.

"I can hold my own with him." I say it more to my boss than to Myles.

A muscle ticks in Ryder's jaw.

"I can see that," Myles chortles. "I admire you for it because not many can."

There's a snideness to his words that has Ryder's shoulders stiffening. In fact, I'm just now picking up on the undercurrent of tension flowing between the two brothers. And I don't think it's all due to the revelation that Myles and I spent a night together. There's something else going on between Ryder and his twin.

"Listen, Gretchen." When Myles steps toward me, I have the irrational impulse to retreat. "I think *boss man* here is right. We should discuss things outside of the office. Would you like to have dinner with me tonight?"

I open my mouth to respond, but Ryder beats me to it. "She's busy," he bites out, coming around his desk. "In fact, why don't you start your weekend early and head home, Ms. Castellanos? You've already completed your work for the day anyway."

My movements are wooden, my thoughts still jumbled. I'm in such a daze that I actually allow him to manhandle me to the door with his hand on my elbow.

"My brother and I have some things to discuss," he says in a low voice near my ear. "I'll see you tonight at the party."

Like hell he would.

As far as I'm concerned, The Oak Tavern is a breeding ground for lepers tonight. I'm not stepping foot inside that building.

"Oh, Gretchen, wait," Myles calls out as he shuffles toward us. "I wanted to get your number—"

Ryder slams the door in my face.

My feet are stuck in cement. I can't move.

I stare at the wood grain of the door like there's a code embedded in the pattern that I'm trying to break. Though sadly, I don't think that's where I'm going to find the answers to solving the mystery of—

WHAT IN THE NAME OF JESUS C JUST HAPPENED?

3

The Bathtub Fortress of Pot Solitude

REAL TALK ROMANCE, EPISODE 16

Kennedy clears her throat. "Okay, so I recently asked all you listeners out there to post the worst scenarios where you run into your one-night-stand on our Facebook page. Here are some of the gems I got:

'Seeing him come out of an HIV support group wearing a nametag.'
'Running into her outside of an OB ward, alone and sporting a baby bump.'
'At a family reunion, where he's introduced to you as your long-lost cousin.'
'You're walking down the street and he's sitting on the sidewalk holding a cardboard sign that says, HUNGRY AND HOMELESS, ANYTHING HELPS.'
And my personal favorite:
'Your father shows up to dinner, holding her hand, and introduces her as your new stepmother—True story.'"

Only delinquents smoke the marijuana, young lady.

I wrap my lips around the joint and inhale.

Deeply.

Let the smoke fill my lungs and hold my breath until my chest burns. As I slowly blow it out, I watch the gray smoke curl above my head and swirl up to my bathroom ceiling. Taking a second drag, I slide further down in my bathtub and luxuriate in the coconut-scented bubbles as they cascade over my body.

Smoking pot in a bubble bath with a glass of wine—it'll cure all your ills.

And mercy me, do I ever need some medicine after the day's rollercoaster of events. Because in my case, my harness wasn't clicked in all the way, and a loopty-loop flung me a hundred feet into the air before I plummeted to the earth with a tragic and sickening *splat*.

I did end up going to Harper and West's celebratory rooftop party at The Oak Tavern in downtown Charleston—thankfully, without running into Ryder—but only long enough to find my girls. If anyone could help me sort out the mess in my head, it's Sloane, Harper, and Quinn. I relayed the whole sordid tale, short of getting too deep into the nitty gritty land of emotions. Baring my soul, even to my best friends, is not something I make a habit out of. I felt uncharacteristically shy when I revealed the secret I've been keeping from them for ten months. That I slept with my bastard of a boss.

Only I didn't.

And that's fucking with my head.

Oh, and drugs *help? Before you know it, you'll be smoking that awful crack cocaine.*

The expense of renovating the master bathroom in my loft last year was exorbitant but so incredibly worth it. Bubble baths are a luxury I refuse to ever give up, no matter where I live. So, the first thing I blew serious cash on after starting at TCG was this badass tub. It's big enough to fit three NFL linebackers inside, with tiled steps leading up to it. It's the kind of bathtub I imagine the ancient Greeks would have approved of.

I sip my wine as I lean against my bath pillow, allowing the weed to work its blissful magic on my muscles. My limbs languidly float in the steaming water, my fingertips tingling with the release of stress and tension.

Then my blasted phone rings.

Nothing disturbs quiet time in my happy place, dammit. Someone is taking their very life into their hands.

I'm seconds away from drowning the thing in the bath water. Replacing it would be a bitch, though. With a begrudging sigh, I set my wine glass onto the wooden tray laid across the tub and place my tightly rolled joint in the ash tray. After glancing at the screen, I answer the call and put it on speaker.

"Did running off that roof in a complete panic not clue you in to the fact that I need to be alone with my thoughts?" I answer in lieu of a greeting.

Sloane huffs over the line. "That's exactly why I'm concerned. Leaving you alone with your thoughts usually leads to me either bailing you out of jail or confiscating all the potential weapons in your loft."

"You can relax, babe. I've locked up all my razor blades and butter knives."

A beat of silence comes through the speaker. "I've just never seen you like that before, Gretch."

I chuckle mirthlessly.

Yeah, she's never seen me lose my shit before. None of my friends have. I'm always chill and laidback, even under the heaviest of pressure. Cloaking my discomfort with inappropriate humor and indifference. That's me. Cool-as-a-cucumber Gretchen. Doesn't get emotional. Doesn't get riled. Never off her game because she's such a pro at playing it.

But at that rooftop bar earlier tonight, I looked like Tony Montana from *Scarface*, minus the machine gun.

"A moment in time, babe," I purr in my *I'm pretending that I'm okay so you don't freak out any more than I am* voice.

I've perfected the act over the past ten years. Throwing up on the inside, throwing out snark on the outside. No one can ever tell the difference. When I don't want to answer questions, I ensure that none need to be asked.

Distract, deflect, disengage.

"It was one small slip," I assure my best friend. "Nothing to be concerned about. I'm dandy now."

"Right," Sloane snorts. "You know, I'm starting to get insulted that you think I don't know you well enough to see when something is bothering you. It kind of hurts that you're always pushing us away, Gretch. Especially when you need us."

Her words are sobering. "I came to you guys tonight to talk."

Which is a big deal for me, considering the fact that I knew there was a strong possibility of bumping into Ryder at that party.

"Yeah, but the second we started asking how you actually *felt* about the situation with your boss and his brother, you clammed up like you always do and lit out of there like your ass was on fire."

I close my eyes in guilt, feeling admonished. "I'm still trying to figure out how I feel about it first. It's still fresh. I'm not ready to discuss whatever emotions may or may not exist in this scenario."

She sighs. "Fine. I'll leave you to process things in your Bathtub Fortress of Pot Solitude. But I've set a timer on your ass, Gretch. And once that timer dings, I'm going to demand some feels from you. There's a real talk session in your future whether you like it or not. Even if we have to tie you down and make you ride the wooden horse like they did during the Revolutionary days. Either way, we're going to get some answers."

I hum in the back of my throat before taking another sip of wine. "Ride the wooden horse, huh? Sounds kinky. Be sure to bring extra rope. I seem to be running low on my supply."

"Done."

"Gotta go, babe. People to see, things to shave. Talk later."

I hang up before she can respond.

It's not rude. That's just how we roll.

It's one reason why I love Sloane so much. Why we automatically clicked as roommates in college years ago. She understands that I'm closed off. That I keep my emotions close to the vest because otherwise, I don't know how to deal with them. An intellectual like Sloane, who needs to verbalize everything in order to understand it, doesn't function the same way. She may not entirely get it, but she accepts it. And she doesn't waste time on pleasantries or sentiments she knows I'll just roll my eyes at.

By the bottom of my wine glass and halfway through my joint, I still don't know how I'm going to handle these Colson brothers.

If you hadn't given the milk away for free in the first place, you wouldn't be in this pickle. Why, in my day—

I mentally slip the old hag an Ambien and tell her to go take a nap.

Maybe I'm making too big a deal of this.

Ryder is my boss. That's where it begins and ends because it's not like anything romantic is going on between us. Even if I was interested in him—which I cannot stress enough that I'm *not*—he's adamant about never getting involved with someone he works with. And since I now know that we never actually slept together, all should be right in the world.

Having said that, his reaction to Myles asking for my number was particularly odd. I mean, he looked like he was seconds away from delivering a knockout punch. To be fair, Ryder's PMS is bitchier than mine some days, so his shitty mood could have been attributed to almost anything. His pen ran out of ink.

The birds were chirping too loudly outside his window. The floppy part of his hair wouldn't lay right. Literally, anything.

But let's focus on the fact that Myles seems interested.

Problem? Possibly.

I honestly don't know if I want to give him my number. If sober sex with him is anything like our one drunken night together, then I'm poised for the most epic hookup of my life. And considering the Countess has been wandering through the desert without food or water for well over forty days, that sounds pretty spectacular.

But what would Ryder think about it?

Why in tarnation do we care?

I don't want to create anymore friction between us than there already is. I don't need more aggravation at my job. A job that I incidentally love and don't want to start hating just because my boss's brother is down for some sweet nakey times with me.

When in doubt, I typically side with conventional wisdom.

And in a case that involves two brothers, one woman, and a workplace scenario, conventional wisdom dictates that you become neutral Switzerland. Say no to everything and everyone.

This isn't *General Hospital.*

It doesn't matter that my one night with Myles was probably the singular best sexual experience of my life. His relation to Ryder makes the situation soap opera-level complicated, and that's a degree of drama I steadfastly avoid.

It's hard to believe now, but Ryder wasn't such a dictating monster in the very beginning. He was...different...my first week at TCG.

"How's your morning going so far, Ms. Castellanos?" my boss asks pleasantly from behind me.

I barely spare him a glance over my shoulder before returning my attention to the contract on my computer screen. I've already skimmed over it once, but I wanted one more read-through before the client meeting in twenty minutes. I have to admit I'm grateful that Mr. Colson here is involving me as much as he is with this new account we're about to sign. Within my first week, he's already asking for my input and seems to be taking my opinions to heart.

But he's still an asshole.

"It's fine," is the only answer I give him. Without turning around.

He clears his throat uncomfortably. "Are you settling in all right? No issues with the software programs or anything?"

I smirk to myself. "None whatsoever, boss."

He makes a noise that's part grunt, part sigh. It's the first time I've detected even a hint of his frustration since I started working here four days ago. "Have I said or done something to offend you? You've seemed a bit...put out by me ever since we met."

We met two weeks ago, dickhead.

When your *dickhead* was inside me.

I plaster on the fakest smile I've got in my bag of tricks and turn to face him. "Not at all, boss. I just don't do a lot of chit-chat when I'm in work mode. Is that going to be a problem?"

He narrows his eyes, a look I've come to recognize as consternation on him. "As long as you do your job and do it well, Ms. Castellanos, I couldn't care less how much watercooler gossip you partake in."

"Good thing I bring my own water bottle with me every day."

His expression remains mostly blank, unreadable. But his voice comes out far less pleasant than before. "Were you able to finish up those PowerPoint slides from yesterday? I realize there were quite a few and I didn't give you a lot of time—"

I toss him a flash drive containing the file with said slides. He catches it against his chest with one hand. "Finished them before I left last night," I tell him flatly. "Let me know if they aren't up to snuff."

His face still doesn't change, with the exception of the slight clenching of his jaw. "You'll learn soon enough that I have no problem delivering constructive criticism."

I quirk a sassy eyebrow. "Neither do I."

He taps the flash drive against his palm, his eyes thoughtful. "Are you always so outspoken with your superiors?"

I experience a brief moment of uncertainty. He can easily fire me without cause if he wants to, and I'm already falling in love with this position. I need to tread carefully here. "I wasn't aware that maintaining a pretense was a prerequisite for this job. And from what I've heard around the watercooler, you value honesty and assertiveness in your employees. You want me to do my job well? Being forthright in my opinions with my superiors is how I'll do it well."

"Some might call that recalcitrant."

I shrug. "I prefer obstinate."

I watch with reluctant fascination as his entire face transforms into something I've never seen from him. It's as if a light has suddenly clicked on inside him. A different version of his personality is peeking through. A smirk begins to play over his mouth. His shoulders relax considerably, and he shifts all of his weight to one foot, cocking his hip out in the process.

"That's just a fancy word for 'bullheaded,' duchess."

My lips part.

What the hell did he just call me?

And why does that change in his voice suddenly bring to mind images of him making me come? Of me making him come? Thinking about that night two weeks ago is breaking my first commandment. Thou shalt not dwelleth on the nighteth thou debased thyself with thy boss.

My new life began four days ago.

And this new version of me never *slept with her movie-star gorgeous boss.*

Realizing that he managed to knock me off-guard, satisfaction crosses his features as his gaze brazenly rakes over me. Which is obvious code for I'm not your boss for these next few seconds. *According to his body language, this six-by-six cubicle is all that exists in the world right now. A place where all titles are forgotten and he's free to be Ryder Colson, man, instead of Ryder Colson, boss man.*

And damn it all, I feel the touch of that gaze everywhere.

Skating along my skin, stroking across my breasts, twining through the strands of my hair. It's incredible. The man I work for actually has the nerve to check me out at my own desk, inside his own office, as if he hasn't already seen what's underneath these clothes.

When his eyes finally find mine again, his pupils are larger and his expression lacks all humor. He points at me with the flash drive. "I'll let you know what errors I find. Be in the conference room in ten minutes. Welcome to The Colson Group, duchess."

Reflecting back, I realize that he at least made an attempt to be polite in those early days. He was cordial, professional. I was the one who bared my teeth and chomped down on his leg. I was short and cold with him. He simply started giving it all back.

Maybe Ryder isn't as bad as I thought.

Maybe I am the sole one responsible for our contentious relationship. All because I was affronted that he didn't remember our one-night sexcapade that I now know never even happened.

Maybe we could actually get along and be…friends.

Eh. Friends might be pushing it.

But maybe we could, at the very least, be civil to each other. I'll accept my role in how things have progressed between us if he can just meet me halfway.

Maybe I could actually like Ryder Colson.

4

The Competitive Edge

Well, that theory gets blown to hell and back on Monday.

Turns out the new client we're quoting wants to start the market research for their product release right away if they sign with us because their overall timeline is pretty tight. The market research really should have been conducted a long time ago, so this is more like a beta test phase. Around two o'clock Monday afternoon, Ryder blows up my inbox with a truckload of items he wants completed by tomorrow in order for us to be prepared for our meeting with the potential client on Thursday.

Which means it's all aboard the Late Night Express tonight. *Choo-choo!*

Hours later, he and I are the only two people left in the office. I've been chained to my desk for four straight hours and I'm wired. Not from the two energy drinks I guzzled down, but from the addictive high of being productive. When I get on a roll like this, I don't stop until my fingers quit listening to my brain and can no longer function.

"Did you book the studio for the commercial shoot?" Ryder asks, sidling up to my desk.

I finish the sentence I'm typing before spinning my chair around to face him. "Yes. They can accommodate the short notice."

His finger swipes over his phone screen. "And the focus groups have been scheduled?"

I wave back at my computer screen. "Done. I'm working on the questionnaire packets now, and Regina was compiling a list of participants all day. Right now, we've got about eighteen locked in for the first one and nine for the second, but we'll get more."

"She managed to get that many in one day?"

My mouth twitches as the voice of our deceptively sweet receptionist echoes in my ears. "Regina's got three kids, remember? She knows how to handle being told 'no' over and over again and still somehow get her way."

Just when I think I might get an itty-bitty smile from him, the man scowls. Lordy day, I'm trying to be amiable here. It's taking all my effort to not revert back to my default behavior and infuse some bite into every word I snipe his way.

But he is *not* playing along.

"Why don't you just come work in my office so I don't have to keep dragging my ass out here to talk to you?" he asks on a frustrated exhale.

"I work better alone. Besides, if we go into that room together, it'll end up turning into a crime scene. And I'm sure you don't want to go through the hassle of replacing your carpet."

What happened to the honey, Gretchen? That was a whole lotta vinegar.

Cut me some slack. I'm new at this nice thing.

With a muffled curse, Ryder reaches forward and snatches all the binders and folders off my desk. "Conference room. Now." Arms full, he pivots on his heel and stalks off.

"Wow, really?" I throw my hands up. "Isn't stealing my stuff a little juvenile? Are you my boss or my older brother?"

He slams to a stop.

Slowly wheeling around, his expression turns livid. *"Never* call me your brother again, duchess," he growls. "Ever."

Stomping off, he violently shoulders the conference room door open, sending it banging against the opposite wall.

Mm-kay. There are two possibilities here.

One, those energy drinks are straight-up rat poison and I just hallucinated that whole thing.

Or two, that actually just happened.

I don't even know how much time passes as I remain frozen in my chair, contemplating the likelihood of the first.

"Get your ass in here, Gretchen!" he yells from inside the room.

Alllrighty dighty.

That's how we're going to play this.

Grabbing my phone and water bottle, I pound across the office, outrage causing my blood to rush through my veins like a raging river. The glare I fire his way when I pause at the threshold to the conference room would fall into the *visual castration* category.

"Did you really just say that to me?"

Calm as can be, he meticulously spreads out my folders and binders on the large wooden table, organizing them in a similar fashion to what I prefer. "I did. You don't like it, report me to HR."

I sneer at his lowered head.

Like I said, I've never been offended by the way Ryder speaks to me, as looney as that might sound. Not to mention, complaining to someone else about my problems implies that I'm not capable of handling them myself.

And...snitches get stitches.

It's actually refreshing that he doesn't mince words, doesn't hide behind subterfuge. I'm a straightforward person, and I like things to be laid out clearly. No bullshit. Ryder is the same way.

It's why we work so well together. He may push my buttons, but he's never crossed a line I was uncomfortable with.

I drop myself into a chair on the opposite side of the table. "Then I guess you'll have to report me to HR for calling you a dick."

He clucks his tongue in agreement. "Only fair."

"I hope the company has a criminal defense lawyer on retainer because I might need it."

"I see those Monday menses are rearing their ugly heads."

"Oh, good. That'll be my defense when I'm on trial for your murder."

An hour later, his suit jacket is draped over the chair beside him, shirt sleeves rolled up to his forearms. My hair is being held up by a pencil, my feet are bare, and the bag of chocolate-covered espresso beans sitting on the table between us is nearly empty. Months ago, during another one of these all-nighters, I was munching on a bag of them at my desk. Walking past, Ryder grabbed it and dumped a handful into his palm. With a mouthful of beans, he mumbled that they, too, were his favorite.

Now, we never work together without that bag between us.

He pushes back from the table and scrubs his hands down his face. "Their Christmas deadline for product release is really pushing it. I think it's too ambitious."

I do, too. But... "They want it on the shelves by Christmas." I roll my neck around on my shoulders. "All that last-minute holiday shopping should drive sales."

"Why did you keep working here?"

My head snaps up, my confused gaze colliding with his. "What?"

His expression is inscrutable, but it's...intense. Whatever is going on behind his blue eyes must be a doozy. "If you thought you had slept with your boss, why didn't you just quit?"

"You really want to talk about this now?" *While sober?*

I do confrontation best with some liquid courage.

He says nothing. Just watches me and waits.

I toss my pen onto the table. "Because if *you* didn't remember it happening, then I could pretend like it never did, too. Clean slate."

When his tongue slowly drags over his lower lip, I can't tell if he likes that answer or not.

I roll my eyes with a huff. "Plus, not to add to your already inflated ego, this is the best market and ad firm in the area, despite your abhorrent people skills. It was a dream job for me."

He taps his finger against the gleaming wood of the table. *Tap, tap, tap.* "You made it clear right from the start that you weren't my biggest fan. Can I now assume that was because you were angry that I, from your perspective, didn't remember us having sex?"

I have no answer.

What the hell am I supposed to say to that? I'm afraid the truth will make me sound like a naïve girl who became obsessed with a guy after only one night.

FYI, I didn't.

Tap, tap, tap of his finger. "But being angry implies that you *wanted* me to remember." A muscle pops in his jaw. "It was that good for you?"

'Kay, *now* I'm rattled.

Because now I know that I never slept with Ryder Colson. My long-time annoyance with him is unfounded, yet it feels as strong as ever and I don't know what to do about it.

"We're not talking about this," I state firmly.

"Why not?"

Seriously? "Because now I know it wasn't you. Which means that none of this is your business. We"—I gesture between us— "never slept together."

Your brother and I did was the unspoken part of that sentence.

He hears it. And his nostrils flare.

"You're right," he admits gruffly. "It wasn't me. Because if it had been me, I wouldn't have forgotten a single detail. Like Myles obviously did."

My face goes slack.

Did he just—? Did I hear him say—?

Ryder just took us into another realm. Another dimension. For the first time ever, he turned a sexual corner with me. One I thought we both silently agreed to never even approach, let alone maneuver around.

But he went there. He put it *out* there.

"Are you saying I'm not worth remembering?"

His face darkens, hardens. "Fuck, no. I'm saying anyone who doesn't remember a night with you didn't deserve to have you in the first place."

I just stare...

...mouth agape...

...and stare some more...

...and drool a little...

I shake my head. Like a dog. What the frig is happening right now?

The old hag knocks back a shot of Pepto-Bismol. *My poor nerves can't take this young man.*

Is Ryder saying that he *wants* a night with me? Or is this just some male chauvinist thing where he has to assert himself as the most virile man in the village because he senses another encroaching on his territory?

He does realize I'm not his territory, though, right?

I'm not his anything. Except employee.

"I'd say it's for me to decide whether or not someone deserves me," I eventually say, my voice oddly hoarse.

Tap, tap, tap. "You never answered my question."

I know which one he's talking about, but I still ask. "What question?"

Tap, tap, tap. "Was it good for you?"

I cross my arms over my chest, assessing him. Okay, fine. He wants to go there? Let's do this. "We're talking about your brother here. You really want to know?"

Tap...tap...tap. "He may not remember it, but you clearly do. It couldn't have been the worst you've ever had."

"What if I said it was the best?"

His face reflects a range of emotions in a matter of seconds that confuses the crap out of me. At first, his eyes crinkle in the corners, as if he's pleased. Then they narrow to slits as banked fury emanates from them.

"Then I'd say that's because *I* haven't had you."

My jaw unhinges like a snake's.

He slowly nods, his eyes burning holes through me. "Yeah, duchess. I said that."

Wariness coils around my ribcage and squeezes. "Maybe you shouldn't have."

He pushes his chair back and rises to his feet. Leaning over the table, he presses his fists onto the surface, his gaze unwavering on mine. "There are a lot of things I probably shouldn't say to you. This isn't one of them."

My heartbeat shoots out of the blocks like it's going for the gold in the 100-meter dash. "What exactly are you saying?"

Heat enters his eyes. Then he *really* says it. The one thing that has the power to change everything. "Whatever you had that night, I can give you better. *I* can give you your best."

Oh, Christ on a cracker.

I know this feeling in my lower belly. I recognize the sensation of lust pooling between my thighs, forcing me to clench them together. The desire for friction rising, my pulse quickening.

My boss is turning me on.

The imposing way he's looming over me, his dominant posture. The sinewy shapes of his biceps flexing beneath his white shirt. The bulging veins in his neck, the whitening of his knuckles against the table. The rippling of his shoulders as they tense in anticipation for my response.

Holy shit.

Language, missy.

I want my boss.

I want Ryder Colson between my legs.

Whatever he's selling right now, I'm tempted to drain my savings and buy up his entire stock. He's never revealed this sexual, demanding side of himself before, and I'm liking it way the hell too much.

After several moments of simmering silence, my words come out in a shaky whisper. "I don't think we should go there, Ryder."

It's the first time I've ever said his name out loud. Usually, it's "boss", "boss man", or "jackass."

His eyes spark with…something. "Duchess, I'm pretty sure we're already there."

I squeeze my hands into fists when they start trembling. "What if I don't want to be?"

He tilts his head to the side. "What if I can change your mind?"

Pretty sure he's already on his way.

My ringtone suddenly slices through the sexual gas chamber the room has turned into. I break our eye contact to glance at the screen, but not before I see Ryder's gaze move in the same direction, glowering at the source of our interruption.

I don't recognize the number, but I need to be rescued from Ryder's magnetism before I climb up on this table and rip my panties off for him.

"Hello?"

"Gretchen? Hey, it's Myles."

My eyes fly to Ryder, who looks wholly enraged. "Who is it?" he demands.

"Hi, Myles," I say cheerily.

Ryder's face blackens into the kind of dark cloud you'd expect to see right before a storm that rains hellfire down on Earth.

"What's up?"

"Well, my asshole brother wouldn't give me your number on Friday, so I called up HR and persuaded them to give it to me." He pauses for a few beats. "Creepy?"

Ryder is glaring so hard at my phone I think he's hoping it will spontaneously combust. "I've seen creepier."

Myles chuckles in my ear. "I'll take it. But it got me talking to you, didn't it?"

"Mission accomplished."

"Not quite," he muses. "My mission won't be complete until you agree to let me take you to dinner."

I rock back and forth in my chair, keeping my face carefully blank. "I'm not sure that's a good idea."

Ryder's cheeks tinge with red.

Why am I enjoying his reaction so much?

Myles grunts. "Because you work for my brother? What if I can promise that it won't cause any problems?"

Not sure you have that power, buddy.

"I don't know…"

Do I really want to go out with Myles? We did have great sex. And obviously, I find him attractive. Maybe we could have more if I give him a chance. But since when do I want more? I'm not looking for a relationship right now, let alone with someone who looks exactly like—and is related to—the man I work for.

"How about we just start with lunch?" Myles suggests hopefully. "Then we'll see where it goes from there."

"I'll have to check my schedule."

Ryder gnashes his teeth. "Gretchen, hang up the phone."

Oh, *no*, he didn't.

My head rears back, aghast that he has that level of nerve.

"Is that my brother?" Amusement laces Myles's tone. "You two working late?"

"You mean is the merciless dictator holding me hostage in the office? Yeah, that's happening."

Ryder shoves away from the table and starts pacing across the room. His hair is soon sticking up in all directions from running his hand through it so many times. Seriously, though. What the hell is his problem? What right does he think he has trying to tell me to do anything? He might be my boss, but he is not my *boss*.

Oh, splendid. We'd really be in trouble if four-year-old Gretchen couldn't make it to this conversation.

Myles snorts. "Typical Ryder. Be sure to let him know I managed to get your number, no thanks to him."

That gives me pause. Something in his voice has me bristling. As if he's gloating. Like a kid shoving the championship trophy his brother didn't win in his face.

I better not be the goddamn trophy.

"So, how does lunch tomorrow sound?"

I study Ryder as he stares up at the ceiling, hands wrapped around his neck, muscles tight with strain. "Lunch tomorrow sounds great."

My boss's head jerks around, his fiery gaze clashing with mine. I'm reading something akin to *over my dead body* on his face.

Mine says *try and stop me, boss man. I triple dog dare you.*

Myles rattles off the name of a popular grill downtown and a time to meet him there.

I smile. "Perfect. I'll see you then."

I hang up, gingerly place my phone face down on the table, and quietly watch the fuming man before me.

He does the same. Until, "You're really interested in him?"

That's when it hits me.

Like getting nailed in the face with a pillowcase full of bricks.

Ryder has never pushed for anything sexual with me in the ten months we've known each other. Now, all of a sudden, he's putting on the full-court press? The timing of his abrupt one-eighty is more than suspicious, and there's only one explanation.

Myles.

Ever since Myles appeared and flirted me up, Ryder has acted agitated, presumptuous, almost possessive, and if I'm not mistaken…jealous.

Uncrossing my legs, I gather all my things and start shoving them into my black leather messenger bag. "Whether I am or not is none of your business. You're my boss. Outside of this office and the responsibilities that fall within my job, you have no authority over me whatsoever."

"Where are you going? We're not done here."

I cut him a scathing look as I slip on my flats under the table. "Oh, believe me. We are. I'll finish the rest at home and email it all to you."

Again, he runs his hand through his hair, gripping the strands like he's about to yank out a handful. He looks on the verge of exploding. But I'll be damned if I get hit by his shrapnel. He can have his little bitch fest with his brother all he wants, but it doesn't mean I have to sit here and witness it. Or become collateral damage.

I sling my bag's strap over my shoulder and turn for the door.

"Gretchen, listen, I—"

"One more thing," I talk over him as I whirl back around. "Whatever game you're playing with your brother, whatever kind of sibling rivalry you two have going on, do me a favor and leave me the hell out of it."

I'm out the door without another glance back.

As I'm pushing through the office's main double doors, I swear I hear a male voice loudly bellow, "fuck!" from the direction of the conference room.

But it was probably just the wind.

5

The Not-So-Evil Twin

I DON'T OFTEN REGRET MY CONSTANT IMPULSIVITY.

But this lunch with Myles is bound to be the most awkward lunch in the history of the world. I feel like a gawky teenager about to face the first boy who ever slipped his hand underneath her training bra.

I mean, Myles and I had *sex*. He apparently doesn't remember much of it. He knows I thought it was his brother instead of him. A brother who happens to be my boss. And Myles looks exactly like the man I've claimed to hate for the past ten months. What do you talk about under those circumstances? Politics? The weather? Which fast food chain has the best French fries?

And how am I going to hold a normal conversation when my mind is still reeling over what happened in that infernal conference room last night?

I walk into the downtown grill and immediately spot Myles sitting at a two-person table near the bar. Even with the large lunch crowd, his height and demeanor—the way he commands a room—tend to separate him from the general population.

Just like his brother.

Okie doke, new commandment. *Thou shalt not thinketh or talketh about Ryder. Period-eth.*

Myles flashes me an easy smile that's completely playboy when he catches sight of me. He's so incredibly good-looking it's sickening. He looks like he was manufactured in a lab, for God's sake.

Just like his—

"I was afraid you were going to stand me up," he says in greeting, rising to his feet.

"Hey, I'm not the kind of girl to turn down a free lunch."

He laughs as we take our seats. "Beautiful, smart, and frugal with her money? Is it too early to propose?"

"Not if you're comfortable with rejection."

He shoots me a sly wink. "I don't think a man could easily get over being rejected by you, so I'll play it safe for now."

After perusing the menu and placing our orders, I'm surprised at how easily the conversation flows, from run-of-the-mill topics like the types of foods we like, to crazy stories we've read about in the news. I learn that Myles didn't go the entrepreneur route like Ryder did and instead, works for their stepfather's steel manufacturing company. He's been working at the main headquarters in Raleigh, but recently moved to Charleston to manage the new factory they opened here a few months ago. He likes to experiment with different barbecue recipes on his charcoal grill, play with other people's dogs as long as he doesn't have to take care of one himself, and...pottery, of all things.

"Like, you're actually sitting at the potter's wheel making vases and bowls and stuff, pottery?" I swallow a bite of my salad, hoping I don't have dressing dripping from my lip. "Like the movie *Ghost?*"

He drops his burger onto his plate, flinging his hands in the air. "Well, there goes that. Do you know how many women I've snared with that *Ghost* line? But you beat me to it and now, I've got no moves left."

I find his candor ridiculously attractive. In that aspect at least, he and his brother have something in common.

"How do you bring it up in the conversation?"

His eyes dance with mischief. "I ask her if she's seen the movie. If she says yes, then I ask if she likes roleplay. I'll be Patrick Swayze, she can be Demi Moore, and I'll give her the best clay sex of her life."

I tip my head back and laugh. "Truly, every woman's wildest fantasy. And what if she hasn't seen it?"

He takes a drink of his water, grinning around the glass. "I let her watch while I make her a vase without a shirt on. Either scenario tends to bring the same results."

"Where was that when we first met?" I try to sound offended. "I believe I'm owed a vase."

His smile dims. "I know I might be blowing my chances here by admitting this, but I honestly don't remember much from that night, Gretchen. I'm not proud to admit that I was kind of trashed."

I barely manage to hide my flinch behind my fork.

I'm not about to let him know how much that stings. Not to sound too much like the virgin who automatically falls in love with the boy who clumsily takes her cherry in the back of a dirty van, but...I really thought we had a connection that night. He seemed different than any other guy I've been with. It *felt* different with him.

Must have just been the vodka gimlets, though.

Because I'm not feeling that same connection now. There's nothing *un*pleasant about this lunch with Myles, but there's nothing earth-shattering either.

Did Gretchen Castellanos actually fall under the boozy sex love spell?

I glance out the window just to make sure there aren't any pigs flying around out there.

"Well, I appreciate you not lying about it," I tell Myles. "I was pretty tipsy myself, so there are some blurry parts for me, too. If you don't remember much, how did you recognize me in Ryder's office?"

He adorably ducks his head in a boyish manner I wouldn't have thought him capable of. "I woke up the next morning and saw a gorgeous woman in my bed. Hard to forget what you looked like after that. But when I woke up again you were gone."

My flinch is visible this time. "Yeah, sorry about that. It's not usually my style to wait around for the bacon and eggs the next morning. I'm actually surprised I fell asleep at all."

He nods in understanding. "You're talking to the poster child here." He huffs, shaking his head at himself. "I'm making quite the impression, aren't I? A philandering potter who likes to barbecue and doesn't remember taking a stunning woman to bed. I should just grab the check now and cut my losses."

His self-deprecating comments are actually endearing me to him. Those plainspoken admissions are sincere, which is one of the most charming qualities a man can have, in my opinion.

"The first thing you should know about me, Myles?" I tip my glass of sweet tea at him. "I don't do filters. Talking to people uncensored is the only way to really get to know them."

He grins. "That I can definitely do."

"Can I ask you a personal question?"

"If you think you can handle the unfiltered, uncensored version of me, then shoot."

I bite my lip, hesitating for a moment. "What's the deal with you and your brother?"

His grin fades. "What do you mean?"

"There's obviously tension between you two. There's history. What happened?"

He plucks a straw wrapper off the table and winds it around his finger. "It wasn't one thing in particular. Our father died when we were too young to remember him. Our mother re-married not long after, unable to support two young boys by herself. Our stepdad is the only father we've ever known, and he's always been a very busy guy. Never had a ton of time to spend with us, but he made the best effort he could when we were young. I guess you could say Ryder and I started competing for his attention at some point, and that competitiveness bled into other parts of our lives."

My face falls in sympathy. "That's unfortunate."

If anyone could understand seeking a father's attention and approval, it's me. But that's not something I openly talk about. With anyone. My relationship with my father is probably the most complicated thing about me, and only Sloane knows the full truth of it. And it took me three years to get that comfortable with her.

Myles shrugs, gaze still on the straw wrapper around his finger. "Our stepfather even encouraged it at times. In his defense, I think he thought he was toughening us up, pitting us against each other in order to make us both stronger. But it just pushed us apart more than anything. We'd get jealous and resent each other if one got more of Dad than the other."

"And now you work for him?"

His expression turns rueful. "It sure as hell wasn't intentional. A few years back, I needed a better paying gig and Dad offered me a job. It just fell in my lap. I didn't have to bust my ass for years like Ryder did."

I purse my lips. "It sounds like you admire him."

"I do. He made something of himself all on his own, just like our Dad did with his steel company. Ryder thinks I started working for him just to rub it in his face. Like, I'm the better son because I'm going to take over the business one day or something. But that's not even sort of the case. I was just desperate for a job at the time."

"Do you want to take over the business some day?"

He cringes. "God, no. I don't even really like the job. But the money is good and what I'd really like to do doesn't come with health insurance and full benefits."

"Pottery," I supply.

His eyes coyly meet mine. "Perceptive little thing, aren't you?"

"I just pay attention."

He sighs. "I've recently started sculpting, too. I'd like to have my own gallery someday. A place where I can feature and sell my work. But I've never been able to make everything come together at the same time."

My heart is melting for this man. I don't know if he normally keeps his guard up around people he doesn't know well, but he's quickly dropped it toward me. In doing so, he's allowed me to see a side of him I doubt many others ever get to.

"Have you told Ryder any of this?"

He tosses the straw wrapper back on the table with a heavy exhale. "Nah. I doubt he'd take me seriously. He just sees me as a kiss-ass and a sellout."

I frown. "I'm sure that's not true. You know, he invests in local businesses. He even helped my friend's helicopter charter business get off the ground. I'm sure if you talked to him, he could help—"

Myles bursts with laughter. "I appreciate the thought, Gretchen. But my brother wouldn't give me money if I was begging for it on the street and living out of a shopping cart."

I can't bring myself to believe that. Ryder might drive me up the wall and back, but he's not a bad person. I think these two brothers are just long overdue for a healthy coming-to-Jesus talk.

Pot, allow me to introduce you to kettle.

I mentally flip the old hag the bird.

"Well, what do you know," Myles mutters sardonically.

My head lifts. "What?"

He nods at something over my shoulder. "What a coincidence."

I turn around in my seat and spot Ryder following the hostess to a table. But oh, he's not alone. Escorting a tall, blonde woman with his hand on her lower back, they wind their way around tables and chairs while she shoots him flirtatious grins over her slim shoulder.

I recognize the slut.

Since when are we catty?

Okay, I don't know where *slut* came from. She probably isn't one. It was just some on-the-spot word association. I took one look at her, at Ryder's hand on her back, at her curve-hugging Donna Karen dress, and *shazam!* Slut. First word that popped in there.

She is, however, a client. Owns a string of hair salons in the area and hired The Colson Group a few months ago to put together an ad campaign for her growing franchise.

Doesn't get involved with anyone he works with, huh?

My Greek ass.

After pulling out her chair for her, Ryder takes his own seat across the table, which happens to face our direction. When he raises his head, his gaze immediately locks onto us. As if he knew we were here the whole time and knew we were watching. He meets my stare head-on, his face stoic, his eyes challenging.

His eyebrow climbs up his forehead. As if to say *you got a problem with something, duchess?*

Ooooh, that motherfu—

"Okay, my turn," Myles interrupts my homicidal thoughts.

I turn back to him apologetically, aware that steam is probably shooting out of my ears.

His expression is thoughtful. "What's the deal with *you* and my brother?"

6

The Business Lunch Face-Off

"THERE IS NO DEAL," I ANSWER MYLES HAUGHTILY, tossing my cloth napkin onto the table in annoyance. "I work for him and our personalities tend to clash."

"Right. Because the look on your face is clearly one of professional indifference."

I bite the inside of my cheek before parroting his words back to him. "Perceptive little thing, aren't you?"

He snorts. "I'd have to be blind not to have seen that. What's the story there? No filter, remember?"

Am I really going to blab to Ryder's own brother about this? A guy I just met? The concept seems strange, but I guess Myles did spill some personal details about his life. It's only fair that I reciprocate.

"I don't know," I confess with undiluted frustration. "I've always had attitude with him because I was under the impression that he didn't remember the two of us having sex. It rubbed me the wrong way when he acted like he'd never met me before on my first day of work."

"Okay, fair enough. But now you know it wasn't him you slept with."

I blanch. "Please, the humiliation was bad enough the first time around."

He chuckles. "Oh, come on. It's an easy mistake to make. Our own mother used to get us confused all the time. We have very few physical differences."

"Well, would it kill you to get a face tattoo or something? Maybe a lip ring?"

His face softens. "For you, I'll consider it."

I slump further down in my chair, pouting. "Not the face tattoo. You're too pretty. It wouldn't be fair to womankind to ruin that."

"Thanks?"

I nod. "Sure thing."

"So, if you know that it was this jackass you slept with that night"—he points at himself—"and not Ryder, then why the death glare?"

I take a sip of my tea, wishing it was more of the Long Island variety than the sweet. "He didn't want me going to lunch with you. He was being a real ass about it. Then he said some things he's never said to me before and..." I squeeze my eyes shut. "Sometimes I just want to throat-punch him."

When I open my eyes again, Myles's features have taken on a measuring quality. Pensive. After too many seconds pass in silence, I clamber for an escape for the first time since I sat down.

"I need to use the restroom. Be right back."

Thank the good Lord the bathrooms are in the opposite direction of Ryder and Slutbag's table. Christ, what is *with* me? I am not that girl. I *never* get jealous. This is probably just sleep deprivation from staying up too late binge-watching *Peaky Blinders* lately. Which would also explain the urge to go on a murderous rampage every time I look at Slutzilla.

Or maybe I just need to get laid.

The Countess is likely to shrivel up and die if the orgasm starvation goes on much longer.

My hand is literally on the bathroom door, about to push it inward, when my wrist is snagged by a much larger hand that drags me into a dimly-lit corner.

"I thought you said you weren't interested in him," Ryder hisses, his mouth only inches away from mine.

Hot momma, he smells good.

And looks good. Anger is a good look on him. Then again, I've seen Ryder pissed off before many times. It's usually the version of him I encounter most often.

This is something else.

Could this possibly be…Jealous Ryder?

After sitting with Myles for the past half hour, I'm definitely noticing the minute differences between the brothers. Ryder has the smallest of dents in the bridge of his nose. The corners of his lips curl upward more than Myles's do. And Ryder has gold flecks in his blue irises that I didn't see in Myles's.

What a shitty day to not wear heels. I have to rise up on my tip-toes just to face off with him. "I believe what I said was, it's none of your business. Which is still true. I'm your employee, Ryder. What do you care who I date?"

He roughly yanks me against his chest, making me gasp. "You're fucking *dating* him?"

"Technically, this is a lunch date. Again, why do you care?"

His eyeballs turn into flaming twin meteors. "Maybe I'm just looking out for my *employee* and trying to save you from Myles's player tendencies. He doesn't usually put others' needs ahead of his own whenever he's going after something he wants."

I jerk back but am stopped by the wall. *When did he push me up against it?* "Like your track record with women is so pristine? Shouldn't you be getting back to Ms. Renard over there?" *Slut.* "I thought you never mixed business with pleasure."

I want nothing more than to bitch slap that smug expression right off his beautiful face. "And why do you care?"

"Just looking out for my *boss*. Ten to one she's sharpening her claws with a nail file as we speak."

His features harden. "It's a business lunch."

I snort. "Does she know that?"

"She called and wants to run another ad campaign. This is the only time she had available to meet."

"How convenient."

When he leans forward, the movement presses our lower bodies together in a way that does some seriously schizo things to my insides. Like, holy horde of cracked-out butterflies. The second I feel how hard he is, I can't rationalize my thoughts to save my life.

All that registers is: *he's hard* and *I want that*.

"Keep talking like that, duchess, and I'm going to start thinking you really *do* care."

I swallow. "I thought I told you to keep me out of your games."

His mouth goes to my temple when he says, "Not a game. Not even close."

"Then why do I feel like I'm being played with?"

He tries to muffle it, but a groan still slips from his mouth. "Trust me, you'll know when I'm playing with you. That's not what this is."

Even though a spark of irritation flickers to life inside me, my hands still clutch his biceps to keep him close. But not too close. "No? You show up to the same restaurant I'm at with your brother, at the same time, and you expect me not to question your motives? I won't be something you hold over your brother's head—"

"Jesus, that's *not what this is*. You're not a prize to be won, Gretchen."

Everything goes still at the tamped rage in his voice. I've known him long enough to recognize when he's telling the truth.

"This has fuck all to do with my brother."

We're both breathing heavily, the sounds blaringly loud in this tiny alcove. Every time we inhale, our chests graze. We notice the contact in the same instant, our heads simultaneously lowering.

And he inches closer.

"Then why now, Ryder? Why are you coming at me like this *now?* Give me something I can believe."

As soon as he opens his mouth, a woman comes out of the bathroom, guiding a toddler by the hand, and almost hits us with the door. She looks up and winces. "Excuse us."

There's the bucket of ice water I needed to stop this madness.

Moment shattered, Ryder steps back with a shaky breath.

He looks at a loss for words, so I save him the trouble. "You should get back to your *business lunch*, boss. Wouldn't want to lose her account now, would we?"

I sneak inside the bathroom before he can deliver the retort I see poised on his tongue. Once I've locked myself safely inside the stall, I walk through the events of the last three minutes.

My boss just rubbed his dick against me. And I leaned *into* it.

You little hussy.

Yeah. Shit's starting to spiral out of control.

7

The Nail and Bail

"YOU ARE SO TOTALLY HOT FOR YOUR BOSS."

I glare at Sloane where she sits in the massaging chair next to me. "Really? Out of everything I just said, that's the best you've got?"

"Your boss is so totally hot for you?" Harper squeaks out cheerfully from the massaging chair on my other side.

I turn my glare on her. "How about a conclusion that might actually yield a helpful solution?"

"If his brother was as good as you say, then Ryder's bound to be a stellar lay, too," Quinn speculates from Harper's other side. "Let him screw you in the break room and find out."

Sue, the nail technician bent over my tootsies, glances up at me with a sly grin.

I groan in exasperation. "You know, I always offer you skanks *useful* advice whenever you're getting your asses kicked by some life crisis. I'm practically Gretchen the Gray with my wisdom and shit."

I feel three heads snap in my direction, but I keep my focus centered on Sweet Sue down there buffing my toenails.

"Uh, you told me to 'pound and rebound' Carter," Sloane points out.

"And you're welcome. Look at all the bowties and suspenders that decision got you."

"You compared the dating pool to a woman's period and told me to take a backseat to my vagina," Harper adds.

"And as your reward for listening to me, you got to have sweaty helicopter sex with your flyboy."

"You told *me* to tickle a man's—"

"Okay!" I cut Quinn off, slicing my hand through the air. "We've established that I'm brilliant and that you three owe me for your smoking hot sex lives. Now, how about something *I* can use?"

Quinn snickers. "I think he's got what you can use."

I roll my eyes. "Clever. Points for Quinnie the Pooh."

"If you're so chalked full of 'wisdom and shit,'" Sloane says, "why are you even asking for our input?"

"Yeah," Harper agrees. "The typical Gretchen approach would be to err on the side of recklessness and not give a hoot and a half."

Quinn nods. "Screw first, don't ask questions later."

"Maybe because I've never dealt with a situation this...delicate before." I sigh. "And maybe because my tried-and-true vagina-driver approach isn't the best course to take here."

We all fall silent as contemplation ensues.

Sloane shrugs in sympathy. "You told me that everyone is capable of having a one-night-stand and it not mean anything. Can you not do that with this one?"

With her porcelain skin and jet-black hair, she could work at Disney World as a Snow White impersonator. She's the studious academic of the group. As a master's student in the history program at Charleston College, she takes her career track just as seriously as I do, so I know she understands my dilemma. Especially since her dumbass ex-husband nearly derailed her entire life. Luckily, she's got herself a sexy, southern gentleman lawyer now who happens to be crazy about her.

"Yeah," Harper interjects. "If you're that attracted to him, why not take one spin on his merry-go-round and get it out of your system?"

Barbie over there hasn't had it easy peasy over the past year either. She might have started her own cosmetics company and given her she-devil mother the heave-ho, but before all of that, she had to live with her then-ex-boyfriend West for six months after they broke up. It was a whole big thing, and it all blew up in dramatic fashion—that I *still* can't believe I missed. Thankfully, they're good now. In love, still living together and all that jazz.

I let out an indecent moan when the massaging mechanism at my back kneads a particularly tight knot. This is an abysmal substitute for sex. I seriously need to get laid. "For one thing, I've already had a one-nighter…with his *brother*."

A low whistle comes from between Sue's lips.

Tell me about it, honey.

"Two, because he's my boss. I have to see him every day. I have to work for him. And I actually love my job. I can't do a nail and bail on Ryder Colson."

No matter how much I might want to.

"What about the brother, then?" Harper asks, closing her eyes in relaxation. "Myles?"

I reflect back on my lunch with Myles yesterday and how much I truly enjoyed myself. I actually liked spending time with him. It weirdly feels like we've known each other for years.

"He seems like a good guy. And he's obviously hot. We got along really well."

Sloane peeks at me out of the corner of her eye. "I have yet to hear the problem. You know now that it was Myles who gave you the best sex of your life, not Ryder. And Myles has suddenly reappeared. How is this even a discussion?"

"The answer seems pretty straightforward to me," Quinn confirms.

Quinnie is our resident horse whisperer. She's short and petite, but she might as well be seven feet tall when she gets up on one of her horses. She breeds and trains equines with her father, and is about as jaded toward love as I am, if not more so. Her father and Harper's mother were married for a brief time when the girls were teenagers. Harper came from money, Quinn didn't, and Quinn resented it. Eventually, the two became besties and their parents divorced. But my guess is that Quinn never really got over growing up poor. I know she's still harboring unpleasant memories from her childhood and there are things she never wants to talk about with us.

And in that, I can relate.

"I'm starting to think I might have beer goggled the unicorn sex," I meekly confess. "I was out celebrating that night with Ross"—my older brother—"because he had just gotten his job with the Coast Guard. I was in a really good mood, and I think I exaggerated how good the sex actually was."

"What makes you say that?" Sloane asks.

Because lunch with Myles yesterday didn't feel the same as our night together did.

Probably because you were sober and not acting like a floosy on the prowl yesterday.

But my girls' heads would explode if I admitted to actually feeling anything that night besides Myles's anaconda inside me. Hell, I might have beer goggled his size, too. If I owned up to feeling something different that night, the interrogation would go on for a week straight.

Oh, my God, Gretchen has feels!

Aw, sweetie, do you think about him all the time? Do you dream about him every night?

Holy balls, you are so going to fall in love.

Blech. No thanks.

Before I met the three of them in college, I was used to having more guy friends than girls. There's no pressure when you're hanging around dudes as friends. There isn't catty chatter, no back-handed competition between each other. Guys are chill and laidback and don't hold grudges the same way girls do.

In fact, that's how it felt being around Myles. Like a friend I go way back with. Talking to him was remarkably comfortable, even companionable. Regrettably, though, not once did I feel the kind of heat I feel with Ryder. There was no throbbing in my nether regions, no desire to maul him like Wolverine.

Conclusion: the sex wasn't what I thought.

Because if it was, wouldn't I feel the remnants of it when I'm near Myles? Wouldn't I sense it? I must have built up the whole thing in my head because the only warmth I felt with him was that of a blooming friendship. I could see myself caring for the man, though never romantically. I could see us getting close in the future, but never intimately.

The way I feel around Ryder, however, is a completely different story.

Out of a completely different book.

It's like apples and oranges. Night and day. Dry and wet.

And speaking of wet...

I can't imagine a world now where I *don't* want to lick the underside of Ryder's jaw just to taste his aftershave. Where I don't fantasize about the other night in the conference room ending with him yanking me across the table and driving into me so hard that we *break* that table. I don't think I'll ever be able to picture those same things happening with Myles. How or why I know that, I can't say.

Intuition, perhaps?

Again, I keep all of this to myself. I don't need the three of them leading me down the yellow brick road to the Wonderful World of Impractical Romantic Notions.

I answer Sloane's question with a nonchalant shrug. "I was just feeling really euphoric that night, with my brother moving back to town and everything. I think it painted the rest of the night's events in—"

Harper bursts into a fit of giggles.

We all look at her.

"Sorry." She wiggles her toes where her nail technician holds a pumice stone. "Ticklish."

Quinn leans around her to look at Sloane. "She's using words like 'euphoric.' Something's definitely up."

"I came here for female advice," I chide, "not a vocabulary analysis."

"You'd never admit to being 'euphoric' about anything unless you were tanked," Sloane says flatly. "We usually get something like, 'I'm gonna start shitting rainbows and unicorns, I'm so stoked.'"

It's rude how well they know me.

"So, there weren't sparks between you and Myles. But there are between you and Ryder."

Like a Chinese New Year parade.

"But he didn't light that fuse until his brother showed up," I point out skeptically. "Now, he's wanting to put in some overtime with me? Awful big coincidence, don't you think?"

"Maybe the jealousy just knocked a screw loose in him," Harper suggests. "After all, he's never had to face competition for you before."

"That's exactly what I'm worried about. Myles admitted to there being a long-standing competitive thing between them. I'm not going to be the toy they fight over."

I watch Sue start applying the first coat of the polish I chose: Rock His World Red. I swear, I didn't notice the name until after I sat down in this chair. Just a wild coincidence that there happens to be a man in my life whose world I want to rock like Ozzy Osbourne at a goth convention.

"Oh, but that playtime would be so much fun," Quinn says wistfully.

Harper purrs like a contented kitty. "Mmm, and you could put them both in timeout when they refuse to share."

Okay, they're making some valid points—

"If we could stop talking like a porno for two seconds," Sloane cuts in. "I don't think that's what Ryder's doing, Gretch. I mean, think about it. Even if there is some sort of competition between them, what happened between you and Myles wouldn't nag at Ryder if he didn't want you for himself."

Even if she's right... "It still doesn't change the fact that he's my boss. If we start something and it ends badly, it could really screw things up with my job."

That's not even skimming the surface of how disturbing my reaction to seeing him with Ms. Renard yesterday was. If we got involved—even if it was just sex—I'm not sure I could handle seeing him with other women. My jealousy at lunch nearly consumed me from the inside out. Like in *Aliens*.

I shudder at the image of a slimy little green monster bursting out of my chest.

And Ryder and I haven't even *done* anything!

"Yeah, that's a hard one," Harper comments.

"That's what Gretchen said."

"Not clever enough, Quinnie," I tell her, disappointed. "I'm deducting points."

Quinn smiles. "I work with what I've got."

"Well, this conversation has been very unproductive," I grumble.

"Oh, I don't know," Sloane muses. "Your nipples are about to rip through your shirt, so I'd say someone has enjoyed herself."

I glance down. She's not lying. Proof positive that merely thinking about Ryder can arouse me. "You checking me out again, Williams?"

"Gretch, those things are like LED headlights right now. People down the street are checking you out."

I blow her a kiss, while making a mental note to wear this shirt around Ryder more often.

First, you're hussy. Now, you're a tease?

The old hag needs to go watch some Wheel of Fortune and stay out of my business.

"Sorry, hon, but I'm not here to be productive," Harper sighs. "I'm here to forget about my worries and my strife. Maybe that's what you should do."

"What? Turn into a cartoon bear named Baloo and go on a honey hunt?"

Quinn starts humming the "Bear Necessities."

"Don't search so hard for answers," Sloane clarifies. "I've learned there isn't a rational solution to every problem."

"What are you saying? That I should do nothing? Isn't graduate school supposed to expand your knowledge base?"

"I think she's saying let whatever's going to happen, happen," Quinn speaks up. "Go with the natural order of things. Sometimes fighting it causes more problems."

"Let me get this straight." Sue curses softly when I lurch forward in my chair, causing her to smear a huge glob of Rock His World all over my big toe. "My Gretchen Gurus, my Saucy *Señoritas*, think I should ignore all the risks, roll over, and just let it ride?"

Quinn nods in approval. "Literally roll over. Onto your back."

"And let Ryder live up to his name," Harper quips.

"If it pleases the Countess," Sloane deadpans, sending them all into cackles.

"Do nothing and give in," I mock. "That's ingenious. Why did I even call this meeting? I could have come up with that all by myself."

Harper reaches over and pats my arm. "Because you'd do anything for a back massage, hon."

"Not true. I wouldn't lick a hobbit's foot."

Quinn makes a gagging sound. "What's with all the *Lord of the Rings* references?"

"Movie marathon on TV this week. And,"—I sigh dreamily—"Orlando."

We all bow our heads in reverence, muttering in unison, "Orlando."

"For what it worth," Sue says in accented English after we all fall quiet. "My vote is for letting him screw you in break room."

A beat of silence passes before we all break out in applause.

I give Sassy Sue a high-five.

Although her words do cause unbidden images of that exact scenario with Ryder to flash through my mind. Of him shoving my skirt up my thighs. Of me tearing off his suit, scattering his shirt buttons all over the floor. Of him biting down on my neck at the precise moment he quietly comes inside me.

The Countess throbs excitedly. Eagerly.

I scoff.

Like it's any mystery where that desperate bitch would cast her vote.

8

The Snakeskin Infraction

"All right, I've got my girls from the Vivacious Vixens cabaret show here in Savannah with me today," Kennedy says, introducing her guests. *"I want to kick off the show by going down the line real quick with your relationship must-haves. What's your biggest requirement in a potential partner? Ready ladies? And go."*

"A nice booty. If my baby don't got back, I'm out."

"If he can make me laugh, sex is almost a guarantee."

"He can't be a dum-dum. One of us has to be the smart one in the relationship and I once got a perm, so…"

"A sweetheart. I want someone who will rub my feet at the end of the day, just because."

"I like a man who's a little possessive of me. Not all psycho controlling, but he'll make other guys in the bar know that I'm taken. A little display of marking his territory goes a long way with me in the bedroom."

"Or a bathroom stall." Silence. "Yeah, don't think we didn't all see you the other night."
All the women break out in laughter.

We have a meeting with our new potential client today, which means it's dress-like-an-adult day for Gretchen.

But because I still have to put my own sassy spin on convention, I pair my form-fitted black pencil skirt that falls just below my knees with a silver satin tank that has a snakeskin print. It's a bit too *trolling the town for some action* for the office, especially with the sexy gold chain that wraps around my neck and holds the material together. Which is why I'm wearing my wine-colored blazer over it. The rich hue happens to match the shade of my new lipstick from Harper's label.

This client has yet to sign a contract with us and if they do, they could become our biggest account. Their decision hinges on today's presentation, as Ryder and I will be going over their budget, timeline, and what TCG can offer them for their upcoming product release, as well as future needs. It's essentially our sales pitch, and we're selling us. TCG. As the senior account manager assigned to this project, I will be leading the presentation.

And if Ryder didn't have to be in the room with me, I'd be hunky-freaking-dory right now. What if I'm incapable of maintaining my composure around him, now that he's basically thrown down the sex gauntlet?

Mute that poison, youngin'. Gretchen Castellanos loses her composure for no man.

Well, if the old hag thinks I can do it, then it must be so.

I'm standing behind my desk chair, bent over as I click the mouse to finish printing out the rest of the documents I need for the meeting, when I hear someone enter my cubicle behind me.

When nothing is said and silence reins over the space, I instinctively know who it is. I purposely snap my head to the side to catch him in the act.

Which I do.

As predicted, Ryder's eyes are shooting laser beams at my ass.

A wicked thrill zings through me. I won't even try to paint on an indignant expression or act in any way like it bothers me. Let him look, let him want. Because I'm looking and I'm wanting, too.

But you're not taking.

When he realizes he's been busted, he doesn't look guilty in the least. He simply closes his mouth, adjusts his cufflinks, and clears his throat. "Ready?"

Turning my head to hide my shit-eating smirk, I grab the last few pages from the printer. "Yep."

Fifteen minutes later, Regina escorts our maybe-clients into the conference room, a Mr. Chadwick and a Mr. Baldwin. Chadwick looks to be in his late fifties, with silver hair and a gold wedding band. Baldwin, however, is lacking both of those. He's a younger man, I'm guessing mid-thirties, with short black hair and a killer smile. Definitely attractive, though nowhere near Ryder's magnetic appeal.

"Good afternoon, gentlemen," Ryder greets them, shaking their hands. He waves to me. "This is one of my senior account managers, Gretchen Castellanos."

"Pleased to meet you, Ms. Castellanos," Chadwick says with a friendly smile. He looks like the type of paternal figure who's happiest when he's in a house full of tiny tots. Like a smooth-faced Santa Claus.

After returning his greeting, I offer my hand to Baldwin. "Very nice to meet you."

He takes my hand, his smile less friendly. It's not *un*friendly. There's just something like...intent regard behind his sharp eyes.

"Pleasure's all mine," he says smoothly.

When he gives my fingers a meaningful squeeze, I know I've got one on the hook that I never intended to bait. After he eventually pulls back to take his proffered seat, I catch Ryder's gaze.

Ohmylantagoodgraciousme.

Boss man did *not* like that.

In fact, he looks like he's performing Darth Vader's Force Choke on poor Baldwin. I'm surprised the man doesn't start clutching his throat and gasping for air. Then Ryder swings that seething glare over to me, his expression accusatory.

And what the hell have *I* done?

He can just stow that fussy attitude and get over himself.

The three men take their seats at the table while I stand in front of the projector screen and go through my presentation slides. Ryder and I both explain what their ad campaign would entail, as well as the kind of return-on-investment they could see with each project based on our market research, broken down by geography and demographics.

As I'm clicking through the slides and detailing every line item, I feel Ryder's eyes dragging down my body, drinking me in. The only time he removes his gaze is when one of the men asks him a question, or he tacks on to something I've said. My palms grow damp around the remote as my body starts to react to the unspoken lust crawling across the table and seeping into my feverish skin. It's a deep, penetrating lust that leaves my mouth so dry I have to stop my speech periodically to take a sip of water. I know my cheeks are flushed because I can feel sweat gathering at the nape of my neck. I don't allow myself to look at him, but it doesn't make a difference.

I *feel* him.

Everywhere.

I also feel Baldwin's gaze. Chadwick is paying more attention to the informational packet in front of him, nodding in agreement and commenting to Baldwin in a low voice. But Baldwin's eyes remain squarely locked on me the entire time. If I wasn't so tuned in to my boss and hate-crushing on him, I'd probably be into the dude. If I met him ten months ago and he made a move, I wouldn't have turned him down.

But that's not even in the realm of possibility now.

For so many stupid reasons.

Once I've finished with my last slide, I sit on the opposite side of the table as Chadwick and Baldwin. Ryder is seated in the head chair, naturally.

"Now, this is just a standard package we've compiled to fit your needs, but it can be adjusted as needed," I explain. "What questions do you have?"

Chadwick immediately starts in with the practical, boilerplate questions I'm used to answering. Despite Ryder's unwavering stare, I'm able to respond intelligently and articulately.

"Your thoughts on our product logo were interesting," Baldwin chimes in, his mouth quirking. "That was my original design."

I force myself not to appear sheepish. It wasn't my intention to offend the man, but I also have a job to do. "And it's clever and creative, don't get me wrong. I just think it could be a bit more straightforward."

Baldwin waves me off. "No, I agree. I like what your team drew up. The lines are cleaner. The message is more succinct. Out of curiosity, was that your design?"

I nod. "I know it's very rough," I rush to say. "I'm not a graphic artist by any means—"

"It's impressive." Baldwin shoots Chadwick an inquiring glance. "I think we might use that instead, actually." Chadwick nods in assent.

A sense of accomplishment warms my blood at their approval. It's nice to have the affirmation that you're doing your job well. I'm not one of those who always seeks validation, but I won't turn my nose up at it when I receive it.

"I thought you could go over this point a little more in-depth," Ryder interjects as he slides his informational packet toward me. He points to a handwritten note in the lower right margin.

Stop flirting with him.

I have to do a double take, just to make sure I haven't suddenly forgotten how to read. My eyes fly up to his. He gives the tiniest, barely perceptible shake of his head. A warning.

The motherfudging *nerve.*

In a client meeting, he wants to pull this crap? *Really?*

Oh, he deserves to suffer for that one.

I paste on a bright smile for the men across from me. "Yes, I agree."

Thinking quickly on my feet to cover up the heated exchange between me and my boss, I do a brief rundown of the potential reach the local billboards and social media ads have. During my breakdown, I casually shrug out of my blazer and drape it over the back of my chair, leaving my arms and shoulders bare in the snakeskin tank.

The armrest of Ryder's leather chair creaks under his tightened grip.

The power move clearly enrages him, especially when Baldwin's eyelids grow heavy after falling on my exposed skin. But in this moment, Ryder's desire is beating out his anger, if the way he's doing the no-hands pants dance in order to adjust himself is any indication.

Another fifteen minutes later, we've wrapped things up and are all pushing to our feet. "We really appreciate you putting this together so quickly," Chadwick says. "We'll make our decision by the end of the week."

Ryder nods. "Excellent. And if you have any questions in the meantime, please don't hesitate to call."

"Do you have a business card?" Baldwin asks me. Not Ryder.

I pat down my skirt. No pockets. "Um, I have some on my desk—"

"You can just call our main line and they'll put you through to me," Ryder cuts in. "If I'm not available, then they'll redirect you to Ms. Castellanos."

Baldwin's gaze darts to Ryder, and they engage in some silent standoff that Chadwick is oblivious to. "You two seem to make a great team."

Ryder's jaw clenches. "We are."

Baldwin glances at me, then back to my boss. "I might have to hire you away from him if anything changes, Ms. Castellanos."

Before I can even open my mouth, Ryder bites out, "It won't."

After several more seconds of their silent standoff, Baldwin eventually nods and trails Chadwick out the door.

I'm *vibrating* with fury. Just when I think his audacity couldn't get more outlandish—more presumptuous—he actually goes and speaks on my behalf in front of a client. If he thinks I'm stupid enough to not pick up on all that man-to-man subterfuge, we don't know each other as well as I thought. And he obviously has much less respect for me than I thought.

"Wow." My voice is dry as I scoop up all my materials and head for the door. "I mean, really...wow."

"What?" Ryder snaps, right on my heels.

"Remind me to bring a tape measurer to the next meeting," I call out as I exit the conference room.

"I don't need one with that little prick. Emphasis on the little."

My feet stumble at the temper sharpening his tone. "That man was perfectly polite."

He's practically on top of me, mouth grazing my ear, when he says, "There's no part of you that man didn't just eye fuck. Since when do you flirt with clients?"

No, the better question is, since when do I get off on my boss battling the green-eyed monster? And devolving into a brutish caveman?

"Who says I was?" I cleverly respond. I drop the stacks of folders in my arms onto my desk with a defiant *thud*. "Besides, if I have to bat my eyelashes a few times in order to score a huge account like this, what's the harm?"

I'm bluffing, but I maintain my poker face. He's right, I never flirt with clients. If I land a new account, I want to know it's because the client is impressed by the reputation and quality of service TCG is known for. Not because they want to become a member of the Countess's court.

Before I can register what's happening, Ryder has me by the elbow and is dragging me through the office at a brisk, albeit forceful, pace. He stands close enough that my co-workers can't see anything inappropriate taking place. And the bastard knows I'm not the type to cause a scene.

He pushes through the double doors and punches the button at the elevator bank. When the doors slide open, he shoves me inside. Then we're enclosed in the cramped space with nothing but our own panting for company. Eyes pinning me in place, he slams his fist onto the emergency stop button, halting the car's descent.

"You've got to be kidding me right now."

"You are not going to flirt with some schmuck just to get his business," he seethes. "I'll fire you before I let that shit happen."

I huff, hands on my hips. "You won't fire me. No one can deal with your intolerable ass better than I can."

His eyes narrow in challenge. "Try me. Take off your clothes in front of a client again and see what fucking happens."

"Stop acting like I just stood up on that table and gave them a striptease. I took off my damn jacket. Big deal."

This car gets a lot more claustrophobic when he launches himself across it and cages me against the elevator wall. His hips mount me to it, his arms trap me in on both sides. His lips are white around the edges from pinching them shut so tightly.

"To Baldwin, you might as well have been shaking your ass for singles," Ryder growls. "Hell, to *any* man. The mere act of exposing this goddamn top was sexual. It was a deliberate move to provoke me, duchess, and you fucking know it."

It's ludicrous how my blood spikes with adrenaline. Nothing has been getting me hotter lately than Ryder being unapologetically direct. And a bit of an asshole. "And why would I want to provoke you?"

His nose nuzzles my jaw. "Good question. Why, indeed? Is it because you like getting a rise out of me?" He gives a sharp thrust of his hips, stealing my breath when I feel his rock-hard erection against my center. "Or because you want to *feel* something rise?"

Houston, all systems are go. We have launch.

And it's fricking glorious.

"This is the second time a man has shown interest in me and you've gone all caveman on his ass. Is there a tattoo on my forehead that says 'Property of Ryder Colson' I'm not aware of?"

His dick jumps against me. "I think that's one of your best ideas yet."

Shock wars with need inside me. It's creating a vortex that's making it difficult to remember why letting him screw me bareback in our office elevator is such an epically bad idea.

"I'm your employee, Ryder. But I'm not *yours*."

"I'll give you a little more time to keeping thinking that."

"What's that supposed to mean?"

A soft rumble comes from the back of his throat as his head lowers over my neck. "You're a quick learner. You'll catch up."

He inhales the scent of my perfume and groans. Against my better judgment, I crane my neck to the side to give him more access. His hot breath caresses my skin, but his mouth never makes contact.

And great balls of fire, how I want it to.

"If this is still about a competition," I rasp, "you said it yourself...I'm not some prize to be won."

He chuckles darkly. "My words were misleading. You are a prize, duchess. Just not the type you win after tossing a ring at milk jugs at the state fair. You're the type you wait patiently for, work tirelessly for. The type that your whole life builds up to. And the type that once claimed, makes everything else you think matters seem superfluous in comparison."

My breath shudders out of me in a gargantuan tidal wave of confusion, distress, and…longing? No, that can't be right. I'm just on edge with the need to release some of this pent-up sexual tension, and Ryder is using all the right moves to get me there. It doesn't go deeper than that.

But his words…

"That's why you make a man want to win you." He stiffens, as if realizing he actually did say that out loud. Then he relaxes again. "That is, if you can ever get past your own stubborn pride and sassy mouth long enough to let him."

"Both have been working well for me the past twenty-five years," I say breathlessly.

Why can't I take a deep breath?

He grunts. "Don't I know it. And every other man who meets you does, too."

"You're really starting to sound like a jealous boyfriend."

Jesus C, did I really just hit him with the "b" word?

He slides his finger beneath the gold chain around my neck and lightly tugs. My head falls against the wall as a hiss escapes my lips. He gnashes his teeth, like he's restraining the urge to pierce my flesh with them.

"If you don't like it, then stop pulling shit like you did in the conference room," he grates out. "I know that move was more for me than it was for him—"

"Think what you want, boss."

He gives the chain another tug, tightening it against my throat. "If you want to show me your body, you do it when it's just the two of us. When *my* eyes are the only ones to see it. Understand?"

"That's never going to happen."

With blown pupils, his gaze travels the length of me, unhurried. "Your body says otherwise. You've been burning up ever since you saw my reaction in that room."

"Did you ever think that maybe I was just hot in there?"

His mouth curls in a crooked grin. "Oh, you were definitely hot. But I don't think removing your jacket cooled you off at all. In fact, I think you're on fire right now."

I wiggle my hips, intentionally nestling his bulge into the notch between my thighs. "Seems I'm not the only one."

"Now who's playing games, duchess?"

The tip of his tongue snakes along the pulse point at my throat. My eyes roll back in my head—

His shrill ringtone severs the heady tension.

He doesn't immediately reach for the phone. Instead, he lifts his eyes to mine, as if trying to burrow inside them so he can read my every thought. Finally, his finger releases the gold chain and he steps back, putting some much-needed distance between our bodies.

Empty.

Already, I miss feeling that heaviness between my thighs.

Jaw clenching, he reaches inside his pocket and answers the call. At the same time, he punches the emergency stop button, sending us careening back up to our floor. He speaks to the person on the other line in clipped sentences, before eventually hanging up without a goodbye.

When the doors open with a *ding*, I'm still stuck to the wall like a smashed bug on a windshield. I'm prepared to ride this baby up and down the floors all afternoon if that's how long it takes to get my shit together.

With his back to me, Ryder exits the car. Doesn't say another word—

His hand flies out before the doors can close.

He glares at my bare shoulders. "Go put your jacket back on, and get some fucking work done."

Then he's gone.

I rush back to my computer to look up the number for a cheap therapist.

Because I need a licensed professional to explain to me why the hell I was *smiling* as I stepped off that elevator.

9

The Shelf Life of Love

THANKSGIVING WITH THE CASTELLANOS IS ALWAYS A SMALL, uneventful affair. With my mom's mother in an assisted living facility down in Jacksonville, we don't see her often. And my father isn't very close with his father, who lives in upstate New York near my uncle and his family.

It's just me, Ross, Mom, and the Major, a.k.a., Dad. We've been ordered to call him that ever since we could talk.

And if that isn't a sign of overwhelming paternal affection, I don't know what is.

Flashing the security guard the special clearance badge I've been issued as the Major's daughter, I'm waved through the gate and onto the Joint Air Force Base on the outskirts of Charleston. My father is a military lifer, born and bred. He enlisted the second he turned eighteen, and I don't think he's ever wanted to know anything else in life. He met my mother in his early twenties when he was stationed in Tampa. She was fresh out of high school and married him right away instead of going on to college.

After they had Ross and I, the Major moved us around the country a lot. We rarely stayed in one city longer than two years. I've only lived in Charleston since my junior year of high school, and I was determined to make a life for myself here after I graduated. It just so happens that the Major was offered a cushy gig at the Joint Base around that time, so he and Mom decided to make Charleston their permanent home base, as well.

Truth? I don't really know my father. Like, at all.

I barely know my mother.

But my brother and I couldn't be closer.

I love Ross so much, I have no idea how I would have survived my childhood under the Major's roof if it wasn't for him. Which is why when Ross enlisted in the Navy at nineteen, I wanted to hate him. I went a little batshit teenager crazy on him, screaming that he was going to end up just like our father—a cold, emotionless cyborg. I ranted and raved that he was carelessly abandoning me, all because he didn't want to disappoint the Major. Everyone knew he had expected Ross to go military at some point.

Thankfully, my panic and hysteria were just by-products of adolescent hormones.

Ross is nothing like the Major.

He had just been wading through the limbo of uncertainty back then. Hadn't yet figured out what he wanted to do with his life and had joined the Navy to at least get his college paid for while he did. Turns out, he actually liked what the Navy had to offer. He completed his term of service and now works for the Charleston Coast Guard.

I let myself into my parents' two-story, cookie-cutter house that looks identical to every other house on the street. Their nine-year-old Australian terrier, Luna, eagerly greets me at the door, nails clacking on the hardwood floor, tail wagging excitedly.

"Hey, girl," I coo, scratching behind her ears. "Mom stuffed you full of roast yet?"

Since she isn't passed out on her pillow that's the size of an innertube with her tongue lolling, I'm guessing not.

"Gretch, that you?" Ross calls from the kitchen.

I shrug out of my jacket and hang it on the coat rack. "Yeah!"

"Would you please get in here and convince Mom that I'm actually capable of stirring the gravy? Since apparently there's nothing else I can be trusted with."

I enter the kitchen, holding the pumpkin roll I bring every year. It's literally the only dessert I can make successfully. I figure if I can bake just one thing amazingly well, it's better than being mediocre at a bunch of others.

"After last year with the cranberries, I can't say I blame her," I say dryly.

Ross's head whips around to me. "They boiled over *once*, and a tiny bit spilled onto the stove."

"The smoke alarms went off, Ross."

"And did anything catch on fire? I don't *think* so."

I catch Mom's eye. "Well, I'm sold. Let's just let him cook the whole meal."

Mom nods as she cuts up sweet potatoes on the butcher's block. "As long as you didn't bring your appetite with you, I think that'll work."

Ross stomps across the kitchen, scowling. With that expression he looks exactly like his father's son. Dark complexion that never has to see the sun. Curly, black hair. And the same shape of narrowed, brown eyes, though the color is from our mother.

"Why don't I just go crack a beer and watch the Major grill outside?" Ross snipes.

I point at him. "*That* you excel at. Stick with what you know."

He grabs said beer out of the fridge and kisses the top of my head on his way out the back door to join our father at the grill where he's smoking the turkey like he does every year. I just had dinner with Ross last weekend, but he always greets me like that, no matter how much time has passed since seeing each other.

When I need a big brother, he's always there.

When I need a surrogate father around, because ours is somewhat lacking in that arena, Ross steps in to fill that role, too.

No clue how he does it, but he always manages to know which one I need him to be in any given situation.

The Major has had a closed-door policy on emotions ever since we started having them. I've never been able to talk to him about anything meaningful in my life, same with Mom. She'll open up to a point, but once things start getting deep, she balks. There are no mushy gushy, "love is free and abounding" vibes in our family. No kumbaya around the campfire. No sharing is caring.

In fact, I can sum up our father's parental guidance with one painful incident. When I was eight, our eleven-year-old German Shephard died from bone cancer. He'd been our family dog since I was born, and as a little girl, I was understandably devastated when he had to be put down. The Major's words to me as I sobbed over my dinner that night were, "Pain and loss build character, Gretchen. They make you stronger. The longer you hold on to a pet you can't bring back, the weaker you'll become."

Needless to say, he didn't get a lot of "Best Daddy Ever" coffee mugs for Christmas.

Part of me resents it.

The other part of me is grateful for it.

Learning how not to be ruled by my emotions has taught me to be a more independent, self-possessed individual. Sloane says it's turned me into a Feelings Nazi.

Can't change your raisin'.

"What do you need help with?" I ask Mom, pushing up the sleeves of my sweater.

Standing next to her, I feel like a giant because she's so petite. In fact, I think the one thing I actually inherited from her was my dark chestnut hair color. My skin tone, eye color, height and general build, and wavy hair are all thanks to those Greek genetics from the Major.

"Um." She looks up from her sweet potatoes to glance around the kitchen. "You got the green bean casserole?"

"It's my jam."

Thirty minutes later, everything is out of the oven, off the stove, and pulled off the grill. As always, Mom and I stick to the safe topics of discussion: our jobs, friends, and the weather. She's a receptionist at a veterinary clinic a few miles away. As long as I can remember, she's worked desk jobs like that, never too far from home. What I've never been able to figure out is why she turned down a music scholarship to follow the Major around everywhere. According to Grandma, Mom was a very gifted violinist in her youth. And when she turned down that scholarship, their relationship was never the same again.

The one thing Grandma couldn't tell me was why Mom did it.

"Gretchen," the Major greets me, gruff and monotone.

Aaaaand that's all the intimacy I'm going to get.

My father is a big man. If you didn't know him, you might assume he retired from a long career in the WWE. Tall, bulky, square jawline that's always free of facial hair, and a buzz cut. When I was a kid, I used to think he looked like an action figure. Especially since his face is always frozen in the same stoic, smile-less expression. When people tell me I look like him, I'm not sure how to take it. His Greek ancestors passed along the dark skin gene to me, sure. Same with the dark chestnut hair.

But do I always look that surly?

The four of us sit down at a table that has far too much food, with a steaming turkey as the mouthwatering centerpiece. Despite the disconnection I feel around my parents, I have no trouble tucking into the homemade meal. Plus, Ross and I are used to breaking up the stifling monotony with sarcastic jokes and incessant sibling ribbing. Our parents have become content to just let the two of us lead the conversation—or carry it entirely—as they sit back and listen.

"How's the promotion going, Gretch?" Ross asks just before shoving a forkful of mashed potatoes in his mouth.

We talk all the time, so he's already well aware of how things are going at TCG. Except for that small issue where my boss has been shoving innuendo down my throat and coming at me like he could devour me in one bite. He's only asking for our parents' benefit.

"You got a promotion?" the Major barks.

His voice always comes out as a bark, so you can never really gauge his mood.

"Yeah, about a month ago. To senior account manager."

Several of the account managers at TCG are under forty, but I'm by far the youngest with the "senior" title. No one can say I haven't earned it, though. In the ten months I've been there, I've brought in six major new accounts, single-handedly. And I'm oftentimes one of the last people in the office. After all, it's not like I have a husband and kids waiting for me at home.

The Major keeps his head down, attention on his food, when he mutters, "You never mentioned that."

Feeling admonished, I squirm in my chair. "Sorry. Been pretty busy since then. New promotion, bigger workload, you know?"

"But you're liking it?" Mom asks.

I swallow a bite of turkey before answering. "I am. We just landed a huge account that has the potential to open a lot more doors for the company." Chadwick called last Friday and gave the green light to have contracts drawn up.

"Good," is all the Major says in response.

The awkward silence that follows requires a subject change. "You still seeing the pediatrician, Ross?"

He shakes his head. "Nope. She's too focused on her career right now to want anything serious. Seemed like we were just wasting our time."

Ross has never been a playboy or the serial dater that I've been. Ever since we were teenagers, he's always wanted to get married and have a big family. He was even engaged once, but they broke it off right before he joined the Navy.

Neither of us can seem to find the elusive One.

Though I'll be honest, I haven't really been trying that hard.

People place far too much pressure on finding the ideal mate at the ideal time in one's life. And if it doesn't go according to their exact plan, stress and unhappiness are inevitable. But newsflash to all you singles with a "plan" out there: you are *not* doomed to a life of misery if things don't follow your playbook, step-by-step. I've always subscribed to the belief that when it's supposed to happen, it'll happen.

"Having a career can definitely get in the way of creating a family," the Major murmurs between bites, keeping his head down. "You're probably better off finding a woman who's not so work-oriented."

This isn't the first time the Major has poignantly brought up this particularly touchy subject in my presence. And like every other time, I instantly bristle. "Women can have families *and* a career these days. Believe it or not, we've come a long way since the suffragettes. It's called progress."

Now the Major looks up. "Watch it."

I grind my teeth, refusing to feel like a scolded child. "Yes, sir."

He sighs, his fork clattering to his plate. "All I'm saying is that a woman will have more time for a family if she's not so devoted to her job. I've never said that a wife and mother *can't* work."

"Devoted to her job like me, you mean?"

The tension in the room amplifies until I hear a buzzing in my ears as my father and I lock horns.

His spine is military-straight, his shoulders rigid. "You've done well for yourself, Gretchen. But you can't deny that focusing on this career path has hindered you from getting married and having children. You couldn't have done both this entire time."

"Because I haven't *wanted* to," I sputter, aghast. "For God's sake, I'm only twenty-five. I got my master's degree just over a year ago. Are you actually saying I shouldn't have gotten my degree and become self-sufficient, which by the way, is something you've always impressed upon us?"

He picks his fork back up and continues to shovel corn into his mouth. "I just don't want you to waste your younger years—"

"On a career that makes me happy?"

"It makes you happy now, but you may not feel the same way when you look back on it in ten years."

At a loss, I look to Mom for support, but she hasn't lifted her head. Hasn't uttered a word. I have to remind myself that she won't support me on this subject because she was my complete opposite at this age. She ran head-first into marriage and motherhood and trailed my father around the country without question.

"There's no rush," Ross steps in, saving me from saying something I'll regret. "Gretchen is becoming successful in her field, she's paying her dues and being responsible, and she's happy with her situation. If it's good enough for her, it should be good enough for everyone."

I owe Ross for countless rescues from our father over the years. I don't know if it's a guy thing or a military thing or what, but he always knows how to put the Major in his place—or at the very least, shut him up.

The Major doesn't say another word. Just stabs a hunk of roast with his fork and chews quietly.

Another grand 'ol Castellanos Thanksgiving.

Ross and I wash dishes together after lunch, standing side-by-side at the sink.

"You really okay?" He hands me a serving bowl to dry. "You seem a little off today."

I wipe the bowl with my dishrag, probably more vigorously than necessary. "Yeah, I'm fine. Just a lot of work stuff on my mind."

"The boss still being a dick?"

Funny you mention dicks. Because I had his bad boy grinding up against me the other day.

Ross has been aware of my combative relationship with Ryder ever since I started working for him. But because I'd rather strap on Lady Gaga's meat dress and go on a bear hunt than discuss my sex life with my brother, Ross has no idea *why* there's been constant quarrelling between the two of us.

"He's actually a little better," I vaguely answer.

His hands pause in their scrubbing. "Yeah?"

What is that in his voice? Curiosity?

I turn away to put the dry silverware back in the drawer. "Yeah. I think we're finally beginning to understand each other."

Or just understand how to make each other super horny.

"Well, that's good." Ross resumes his washing. "Glad to hear it."

Several minutes pass where silence engulfs the kitchen, both of us seeming too lost in our own thoughts to break it. As I glance out the back window, my gaze falls on Mom and the Major sitting in the screened-in porch, doing what they do best.

Not talking.

The Major's watching football and Mom's reading a book. Not sitting beside each other. Not even looking at each other. I can count on one hand how many conversations I've actually heard them have over the years. Probably because they have next to nothing in common, at least from what I can tell. It's like they've spent their entire marriage living in a silent movie from the 1930s.

"I'll never understand them."

Ross raises his head to follow the direction of my gaze. And sighs. "Me either. But marriage looks different to everyone. Whatever their relationship is, it's worked for them for thirty years."

"Or Mom has just never had the courage to leave him."

"Do you really think she wants to?"

I wave at them. "How can she be happy? She never acts like it. Hell, he doesn't either. He's more robot than human, and she's never had a backbone. Where is the appeal for either of them?"

"Who are we to say there isn't any?"

Playing devil's advocate has always been one of Ross's strengths.

"We might be their kids, but we're still outsiders. No one knows what goes on inside their marriage except the two of them."

I smirk, bumping his shoulder with mine. "How is it that you're a bigger romantic than I am?"

He snorts. "Because you got more of the Major's personality traits than I did. And I don't mean that as an insult," he quickly adds when I open my mouth. "I just mean you're a tougher nut to crack."

"And what are you? The gooey caramel center?"

He puffs out his chest. "Damn right. Women like some sweet with their salty."

I shake my head, grinning. "All I'm saying is if that's what marriage looks like, I'm certainly in no hurry to tie the knot."

In fact, I'm starting to think that romantic love might have a shelf life. It only stays fresh for so long. And in my parents' case, the expiration date probably fell around the ten-year mark, and then it all started to fade. I believe it was Marilyn Monroe who once said:

"Love is rare. Life is strange. Nothing lasts and people change."

A bit bleak, perhaps, but the woman knew what she was talking about.

"Why do you think I refuse to settle?" Ross asks. "I'll wait until I'm fifty to get married if that's how long it takes to find the right woman."

"Do you think that's what it is? They both settled?"

He shrugs, his hands still submerged in the sudsy water. "Who knows? They haven't told us anything about themselves when they were young. It's anyone's guess what brought them together."

My mind inadvertently goes to Ryder and our confusing, bipolar relationship. All the twists and turns it's taken. I have to admit we seem to have some things in common, at least in terms of our work ethic and professional mindset. Other than that, I know approximately zilch about the man, except what Myles has told me.

Myles.

This is where it gets hella confusing. As I told the girls, I could see us actually becoming friends.

But Ryder...I could see us having mind-blowing sex.

Is it just the whole taboo of sleeping with my boss that has me pumped, primed, and ready to go? Is all this pent-up lust due solely to the excitement of doing something I know I shouldn't? Is the wicked notion of getting caught with our pants down in the office fueling all the fire between us? Because if so, the typical pattern dictates that once I have what I'm after, I'll immediately lose all interest in it. The thrill will be gone, and I'll be forced to move on. Same goes with him.

Two men. Who look exactly alike.

One is comfortable friendship.

One is passionate heat.

Of course, the latter sounds more fun in the present, but the former is safer long-term. Stable. Secure.

It's easier to build a foundation on friendship than sex, right? Passion and lust can fade. But companionship, once solidified, can withstand far more. I felt some kind of connection with Myles that night ten months ago. Looking back on it, maybe it was nothing more than the platonic intimacy I felt during our lunch date. But for me to constantly reflect back on it tells me that it meant *something*.

I can work with something.

To not pursue that connection feels like a waste. Like I'd be giving up. What if I just haven't looked deep enough with Myles yet? What if I'm missing out on something incredible?

So, when Myles calls me the very next day to ask me to dinner, I agree.

While ignoring the fleeting disappointment that it's not Ryder's voice in my ear.

All that means is that I seriously need to get laid.

And call that therapist.

10

The Jazz Club Scuffle Shuffle

REAL TALK ROMANCE, EPISODE 9

"Today is all about first dates, folks," Kennedy *announces* *enthusiastically. "The critical, make-or-break moment in a couple's existence. We're going to go through the dos and don'ts of those first impressions later, but right now, I want to hear your worst first date stories."* Click, click. *"I've got Myra on the line with her traumatic tale. Let's hear it, girl."*

"Hey, Kennedy," Myra *says in greeting. "So, I was out on this first date a few years ago with a guy I met online. He seemed nice enough during dinner, if not a little shy. I could tell he didn't get out much, but I'm fine with the reserved types. It was when he brought me back to his apartment that shit got real weird."*

Kennedy *chuckles. "Oh, I like where this is going."*

"He turned into a completely different person," Myra *goes on. "Started talking relentlessly about his cat that had just died two weeks before, and apparently, he was still pretty depressed about it. Kennedy, he would* not *stop talking about the cat. I mean, it was* constant. *Like it was his child or something. And*

sure enough, there was a shrine to the cat in his living room. Eventually, I went into the kitchen to get a glass of water. And when I opened the freezer to get some ice, you will never guess what I found."

"His mother's severed head," Kennedy tosses out.

"His cat!"

Kennedy explodes with laughter.

"I am not making this shit up. His dead cat's frozen body was stuffed into the freezer, right next to fucking ice cream!"

"What did you do?" Kennedy asks between wheezes.

"I told him that dogs rule and cats drool and I got the hell out of there."

Myles's eyes run over me when I open the door for our date. And I feel…warm. But no tingles, no stirrings.

No heat.

My shoulders slump in dejection, but I'm not giving up yet. It's not that I'm actively chasing down a relationship with anyone. It's just that everything in my head would make so much more sense if I felt something deeper for *this* man.

I lift my chin. "'Sup."

"Yo." It takes him a moment to pry his eyes off my body and connect them with mine. "You look amazing."

"So do you."

And he does.

His gray Henley molds to his sculpted pecs and broad shoulders. His sleeves are shoved up to his elbows, the silver watch on his wrist glinting under the light of the sconces outside my door. His dark jeans are crisp and in like-new condition, giving the impression that he doesn't wear them often. I suppose managing a steel manufacturing factory wouldn't require three-piece suits.

I chose a charcoal poly/wool blend dress with a flared skirt. The neckline is cut into a V, showing a hint of cleavage. Being the end of November, there's a little bite to the air, but because it's Charleston, my thin black stockings and leather jacket are enough to keep me warm. My suede ankle boots place my face at his throat, but I still have to crane my neck to look at him. I twisted a small portion of my hair into a bun on top of my head and went all out with the makeup. The smoky eye highlights my silver irises, and the berry lipstick infuses the right amount of color into the look.

His grin is lopsided and adorable. Ryder doesn't have many adorable grins like that. What he does have is about four different versions of a *I'm going to fuck you so hard you'll feel the imprint of my dick inside you for a week* grin.

Second commandment.

Right. I'm on a date with Myles, so I'm going to be on a date *with Myles*.

"I feel like this is the part where I should extend my arm and say something gentlemanly like, 'Nice night for a stroll, milady. Shall we?'"

I clasp my hands together and rock back on my heels. "And are you going to?"

He shrugs. "Eh."

Then he just saunters off without waiting for me.

A laugh bubbles up my throat as I lock my door. "Ass."

"Heard that!" he says over his shoulder.

"You were supposed to!"

He barks out a laugh that echoes off the brick walls of my building. By the time I reach his truck parked along the curb, he's holding the passenger door open for me. I lift an inquiring eyebrow.

He winks. "Well, I can't be completely predictable. Got to keep you on your toes."

"I wouldn't recommend it if you're planning on buying me drinks. I turn into Calamity Jane after I've had a few."

"Then let's see how quickly we can get you to a few."

❖

Myles takes us to a swanky new jazz club downtown that opened a few months ago. I've been dying to come here, but haven't had time with work lately. We're squeezed into a small table just off the side of the stage, in the middle of a packed house.

"Great choice." I drape my purse strap and jacket over the back of my chair. "How did you know I like jazz?"

His look of surprise answers my question before his words do. "I didn't, actually. I've just been hearing great things about this place, so I figured we'd try it out. I'm not even a huge jazz fan."

I make a *pfft* sound. "Poser."

"Hey, I can appreciate the sound without loving the genre."

As I incline my head in agreement, I can't help but recall how much Ryder enjoys jazz. More than once he's had it playing through a speaker in his office when we've worked late nights together. We even favor a lot of the same artists.

"I'll go get us some drinks," Myles says, standing up.

After relaying my order, I hunker down in my chair to listen to the set. It's a local band I've never heard of, but they've got a smooth hook to their rhythm. I'm already digging their style and making a mental note to pass their name along to Ryder.

My phone buzzes with a text from my dress pocket. Normally, I wouldn't look at it while on a date, but since Myles hasn't returned from the bar yet, I figure I'll make it quick.

When Ryder's name pops up on the screen and my heart does a little kick, much like the percussion of the drums onstage, I know I'm in deep shit. Nothing has kicked around inside me with Myles all night. Not even a slight poke. But just seeing Ryder's name is like feeling the kickback of a twelve-gauge shotgun.

RYDER: *Check your email. Just sent you the updated spec sheet for the Chadwick account. They want to add a local radio spot.*

As much as I itch to check my inbox because I'm obsessed with my job—and possibly with my boss—I refrain.

ME: *Can't right now. Busy. Will check it later.*

RYDER: *You're busy, yet you're texting me...*

To make my point, I set my phone back down on the table and don't respond.

Until another text comes through.

RYDER: *Busy doing what?*

ME: *None of your business.*

RYDER: *Are you on a date, Gretchen?*

Why do I feel like I should apologize? I'm not doing anything wrong, dammit.

ME: *Again, NOYB.*

RYDER: *Is it with my brother?*

I flinch.

Even in my own head, I read that in a curt tone, imagining exactly how Ryder would voice the question. Responding would send this exchange plummeting down a dark, dank sinkhole. Nothing good can come from that. So, I don't reply.

As if *that* brilliant plan was going to work.

RYDER: *Fucking ANSWER ME.*

Yeesh. Someone needs to change his tampon.

I decide to give him his precious little answer because I've got nothing to be ashamed of. After all, what the hell is he going to do about it? Fire me for dating his brother?

ME: *Yes.*

Myles returns to the table, drinks in hand, right as I send that. "Belly up. I'm dying to meet Calamity Gretchen."

Ain't gotta tell me twice. Just need to pop a Prilosec and it's down the hatch.

I tip back my glass, needing the burn of the liquor to numb every sexually-charged neuron in my brain. Myles's own glass freezes halfway to his mouth as he watches me gulp down the gin and tonic. When his phone chimes with a text, I pour even more down my gullet without pausing. I have a feeling I know exactly who's messaging him. He pulls the device out of his pocket and quickly scans the screen.

His eyes shoot to mine.

Bingo.

A satisfied smirk overtakes his features as he types out a response before stowing the phone back in his pocket. I don't bother asking who it was or what was said, and he doesn't offer the information. I'm determined to enjoy the rest of the night with a perfectly nice guy and my perfectly nice drink, without thinking about my perfectly douchey boss.

Our conversation after that moves from one random topic to the next, our banter flowing as easily as it did at lunch last week. He makes me laugh, I make him smile, and my drink makes me forget Ryder's bullshit.

For a little while anyway.

By the end of the band's set, I've heard Myles's phone go off at least a dozen times. Once the band exits the stage and the room has quieted down somewhat, Myles blows out an annoyed breath and yanks the device out of his pocket once again.

"Oh, for fuck's sake," he mutters under his breath.

"What's up?"

His mouth tightens into a firm line. "Nothing. I'm sorry, but is it cool if we call it a night?"

I frown. I was just starting to really relax. *Thanks, buzz. You're always there for me when I need you.* "Sure. Is everything okay?"

There's a wry curl to his mouth. "I guess we're about to find out."

Wha-wha-whaaaat does that mean?

Ah, even the old hag is tipsy. She's a fun drunk, that one.

Myles drives me back to my loft, his behavior a complete one-eighty from when he picked me up. His hand has a death grip on the steering wheel, and a vein keeps popping out on his neck. No longer smiling or teasing, he's well and truly miffed about something.

What am I missing here?

He pulls to a stop at the curb and throws the truck in park. Something grabs his attention down the street. "Are you fucking serious?"

"What is it?"

I look in that direction but don't see anything out of the norm.

He gets out of the truck without answering me and comes around to my side. I'm experiencing such whiplash over how drastically this night has shifted gears that I'm in a daze whenever he throws open my door and gingerly helps me down.

"Myles, did I do something to upset you?"

Tipping his head up at the night sky, he releases a long-suffering sigh. "Not at all, Gretchen. I'm sorry for how the night ended." Something over my shoulder again catches his eye, igniting a mischievous sparkle in it. "But I'm not sorry about this."

"About wh—"

My eyes shoot wide when he stamps his mouth over mine.

I mean, the man's lips feel great and all, but—

His mouth is ripped away as a ferocious, yet very familiar, growl reaches my ears.

"You mother*fucker*."

The next thing I know, I'm staring at Ryder's back as his fist flies through the air and cracks against his brother's jaw.

11

The Stamp of ~~Ownership~~ Denial

REAL TALK ROMANCE, EPISODE 25

"What's your stance on jealousy?" Kennedy asks her best friend. "Is it the ugliest of emotions, or can it be a reflection of a person's commitment to a relationship?"

"I think there are degrees of jealousy," her best friend answers matter-of-factly. "There's territorial jealousy, where an individual stakes his or her claim on you in public, warning others to back off if they get too close. Then there's possessive jealousy, where the individual wants you all to themselves and doesn't want to share you with others. Then there's paranoid jealousy, where they go ballistic over the smallest things and do their best to completely cut you off from the outside world. They'll take whatever action is necessary to remove you from any other relationship you have because they're always panicking that you'll leave them."

"Then is jealousy good or bad?"

"I think it depends on what motivates it. If the emotion stems from love for the other person, then it can be a justifiable reaction. But if it's simply a means of asserting control over the

other person, or just a show of dominance toward a competitor, then it can be unhealthy."

"So, whenever you tweeted a dick pic of your ex after he was seen talking to his ex-girlfriend, was that the healthy kind of jealousy or the psychotic kind?" Kennedy asks, choking on her laughter.

"That was constitutional retribution, not jealousy," her best friend snaps. "Because they didn't just talk. He told his buddies later that she jacked him off in the bathroom."

"Then posting that tweet was your first mistake. When you're planning a murder, you never leave a paper trail."

"Not if killing his social life was my plan all along," her best friend retorts. "I don't think he got too many hand jobs after that tweet."

"Why do you say that?"

"Let's just say that the man's ego was his biggest attribute."

I'm frozen in horror as Myles's head snaps to the side from the force of Ryder's punch, sending him stumbling back a step.

"Ryder, stop!" I rush forward and clamp my hands down on his arm to prevent him from delivering anymore blows. "What the hell are you doing?"

Ignoring me, he stabs his finger in Myles's direction. "I *told* you to stay the fuck away. You knew what I would do if you touched her."

Uhhhmmm...

I gape at my boss like he just grew pointy ears and started speaking Vulcan.

When Myles straightens, he's...smiling? With a bloodied lip, he looks at his brother with unbridled pleasure. "I've never been a good listener, though, have I? I've got years of report cards to prove it."

"Jesus, are you okay?" When I move to inspect his lip, Ryder's fingers close around my wrist in a lightning-fast move. I glare at him over my shoulder. "Back off, Ryder. I mean it."

He lets go without taking his eyes off his brother. When I pull a tissue from my purse and dab at Myles's lip, he doesn't even flinch. Just continues watching Ryder in some sort of secret staring contest I don't seem privy to. Honestly, I'm not sure I even want to understand what the hell's going on here.

Myles gently pushes the tissue away, smiling softly down at me. "How do you feel about men with scars?"

"I'm sorry," I whisper, for once not feeling the joke. "I don't know what just happened. I didn't mean for the night to go this way."

His thumb caresses my cheek. "You've got nothing to apologize for. I knew what I was doing."

By taking me out? Or by kissing me?

I don't get a chance to ask either question because Ryder goes all asshole again. "You're done here, Myles."

"What the hell is your problem?" I glare at Ryder so hard I worry I'm going to pull a muscle in my face. "We were having a great night before you showed up and ruined it."

His eyes blaze with fiery rage as they swing back to Myles. "And now the night's over."

"*Excuse* me—"

"It's fine," Myles insists, his hand rubbing down my arm in reassurance. "Tell Calamity Gretchen I'll take a raincheck. We'll talk soon, okay?"

"Stop touching her, goddammit."

When Ryder bares his teeth like an animal, I'm tempted to smack him upside the head with a rolled-up newspaper and treat him like one. "Myles, you don't have to go."

He chucks me under the chin, winking. "I've got an early morning anyway. I had fun tonight. You might have actually turned me on to jazz."

That manages to pry a smile from me, though it's weak.

He shoots Ryder one last stormy look before getting into his truck and driving off. My fists clench at my sides as I watch his taillights disappear, my nails cutting into my palms. Mount St. Gretchen is about to erupt all over the goddamn place and burn Ryder's ass to a crisp.

I spin around and shove him. He's so much bigger than me, I know I couldn't move him if he didn't want me to. But he takes it. "What the *fuck* was that? Huh? What are you doing here, Ryder! Why are you suddenly all up in my business all the damn time?"

I shove him again. He takes it again.

"You're not his to have, duchess," he says baldly.

This shove is the hardest.

"Christ, I'm not yours either! You and I are nothing to each other. If this is all still about that bullshit competition between you two, it stops *now*. I won't be pulled into this again."

Unable to formulate any thoughts that don't end with me stabbing him with my nail file, I push past him and whip open the door to my building. I've been screaming like a madwoman on the sidewalk of a residential area. It would be just my luck to have one of my neighbors call the cops.

Then again, seeing Ryder hauled away in handcuffs does have a certain appeal.

His footsteps pound inside the building after me.

I pick up my pace toward the stairs. "You can let yourself back out."

"Not a fucking chance."

I've barely reached the first stair when Ryder's hand grips my upper arm and hauls me backward. He pulls me around to the darkened cranny beneath the stairs and roughly shoves me against the wall.

"When are you going to get it through your head, duchess?" he hisses through clenched teeth. "This has never been about some fucking competition. Not for me."

The second the last word leaves his lips, he slams our bodies together, nearly knocking the breath out of me. His mouth covers mine, silencing my litany of four-letter words. He swallows them all into his mouth with a masculine groan of unadulterated relief.

The filthy, demanding kiss lacks all smoothness—the desperation in it overpowers any need for finesse. His tongue assaults my mouth, thrusting past my lips and driving straight to the back of my throat. His hunger is voracious, needy, and so intoxicating it's all-consuming. Whatever techniques he's honed over the years are completely thrown out the window and are replaced by the kind of greedy, unyielding passion I've longed to feel my entire life.

Heaven is real and I'm standing at the pearly gates.

Lord, blessed be the day.

It's like I've been holding my breath for ten straight months. Now, I'm finally allowed to let it all go.

And let it go I do.

I throw myself into his arms, into his kiss, against the hard ridge in his pants. I don't think anything has ever felt more blissful than shamelessly dry-humping his straining erection against this wall. I need that buried inside me to the motherfrigging hilt. I've never needed a good hard thrust so wildly that it's made me mindless.

Ryder rips his mouth away. "Fuck yeah, duchess. Don't go easy on me. Make me work for it."

His words spark yet another match inside me, and I pull his mouth back to mine. Our lips slide together in a breathless melding of frenzied biting and sucking. I can't get deep enough inside him, can't feel enough of him around me.

I'm on *fire* for this man.

I whimper when he tears his mouth away again. "Ah, duchess, I knew you'd be like this. Can't control yourself right now, can you?" He palms my ass, pulling me tighter to him. "Good. I want you totally free. Go fucking crazy for me. Rub more of that heat all over my cock. I want to take your smell home with me on this suit. It'll never see a dry cleaner again."

If I hadn't already learned in the last few weeks that Ryder has a dirty mouth, I sure as hell know it now. I obey his command and drive my hips into him, thrusting my center against his jutting shaft. He's so hard that when his tip bumps my clit, I nearly combust.

I'm well, *well* overdue.

His fingers fumble at my back, searching for the zipper on my dress. He yanks it down, nearly ripping the garment in two. Impatient, he shoves the dress off my shoulders and down past my breasts.

"Need to see these," he rasps, sounding at the mercy of his body, his mind no longer in control. "Need to see my hands on these." When my red demi cup bra is revealed, he leans back to take his fill. "Fucking beautiful." Then his eyes darken. "But I never want to see this bra again. You wore it for *him*, not for me."

"It wasn't for anyone," I pant. Why I feel the need to reassure him, I have no idea. "I had no plans to sleep with him."

He looks marginally appeased by that, but not enough for the anger in his expression to dissipate. In the next breath, he's shoving the bra cups aside and holding my breasts with disbelieving reverence. As if he never thought he'd actually get to feel them in his hands. Falling forward, he pushes his tongue back into my mouth just as his fingers simultaneously twist both of my nipples.

There's sensation coming at me from all angles.

My lips, my chest, between my legs, even my toes are tingling with impending release—one of epic proportions. There's so much arousal coursing through my body it's going to start oozing out of my ears.

"How tight are you gonna be, duchess?" he breathes, his fingers working my distended peaks. "How snug is it gonna be inside that pussy? The pussy I've fantasized about having wrapped around me for ten…fucking…*months*."

I take hold of his hand and guide it under my dress. "Find out for yourself."

His agonized groan echoes off the walls of our tiny alcove. His hand dips inside my panties. I wrap a leg around his waist, spreading as wide as I can for his ministrations. Then he plunges two fingers deep inside, eliciting a throaty moan that leaves my voice hoarse.

"Just like I thought," he growls. "Drenched. You've been wanting my cock here, haven't you? We've tip-toed around this for too damn long."

I'm hearing what he's saying, but I'm not really listening. Nor am I considering the ramifications of what we're doing because *who the hell cares*. I need him to take this unrelenting edge off before I unravel into a horny mess right here on this dirty floor.

And *dirty* is exactly what Ryder gives me.

His mouth laves my jaw, my neck, my breasts, as his skilled fingers take me with reckless abandon. Our breathing is labored and loud, our skin on fire with lustful fever.

"I *never* want to hear you say that you and I are nothing," he snarls against my parted lips that are swollen from his kisses. "Never again, Gretchen."

With those puzzling words hovering in the air, his mouth glides over my sweat-dotted skin and takes my nipple into his seeking mouth.

I arch into him, my hand automatically clutching strands of his hair. "Oh, *God*, yes."

His guttural grunts vibrate against my hyper-sensitive flesh. His tongue expertly flicks across the puckered tips, wetting them, sucking them into his hot mouth. My breasts usually aren't powerful pleasure points for me. But he is *doing* something to me right now. It's like he's re-programming my body—hell, my entire brain. He's loving my breasts with almost tender affection while his fingers mercilessly pump inside me, so ravenous in their pursuit of my release. The contrasts are making all my internal organs go haywire.

How does he know exactly how I need it?

Once his thumb presses down on my clit, I achieve the screaming climax he's been steering me toward. He muffles my exaltations with another turbulent kiss. It leaves me with the uneasy feeling that I might never be satiated with Ryder. Fulfilled, yes. Satisfied, fo sho. But I don't think I could ever get enough of that. Of *this*.

Even all of him would never be enough.

What a terrifying thought.

"Let me fuck you." He carefully pulls his fingers out of me. "Put me inside you, duchess. Here. Now. *God*, I need it so bad."

I actually want to cry. I knew from the moment we locked lips that this is how it would end. How it *needs* to end. I knew we couldn't go that final distance, not without some serious consequences. Consequences I don't think he's fully comprehending amidst the thick fog of lust permeating the space around us.

I place my hand on his chest. "I can't. *We* can't."

He tenses beneath my palm. "Why not?"

"Because nothing's changed." My voice sounds forlorn, even to my own ears.

His head rears back. "Uh, I'd say a whole fucking lot just changed."

I shake my head in denial. "You're still my boss. I still work for you. Which means we can't do this."

He grasps the nape of my neck, forcing me to look at him. "Well, I'm your boss and I say we can."

My fingers wind themselves around his wrist. "That's not how I'm going to get ahead in this company or in this industry. Whether you realize it or not, sex will change things. It'll influence your decisions toward me. And if anyone found out, I'd forever be known as the woman who slept her way to the top."

His eyes narrow to slits. "I won't allow anything that happens between us to affect our business relationship. It's not like I'm going to be discussing it at staff meetings."

Desolation settles in the pit of my stomach. "There's a reason why you have that rule of not dipping your pen into the company ink. Things at the office would eventually get complicated if we started having sex. This is a bad idea, and you know it."

"Maybe I did think that at one point," he concedes. "But I've had a long time to consider it, and I think we can handle it. To hell with what anyone else says."

"You don't have as much to lose. My entire career would be on the line if anyone found out I was sleeping with my boss."

His face crumples as if he's in pain. Then it hardens into the kind of determination he wears when negotiating a contract with a client. "We've resisted this long enough. I don't think we're capable of brushing it off anymore. We're risking more by *not* addressing it. By letting it build up to the point where we can't control ourselves. I'm past the point of denying it. I *need* you to give me the right to touch you."

Please don't say that.

I don't know what else to say except, "I just can't. I'm sorry I let this happen."

He chokes on his mirthless laughter as he hangs his head. "You're sorry. I suppose the next thing you're going to tell me is this was all a big mistake."

I decide to let that comment go. As I lower my leg, it brushes against his still-hard bulge. My chest swells with sympathy when I take in how far his zipper is being tested.

I reach for him. "Just this once I can…"

He knocks my hand away and steps back. "*No.* The first time I come with you is not going to be in your fucking hand."

"But you didn't—"

"I've survived it for ten months. I can make it a little longer until your head is right here with me. I want you all in when I finally take you. I won't accept anything less."

I'm so taken aback by his fervent words, I barely notice when he straightens my dress and pulls the zipper back up. Gently taking me by the arm, he guides me upstairs to my loft. At my door, I even let him cup my jaw and lay a searing kiss on my mouth that baffles and bewilders in equal measure.

Because it feels like a stamp of ownership.

But didn't I just say this couldn't happen?

"I'll see you Monday morning, duchess," he whispers. "Don't go on anymore dates before then."

I don't blink until he's down the stairs and out of sight. Either I just had a total out-of-body experience…

Or I just hooked up with my boss.

Oh, shiiiiiiiiit.

First thing I do after locking the door behind me?

Light up a joint.

And pray it causes memory loss.

12

The Helicopter and the Harpy

DEFINITELY WEARING PANTSUITS TO WORK FROM NOW ON.

No more skirts for this girl.

Because the way Ryder's incinerating my stockings clean off my legs with his eyes is not conducive to productivity. Watching the muscles in his shoulders lock up from arousal is a new, extremely distracting, development in our working relationship. Since last Friday night, it feels like everything's changed.

The dam has ruptured.

Whatever's between us that's been chained up in the dungeon for the past eleven months has broken free and is terrorizing the entire village.

My boss is hiding *nothing* now. In the looks he's leveling my way, the distance he's no longer maintaining between our bodies, Ryder is making it abundantly clear that he won't be forgetting what happened the other night—much to my dismay. I came into work Monday morning hoping for the impossible: that we were actually capable of hitting the rewind button. Pretend that we never had our tongues halfway down each other's throats, that he never had his very talented mouth around my nipples. Go back to business as usual.

Fat. Fucking. Chance.

He's not interested in keeping the status quo between us, if one even exists anymore. What I said under the stairwell Friday night still holds. I don't want to jeopardize everything I've worked for by having an illicit affair with my boss.

But I also can't deny that I thought about it the entire weekend.

Constantly.

Flicked my bean to it a few times actually.

I haven't heard from Myles, and I'm afraid to text him. I feel enormously guilty for inadvertently getting him punched in the face, then making out hard with his brother seconds later. Regardless of whatever the hell was going on between them that night, I don't think it's a good idea for Myles and I to see each other anymore. At least, not in a romantic capacity. For me, it would just feel...forced.

My phone vibrates in my hand. I drag my attention away from the fluffy white clouds whizzing past the helicopter window to check the text message.

RYDER: *Are you wearing garters with those stockings?*

Like I said, *pantsuits.*

Because the royal blue pencil skirt, patterned black stockings, and four-inch heels were a fantastically stupid idea. I try to cover more of my legs with my coat, but it does no good. From his seat across from me, Ryder's eyebrows go skyward as he waits for an answer.

ME: *You'll never know.*

After reading the message, he huffs arrogantly. His fingers fly over his screen as he types out a reply.

RYDER: *Won't I? Spread your legs, duchess. Show me what you've been hiding under there all this time.*

His words kickstart all my erogenous zones. It's the same thrill I felt when he nearly ripped my bra off Friday night trying to get to my boobs. The one I revisited in my mind as I touched myself over the weekend. The one I've been jonesing after for the past two-and-a-half days.

I'm already feeling the stirrings of addiction.

The old hag tuts her tongue in my ear. *Trouble's a brewin'. I feel it in my bones.*

We're riding in the cabin of West's helicopter on our hour-long monthly charter to Charlotte, where we have an important client we have to hold regular in-person meetings with. Due to the noise of the whirring blades above our heads, the only way we can speak to each other is through the mouthpieces attached to the bulky headphones we're wearing.

Hence the texting.

Because I'm not about to drop any nuggets for West to pick up regarding the situation between me and my boss. He'd immediately tell Harper, and my phone would be blowing up before we even land.

ME: *I told you this isn't happening.*

RYDER: *Little late for that. My cock has been hard for you ever since your pussy rode my fingers.*

ME: *You are my BOSS, Ryder.*

RYDER: *I DON'T CARE, GRETCHEN.*

I'm forced to sit here and seethe, his body language mirroring mine. The realization that he might be struggling as much as I am to breathe through the suffocating sexual tension electrifying the space between us calms my racing heart. Barely.

He glances away long enough to type out another message before his dark blue eyes once again find mine.

RYDER: *Stop fighting this. The other night never would have happened if you weren't feeling it, too. We can't turn back the clock. It doesn't work that way.*

RYDER: *And don't ask me to try because I can't.*

ME: *I'm trying to be smart for both of us. If you were literally anyone else, yeah, I'd ride you in that seat right now.*

Whoa, cowgirl.

What the hell made me say that? As if encouraging his sexting is going to help anything.

His eyes flare wide with desire. The hand resting on his knee clenches, his fingers digging into his slacks.

RYDER: *Do it. Right now. We'll have enough privacy if I close the partition.*

Thanks to the headphones, I hear my pulse quicken in my ears. My gaze flicks over his shoulder where said partition remains open, allowing me to see West inside the cockpit, piloting the craft. We never close that partition during these charters, so he would know something was up if we suddenly did.

RYDER: *You have no idea how much I want you. It's your fault I'm hard as a fucking rock. Get your gorgeous ass over here and come sit on it.*

Galvanizing what remaining self-control I have left, I punch the tiny buttons on my phone with shaking fingers. I might as well be a starving lioness and he's the fresh meat being dangled in front of me.

ME: *Like I said, if you were anyone else. But we don't have the luxury of ignoring the risks.*

Something enters his eyes that dulls the vibrant blue hue. I re-cross my legs as a nervous energy swarms me.

RYDER: *Anyone else…like my brother?*

When I glance back up, his jaw is steel, his expression stern.

ME: *I already told you that nothing happened.*

RYDER: *Yet you went on a date with him. Have you talked to him since Friday?*

Despite how much he's overstepping, I decide to throw him a bone. After all, he did give me an orgasm. And in return, I'm pretty sure I'm giving him another case of blue balls.

ME: *No*

His shoulders sag, though he doesn't appear entirely satisfied.

RYDER: *If he touches you again, he'll get another black eye. Just so you know.*

His behavior has been so erratic and confusing. I can't figure out where this sudden possessiveness is coming from. Has it always been there and Myles's kiss just brought out Ryder's inner beast? He said it had nothing to do with sibling rivalry, and strangely, I believe him.

ME: *And what if another man touches me? How did you think this was going to work? You going to beat up every guy who flirts with me?*

His nostrils flare in anger.

RYDER: *If I have to. But you'll eventually come to your senses and realize that my hands are the only ones you want on you.*

It's my turn to raise my eyebrows.

ME: *That's mighty presumptuous of you.*

RYDER: *No, that's perceptive of me. I KNOW you, duchess.*

My heartbeat stutters at his self-assuredness. I admit I've let down my guard with him more than with most people in my life, but that's because we've been forced to spend so much time together. I don't let many people really *know* me. My inner circle is practically microscopic. I haven't let Ryder become one of those people.

Have I?

Because if that's true, then he knows my fears, my weaknesses, my insecurities. He knows what I'm working toward and what I'm fighting against.

Impossible.

We've never opened up to each other like that. We haven't revealed intimate details of our pasts, our childhoods, our dreams. He doesn't know anything.

I'm in the process of typing out that exact message when West's voice comes through our headphones. "We're about to begin our descent."

How appropriate.

It feels like all I'm doing in Ryder's presence these days is falling.

Our client is an attractive redhead in her early forties who started a bakery delivery service that now has branches all over the Southeast. She hired The Colson Group to run an ad campaign when she opened a branch in Charleston, which she's since initiated at all of her other locations. Honestly, I think she keeps extending her contracts with us because she wants to diddle my boss.

I hate her.

Thank God she's married.

Although older than Ryder by ten years, she looks closer to his age. She's pretty and fit and sophisticated, not to mention wealthy. He's a beautiful, red-blooded man who would snag female attention if he lived in a dumpster. I can't help but wonder if he would go for her if she was single and not a client. I've never seen Ryder with a girlfriend, so I don't know what his usual type is.

Me?

Try not to sound too hopeful, dearie.

"Mrs. Mercer," Ryder greets her with a charming smile. "It's good to see you again."

She leans in for a cheek kiss that clearly takes him off guard. She's never offered him anything more than a flirtatious handshake that lasts a few seconds too long.

"Lovely to see you, too, Mr. Colson. But I'm afraid it won't be 'Mrs.' for much longer." She heaves a half-hearted sigh. "Mr. Mercer and I are divorcing."

Real subtle, lady.

She sounds super broken up about the split.

"I'm sorry to hear that." Only someone who's been around him as much as I have could tell how uncomfortable he is. Clearing his throat, he gestures to me. "You remember Ms. Castellanos."

Her smile is much icier when it's aimed at me.

Right back atcha, bitch.

"Of course." She gives me a stiff nod. "Pleasure. Well, should we get down to business, then?"

An hour later, I'm close to snapping my pen in half and letting the black ink explode all over the soon-to-be-ex Mrs. Mercer's silk blouse. Like an octopus when it feels threatened. She hasn't stopped smiling at Ryder, can hardly keep her hands off Ryder, and keeps shoving her medically-altered cleavage at Ryder.

Maybe I'll just stab her with the pen instead.

For his part, Ryder's maintained professionalism, despite her advances, though his voice hasn't exactly been cold and aloof. Granted, Ryder's voice is naturally sultry and provocative. It's as if he has no control over the way every sentence comes out as a seductive purr that's being whispered in your ear.

Mrs. Mercer here is taking it as an invitation.

So many times I've wanted to lay my hand proprietarily on his arm. To let this cougar-on-the-prowl know that this one is taken and warn her to back the hell off unless she wants me to rip out her weave and strangle her with it.

Damn professionalism. Damn this man for making me feel like a territorial shrew. Damn him for making me jealous, an emotion I truly detest. And damn him for making me care in the first place.

By the time the meeting concludes, I'm a fuming hot mess of boiling anger.

Mrs. Mercer leans back in to give Ryder a goodbye cheek kiss, her hand drifting down his arm in a wildly inappropriate move. "Call me when you have these new quotes ready, will you? Feel free to use my personal line."

The old hag snorts condescendingly. *When hell freezes over, you home-wrecking harpy.*

Unconcerned if Ryder is following or not, I stomp out of that office, out of that building, and toward the taxi I immediately flag down on the street. Once he catches up, he gives the driver the address of the helipad where West is waiting to fly us back to Charleston. Thankfully, Ryder gets a phone call that he remains on for the entire drive, saving me from having to speak to him. Instead, I spend that time waging an inward battle that seems more and more insurmountable with each passing minute: locking up everything I feel toward this man—except maybe annoyance—and throwing away the key.

"Something wrong?" Ryder asks once we arrive at the helipad, having finished his call.

"Nope, just peachy."

Hearing my arctic tone, he doesn't say another word.

He helps me into the aircraft, quirking an eyebrow when I intentionally choose the seat closest to the privacy partition. This puts my back against the wall that separates us from the cockpit, which is Ryder's usual spot.

I ignore the questions in his gaze and put on my headphones while he takes the seat opposite me, facing the cockpit. As West goes through all the pre-flight checks and tower clearances, our gazes never stray from each other.

Something entered this cabin with us.

Something dense. Something carnal.

Something I can't shake. Like a bad habit. There's no doubt in my mind that Ryder would be the *worst* kind of habit I could pick up. Worse than smoking. Worse than drinking. Because neither of those affect the most vital organ in the body like this man could: the heart.

His brows knit together in confusion. Then I see when he picks up on my energy. Like he knows exactly what I'm thinking, and he's waiting for me to make my move.

I don't know if it's my jealousy from watching Mrs. Mercer come onto him that's driving my need for payback, or if it's the memories of his kisses from Friday night that's fueling my desire for more. Either explanation demands action.

Channeling my inner Sharon Stone, I slowly uncross my legs. And spread them.

His furtive gaze dips to my thighs, his lids growing heavy with lust.

I watch in rapture as he mouths the word *fuck*.

13

The Spiral Into Madness

"My guests today are all male bartenders who work in the downtown Savannah area," Kennedy starts off the show. "The subject of this session today, gents, is all about teasing. When is it appropriate, when is it not, and how do you feel about girls who are relentless teases?"

"As long as it's considered foreplay and eventually leads somewhere, I like it."

"But there's a big difference between flirting and leading a guy on. Don't let a man think that sex is on the table if it's definitely not."

"See, women don't realize how difficult it is for us to walk around with a boner when we can't do anything about it. There comes a point where teasing is cruel and blue balls become a medical emergency."

"And women who constantly get off on inflicting that pain are just plain sadistic."

"So, how long would you consider teasing appropriate before you expect her to put out?" Kennedy asks.

"Three to four hours, tops. Depending on where we're at."

"But if we're just talking a handy or oral, probably two."

"There you have it, for all you teases out there," Kennedy interjects. "The moral of today's lesson: work on your follow-through or don't bother swinging at all."

As I take the hem of my skirt between my thumb and index finger and slowly inch it up my thighs, Ryder's eyes avidly track every movement. When the lace garters come into view, his forehead scrunches, his eyes momentarily squeezing shut. I'm utterly fascinated by the ferocity in his reaction. Reveling in it. His lips move as he appears to talk to himself. Like he's giving himself permission to look again.

And he does.

His loud groan can be heard even over the whooping blades overhead.

I push my underwear aside and run my finger over my swollen opening. His Adam's apple bobs, a tantalizing sign of his hunger. I know my slit is shiny with arousal because I can feel how wet I've become. Can feel how soaked playing with myself in front of him—*for* him—has gotten me.

His tongue drags across his lower lip as he watches my finger.

God, I love that.

Love that his mouth is watering at the mere sight of me. That he's been reduced to a near-drooling state. Like he wants to replace my finger with his tongue, my hand with his face. Is he wondering how I taste? What my triggers are?

Using my free hand, I type out a text and send it.

ME: *See something you like?*

118

His screen lights up with my incoming text, but he doesn't immediately check it. He acts loathe to even blink, like he's afraid he'll miss something. After several moments, he reluctantly moves his gaze to the device.

RYDER: *I'm two seconds away from burying my face in that and making out so hard with your clit.*

I almost come on the spot.

I glance behind me to make sure that West can't see anything I'm doing. But nothing is visible below my shoulders through the opened partition. Even if he wasn't completely focused on the controls in front of him, he wouldn't be able to see my splayed thighs.

When I face Ryder again, his mouth has pulled into a wolfish grin.

He knows he's got me.

Whatever. I'll let him think as much. Because while I might be the one giving him a show, he won't be winning this round. He thinks he's got leverage now, but that'll all change by the time I'm done with him. And short of West crashing this bird into a field, nothing could stop me now.

Ryder's eyes flick down to my hand and back up. He doesn't need a text for his message to come through loud and clear.

Get back to work, duchess.

Dropping my head back against the seat, I give myself over to the wicked act. He spreads his own legs wider, surely to accommodate the growing bulge between them. His mouth is parted, sweat dotting his upper lip, as his hand scrubs over his chin.

RYDER: *You like it when I watch?*

Nerves too frayed to reply, I simply nod.

RYDER: *This is the image I'll be fucking my own hand to in my office later. I'll be jerking off while you're filling out expense reports.*

His desperation stretches across the cabin and touches me like a caress. I put pressure on my throbbing bundle of nerves, careening closer to ecstasy, as my hips unconsciously undulate.

Through my headset, I hear his breath hitch. My fingers work faster, circling, seeking.

RYDER: *I see how close you are. You need my tongue. Let me lick you.*

Before I can fully prepare myself for lift off, my feet are no longer touching the earth. I'm picked up by a cyclone like Dorothy, weightlessly trapped in a never-ending spiral. Somehow, through the disorienting haze, I manage to push my mouthpiece away before West hears my ribald panting over the line.

RYDER: *You better soak those fingers, duchess. You won't let my fingers or mouth get in there? Fine. Then fuck your pussy like I did the other night.*

The phone slips from my fingers as those words drop me smack dab in the middle of Oz, where I merrily skip down the yellow brick road to meet the man behind the curtain.

Helloooo, Mr. Wizard.

By the time my breathing slows and my legs have stopped trembling from sensation overload, Ryder looks a tormented mess. He adjusts himself in his pants, wincing in pain. As if he can't help himself, he drags his palm up and down.

Over and over.

Again and again.

Never looking away from my fingers.

Is he going to treat me to the same show? I bite my lip in excitement. Even though he brought this on himself by sexting in the first place, I don't like the idea of causing him pain. In fact, I feel a sense of pride at being able to relieve his ache. Of possessing the key to unlocking his fulfillment.

That erection belongs to *me*.

I'll be damned if I let some other woman accept the plaque with my name on it and take all the credit for *my* work.

Nope. If I get him hung, *I'm* the only one who's reaping the rewards.

But I don't get the chance. His phone rings as we're making our descent into Charleston, and he's on it for the entire drive back to the office. As much as I want to turn the tables in the elevator and push that emergency stop button on *him*, I know he's only got a few minutes before his next meeting.

As I follow him into the office and past reception, I get stopped by Woods, one of our graphic artists that we recently recruited from SCAD—Savannah College of Art and Design. While answering his questions about the layout for a promo we're running in the next edition of *Charleston Living*, a southern lifestyle magazine, I hear Ryder's booming voice come from the direction of my cubicle.

"Excuse me, can I help you?"

Oh, geez. What now?

Promising Woods I'll catch up with him in a bit, I scurry across the office. I can't imagine what could possibly be upsetting the man now, but I'm sure that whatever it is, I'm likely the cause of it.

When my cubicle comes into view, I stop short.

Ross is sat at my desk chair, looking up at Ryder with a bemused, if not slightly annoyed, expression. Ryder's form is imposing as it towers above my brother. Being a former Navy man, Ross is certainly no slouch. But that doesn't mean I want the two of them coming to blows right here in the freaking office. After witnessing Ryder punch his own brother in the face, there's no telling what he'll do the next time something sets him off.

"I'm looking for Gretchen Castellanos," Ross calmly tells him, with a tinge of innocence.

"And who are you?" Ryder bites out.

"Someone who's looking for her."

It sounds like Ryder chokes back a growl. "Ms. Castellanos is busy."

When Ross glances around the room, his gaze catches on me. "Apparently, not too busy."

Deciding I need to end this before Ryder starts acting more territorial than is appropriate for a boss, I approach them. "Hey, what are you doing here?"

"Had a training session that got out early," Ross answers, pushing to his feet. "Thought I'd see if you were free for lunch. And I realized I've never seen where you work." Under his breath, he adds, "Though I'm starting to understand why."

Stifling my chuckle, I turn to face my boss, who looks like he's about to bodycheck Ross through my cubicle wall. "Ross, this is my boss Ryder Colson. Mr. Colson, this is my brother Ross."

After both men are introduced, they have remarkably different reactions. Ryder's shoulders noticeably relax, and the frown lines around his eyes and mouth smooth out. Ross, however, rises to his full height and scowls.

I recognize that move.

And I cringe.

He's going all *I was an officer in the Navy and know about twenty different ways to kill you with that pencil on my sister's desk* on the man I've complained to him about countless times. Ross has heard me call Ryder every name in the book. Once, I referred to him as a "callous overlord who wouldn't know a compliment if it came up and sucked on his schlong like a two-dollar whore."

That was Fourth of July and I was stone cold hammered. Don't judge.

For the first time, guilt gnaws at me for all my Ryder-bashing to my always-ready-to-throw-down-for-his-little-sister brother.

"Brother," Ryder reiterates. Visibly shaking himself, he holds out his hand and switches to Charming Ryder right before my eyes. "Sorry about the confusion. I thought you were someone else. It's a pleasure to meet you."

Ross studies him with a shrewd eye as he shakes his hand, reminding me so much of our father it's frightening. "Yeah, likewise. Heard a lot about you."

I grimace. *Thanks, bro.*

Ryder isn't stupid, despite my frequent testimony to the contrary. If I've talked about him to my family over the past eleven months, he knows it couldn't have been pleasant. After all, it's only been a few weeks since things really started to change between us.

His face falls a little as his eyes dart to mine knowingly. "Well, I hope it wasn't all bad. Suffice to say that your sister here is one of the most passionate people who's ever worked for me. Our debates can get rather heated."

My eyes widen. He just complimented me and admitted to something deeper in the same breath. Even if Ross doesn't pick up on the "passionate" part, *I* know what Ryder means by that.

Ross barks out a laugh. "That's generally how we describe her in our family. Though we usually replace the word 'passionate' with 'stubborn and pig-headed.'"

I glare at my brother, suddenly feeling ganged up on.

Ryder shrugs at me. "He said it, not me."

I roll my eyes, flabbergasted at how easily he manages to charm the pants off of everyone he meets, including men. Even my brother, who's heard me call Ryder a "condescending crotchbag I'm nominating for the Asshole Boss of the Year Award."

And I was sober for that one.

"But if I'm being entirely honest," Ryder continues, looking back at Ross. "I have to admit that her clever intellect can be a bit intimidating. She challenges me every day to hold my own against her. Don't get me wrong, it's a good thing. But it does tend to incite my competitive side."

Ross throws his arm around me. "Shit, you're preaching to the choir, man. This girl hates to lose. I'll have to tell you about the Monopoly Meltdown of 2014 sometime."

I groan as Ryder chuckles. "Yes, you will." He glances down at his phone when it starts ringing again. "I'm sorry, but I have to take this."

"Don't forget you have that meeting with Forrester & Sons in fifteen," I remind him.

He nods. "Right. Printouts?"

"Are on your desk, and I wrote down a few things that need clarification on their end."

"Got it, thanks." He shakes my brother's hand again. "Really nice to meet you, Ross. The three of us will have lunch soon."

I shake my head, panicking. I do *not* need these two falling into a bromance. "No, we shouldn't—"

Ross gives me a hard squeeze. "We'd love to."

Ryder puts his phone to his ear and rushes off toward his office.

My brother releases a low whistle as we watch him walk away. "After all the crap you've told me about him over the past year, it's finally starting to make sense."

I warily meet his eyeline. "What are you talking about?"

"I know why you've been acting extra weird lately."

"Excuse you, I've been acting my normal level of weird."

Ross tuts at me in admonishment. "Shame, shame, sis. You've got a thing for your boss."

The laughter that bursts out of me sounds manic. Like a hysterical clown. *Bring it down a notch.* "Are you kidding? You think I have a thing for the man I once said was 'a swaggering jackass who needs a vasectomy before he manages to sire a new generation of swaggering jackasses?'"

Ross goes on like he didn't even hear me. "But since I now know the feeling is mutual, I won't have to punch his teeth through his skull. I'm guessing you probably like them right where they are."

I gape. "Have you been stealing from my stash again? You know you can't smoke that shit in the Coast Guard."

He rolls his eyes. "That man likes you, Gretch. There's no way you're that blind."

And there's no way my brother was able to figure all that out in two minutes.

Wild guess.

He slaps me on the shoulder. "Now, come on. You're buying me a plate of fajita nachos." As he turns to walk away, I hear him mutter, "Clever intellect, my ass."

14

The Wine-ing and Pine-ing

"THIS TASTES LIKE CIGARETTE ASH." I scowl down at the red wine monstrosity in my glass.

Sloane holds her own glass of red up to the light, examining its richer color. "And you called us 'wussies' for ordering from the sweet end. How's that burnt ciggie butt treating you over there, Gretch?"

I frantically look around the winery's tasting room. "This place has a full bar, right?"

This winery in Mount Pleasant opened earlier this year, but none of us have had the chance to stop in for a tasting before now. Having now had my first sip of their label, I've concluded that they're spending far more money on their interior design than on their wine production.

The building is less than a year old, and the fragrance of new lumber still wafts in the air. The tasting room is decorated in a mountain lodge theme, with lots of cabin-style furniture made out of logs and antlers and pinecone accent pieces. A humongous bearskin rug lays in front of the gargantuan stone fireplace in the center of the room. And because we're two weeks away from Christmas, the place is decked out, top to bottom, in holiday foliage. Tasteful white lights hang from the ceiling. Lit winter garland is wrapped around each column and framing every arched doorway. Poinsettia centerpieces decorate the table surfaces, and buffalo plaid is everywhere.

It's actually kind of…romantic.

Good thing I'm here with the three great loves of my life.

Harper takes a sip of her white wine and makes a few notes on her tasting sheet. "Hon, I think the more important question is, when was your last waxing?"

I attempt a reproachful look that doesn't land because everyone at this table knows I can't reproach anything.

She looks up from her sheet, grinning sheepishly. "Oh, don't give me that look. You know you're going to bang Ryder. Everyone at this table knows you're going to bang Ryder. I'm just trying to look out for my soon-to-be-banged friend."

"I disagree," Quinn speaks up, just before swirling a sip of her semi-dry rosé around in her mouth.

"Lookee there," I wave my hand at Quinn. "Jockey Robinson is on my side."

"The most important question is, where are they going to shag first?" She raises her hand like she's waiting for the teacher to call on her. "My vote is his desk, since he's the boss and all. Symbolic, you know?"

Sloane shakes her head, sending her long raven hair swishing around her pale shoulders. "Nah. Do it at his place the first time. Easier escape route in case you need to bail."

I think there's a greater risk of the opposite happening. If I got Ryder on top of me—or beneath me or behind me—I might never want to leave.

"Helicopter sex is pretty killer," Harper throws out. "But West might get squicked out if you lose your chopper cherry in his bird, so maybe not that."

Would he be squicked out if he knew I diddled myself dirty in the back seat?

"Slow your roll, you cronies. I never said Yes to the Sex."

Quinn stares off into space, nodding consideringly. "I'd watch that show."

"So, I'm guessing Myles is out of the picture?" Sloane asks.

Quinn snorts. "If he doesn't want to head-butt Ryder's right hook again, I'd say he is."

"That's so hot." This from Harper.

I try another sip of my ash wine. Maybe I just didn't cleanse my palate enough before that first drink.

I gag.

Yeah, nope. It still tastes like it was poured from the Grinch's sweaty socks before they crawled away from him.

"It was not hot," I squeak on a hiccup. "It was barbaric and way too *I drag you back to my cave and we mate* for this girl."

Sloane tosses me a *really, you're gonna play your girls like that?* look. "Don't even try to tell me that no part of you wanted to bump uglies with that hunk-a-dunk after watching him hit another guy for kissing you. You said yourself you practically climbed him like a spider monkey underneath that stairwell."

"Last Christmas" by Wham! comes over the room's speakers, sending my foot tapping against the leg of my bar-height chair.

"All right, I admit I'm a sucker for *some* displays of male aggression," I confess. "But my judgment was clouded due to being seriously overdue."

Harper drops her pen in shock. "*You?*"

"I will smack your cute button nose right off your face, Barbie," I threaten.

The blonde witch giggles before picking up a glass of red from her flight and taking a sip. "I'm tasting some cherry."

Sloane snatches it from her and drinks. "No, that's definitely blackberry in there."

Quinn snags it out of Sloane's hand and lifts it to her mouth. "I don't know what you two are drinking because all I'm getting is stale oak."

Harper huffs. "We suck at this."

"Would I be completely crazy to boink my boss?" I bluntly ask.

In response, I get:

"No."

"Define boink."

And, "Only if his dick is small."

"Great, that helps."

I gulp down more of my tobacco wine, noting that it tastes less like the bottom of a fire pit and more like cigar ambrosia now. A slight improvement.

"Okay, let me rephrase that. Would I be losing all my dignity if I boink my boss?"

This time, I get:

"Not *all* of it."

"You mean you still have some?"

And, "Again, only if his dick is small."

"Bunch of hoes," I mutter before sucking down another mouthful of liquid charcoal while they turn into cackling banshees.

After Sloane catches her breath, her expression turns serious. "Has he honestly ever made you feel like you would?"

Thinking back on my entire relationship with Ryder—spanning from when we full-on detested each other, all the way up to the jealous, hate-crushing of the past few weeks—I have to say, "No. Never."

The one thing Ryder has never done is disrespect me. Even since things started shifting between us, he's never made me feel like I'd be compromising my integrity if things got more rough and tumble between us. He's always treated me as his equal, his peer. And when we've been intimate, I'm just a woman to him. Not his subordinate, not his employee. For him, that doesn't seem to enter into the equation when he has his hands on me.

"What about the night you got all biblical with his brother?" Quinn inquires.

I wave that off. "Nothing more than a voodoo batch of vodka working some weird juju on me. It wasn't what I thought it was. Nothing at lunch with him that day..." I trail off, knowing this is going to sound so high school I could die.

"What?" Harper chirps, equally high school in her enthusiasm.

"Tingled," I finish on a sigh. "He never made me want to climb him like a spider monkey."

Sloane and Harper both nod in understanding. And surprisingly...so does Quinn. Like she *knows*. What's up with that? Is there someone she wants to climb like a spider monkey that she hasn't told us about?

"Is that all it is with Ryder?" Sloane asks in a contemplative tone. "A case of the tingles?"

I have to remind myself to be patient with her because she's always patient with me. She's the type who needs to discuss every little detail, every feeling, every emotion, or else her brain will twist itself into knots.

"He's got the personality of a garden snail," I lie. "So, yeah, I'd say it's just about his dick."

She watches me with her snowy wolf eyes. The girl is far too damn intelligent for her own good. "The timer's almost up, Gretch," she murmurs in a voice that only I can hear.

In other words, *be prepared to be waterboarded if you don't give me some real feels soon.*

I wink at her. "Then you better be ready to pull those cupcakes out of the oven."

"As long as you guys are careful and he can keep it quiet, I say go for it," Harper says, surprising me.

She used to be the non-risk-taker of the group. The one who, after going 'just around the river bend', always chose the smoothest course. West has clearly been a good influence on her, not that I didn't already know that.

"It's a risky move." Quinn tips her glass in my direction. "Keeping it a secret from everyone, constantly sneaking around..."

Harper looks at her ex-stepsister incredulously. "Isn't that the whole fun of having an affair?"

I throw my hands up, silencing them. "Let's nix the word 'affair,' shall we? We're not hooking up in sketchy, pay-by-the-hour motel rooms. This is simply about the two of us working this insanity out of our systems. And bonus, breaking my dry spell at the same time is killing two birds with one stone. Once the mystery is gone, we can move past the whole moronic thing."

Sloane's expression is skeptical. "And what if it makes everything awkward at the office?"

I shrug, unconcerned. "We've always had an unconventional work relationship. I don't think doing the squeeze and squirt together can really make it worse." Harper chokes on her wine. "Especially since up until recently, I thought we'd already done that. It might actually help if the sexual tension is gone once and for all."

"I'm not so sure, Gretch." Sloane's voice is soft, sympathetic. "If this is all just about getting some afternoon delight, you can end your drought with anyone. Is it really worth sacrificing a job you love and a career you've only just begun?"

I slam my forehead down on the table, groaning.

She's right, damn her. I can go to a bar tonight and pick up a guy to take home. It's my own fault the Countess has been surviving on bread and water lately. I can change that anytime I want. Whatever's going on between me and Ryder is fleeting, but I plan to be in the advertising industry for years.

A penis is easy to replace.

A job you adore, not so much.

"You're right," I tell her, the table absorbing my dejection. "It's just that I've never been the sacrificial type."

Harper sighs, sounding crestfallen.

"Probably wise," Quinn says. "I mean, historically speaking, when has a woman sleeping with her boss ever not ended in disaster? You don't want to be the woman at the end of the day with a stained dress and a tarnished reputation."

Yuck.

Just the thought of the people I work with losing all respect for me because I let Ryder pop me with his corkscrew is enough to turn my stomach. *Or maybe that's just because you're drinking soot.* If people found out, they would talk. Rumors would fly. My recent promotion would come into question. The other senior account managers would gladly take the larger accounts I've brought in off my hands. Hell, an ugly pall would be cast over my entire time at The Colson Group.

"And we're done with me." I close out the subject with a salute of my cinder wine, just as Brenda Lee's "Rockin' Around the Christmas Tree" starts playing. "How about we discuss strategies to get Quinnie laid?"

"Pass."

"You know what I've been thinking," Harper says, shooting our little rodeo queen a sly look. "Gretchen should set Quinn up with Ross."

Quinn spits out her wine.

I gape at Harper before moving my attention to her ex-stepsister, who's swiping a napkin over her chin.

Ross and Quinn as a couple would never have occurred to me in a million years, but I consider it for a moment. They're two of my favorite people in the world, they're both outdoorsy and like to stay active, and they're both a bit jaded toward relationships, though for different reasons.

It's possible they might actually work.

"Absolutely not," Quinn says emphatically.

"Why not?" I ask curiously.

I'm still not sold on the idea, but I want to hear her objections. I've sensed something off with her the past few months. Ever since she worked at some rich guy's estate over the summer. She and her father were hired to train show horses there and ever since then, she's been acting different.

"Are you all wine-drunk?" she sputters. "He's your brother, Gretch. That's the highest level of off-limits territory. I don't want anything to jeopardize our friendship or your relationship with him. The answer is a big, fat no. Never going to happen."

Okay, point taken.

But something still niggles at the back of my mind. Something in her voice and expressions lately. I'm beginning to think there's another reason why she doesn't want to hook up with Ross. Why we haven't heard of her going on any dates for a while. I'm thinking Quinnie the Pooh here has a secret man toy she's been keeping under wraps. Or under the sheets.

But who?

I silently listen to the conversation around me when Sloane and Harper start discussing what they got Carter and West for Christmas. Hearing them talk so candidly about all the sweet things their men do for them has me a little wistful, I'll admit. Especially since I ate my dinner over my sink last night. Alone.

I find myself drifting off to one particular day with Ryder a few months back when he was being uncharacteristically sweet...

My boss answers his phone on the fourth ring. "You better be calling from the hospital," he says curtly. "Because bodily injury or illness are the only acceptable excuses for being this late."

I rub my temple, trying to fend off the lingering headache. "I am."

"You're what?"

I sigh, exhausted from the morning's events. "Calling from the hospital."

Silence. Then, "Wait, you're serious."

"Yep."

"What happened? Are you okay?"

I'm taken aback by how worried he actually sounds, but I don't have the energy to dwell on it. "I was rear-ended this morning on my way to work and I hit the truck in front of me. FYI, they aren't lying when they say those air bags really punch you in the face. Anyway, I'm doing better than my car is—"

"What hospital are you at?" he interrupts.

I hesitate. "Why?"

I can practically hear him grinding his teeth through the line. "Gretchen... What. Hospital."

I tell him the name, confused.

"What building?"

Again, I tell him, wary now.

"I'll be there in ten minutes."

I inspect my phone to make sure I dialed the right number. "Why would you come here? I was just calling to tell you that I'll probably be another hour or so. I should be in the office by eleven."

He hangs up without another word.

I've never felt such a potent dose of stunned bewilderment in my life than I do whenever Ryder walks into that emergency room and makes a beeline for me. He looks stressed and a little panicked when our gazes clash. And when he carefully sits down next to me, he acts like I'll shatter to pieces if he so much as blinks too hard.

"You okay, duchess?"

His voice is so soft as he inspects the darkening bruise on my forehead where my head slammed into the car window that I almost don't recognize it.

"Um..." I have to clear my throat. "Yeah, I'm okay. Just a few bruises."

He frowns. "You don't usually go to the hospital for bruises."

My hands fidget in my lap at this unusual interplay. In all the months I've known him, he's never once acted concerned about my well-being. "My doctor just wants to make sure that the rods in my back weren't damaged from the impact of the collision."

His eyes fly to mine. "You have rods in your back? From what?"

Since when does he care about any details of my life?

"I had scoliosis surgery when I was nine," I answer numbly. "The metal rods in my back keep everything straight and aligned. I'm having a little discomfort along my spine, so my doctor wants to make sure nothing moved around."

His hand reaches out, as if he might touch me, but he pulls it back at the last second. "You're in pain?"

I can't take my eyes off his forehead. It's scrunched in a way that I recognize. He only ever makes that face when he's upset. Usually when he's angry or...troubled.

"Not much." Why am I whispering? *"Just minor aches. I'm sure everything is fine."*

"Did you call anyone to be here with you?"

I shake my head. "I'm not going to worry anyone with this. The X-rays won't take long. I'll probably be in and out in twenty minutes."

He swallows thickly, looking unconvinced.

The silence makes me uneasy, and I squirm in my chair. "You don't have to be here, boss. I'm sure you have a ton of work to do."

He prolongs the silence by studying my expression with unwavering intensity. He's never looked at me this way before and it's unnerving. Like he's acknowledging that I'm more than just the person at the office he bounces sarcasm off of.

Then he schools his expression with his trademark cocky grin. Pulling his phone out of his pocket, he leans back in his chair and crosses one ankle over his knee. "Well, that's the great thing about cell phones, duchess. Makes it easy to do work from anywhere. So, let's discuss the Brower account..."

I'm actually grateful for the distraction. Our normal routine of exchanging insults, while at the same time getting things accomplished, takes my mind off the aches in my back and that small concern that it could be more serious than I think. That worry is there any time I feel the slightest twinge along my spine.

This dysfunctional normalcy with Ryder, I know.

What he was doing before, acting like he has some sort of vested interest in me, I don't *know. His concern is entirely foreign and unprecedented. I would need Captain Ahab at the helm to help me navigate those uncharted waters.*

When I return to the waiting room forty-five minutes later with a clean bill of health from my doctor, Ryder is still sitting in the same chair, waiting for me.

I've never been so happy to hear the voice of Mariah Carey in my life.

Because when "All I Want for Christmas Is You" starts blaring over the speakers in the winery's tasting room, I put all my energy into forgetting about Ryder's sporadic displays of humanity and focus entirely on our spontaneous table karaoke.

In fact, the four of us are singing so loudly and enthusiastically that the entire tasting room joins in and is belting out the lyrics with us by the time Mariah goes into her falsetto that everyone hilariously tries to match. I'm surprised every wine glass in the place doesn't shatter.

I end up buying four bottles of the ciggie butt wine.

That shit's not bad.

15
The One Night Proposal

"News from the world of sociology, folks," Kennedy says. "A recent survey was conducted by a research team at the University of Colorado that asked participants about their views on dating a co-worker:

19% of people believe the workplace is a great environment to meet your future spouse.
43% say hooking up at work is fun and exciting, but it's best to keep it casual.
And 38% think getting hot and heavy with a co-worker is a disaster waiting to happen.

You know, I have to agree with the last group. I mean, the only industry I can think of where hooking up with a co-worker wouldn't be awkward as hell is the porn industry. They probably just consider it the dress rehearsal, right?" Pause. "Or the undress rehearsal."

My cubicle can be a giant pain in the ass.

Because it doesn't have a door I can slam in people's faces.

As much as I love my co-workers—sometimes I want to pinch their cheeks a little *too* hard—every now and then, I just need my space. A quiet, peaceful place to get my job done without interruptions. Which is why I tend to barricade myself in the focus group viewing room in our office. It's dark, it's soundproofed, and no one knows where to find me.

Next to smoking a blunt in the bathtub, this is where it's at.

Slightly bigger than a closet, it's empty but for a single table and a few chairs for us and our clients to monitor the focus group discussions. The large two-way mirror that extends the length of the wall looks in on our focus group room, where the participants gather to offer their honest opinions and reactions about various advertisements, products, and services, depending on our clients' needs. Usually, it's the client and coordinating account manager sitting in this room during a session, along with Ryder, who typically oversees all focus group events.

Tonight is the first focus group for the Chadwick account, so I've been balls-to-the-wall for the past six hours in preparation. Ryder has been at a client meeting in Atlanta all day, so I haven't seen him.

But he should be walking through that door any minute.

It's nearing six o'clock and the participants are starting to trickle in. Sonja, another senior account manager, escorts them into the room. One by one, each of them takes a seat around the large table, speculating over why they're here. The participants never know the topic of the session prior to arriving. They've merely been asked to offer their opinion on a subject our

137

records indicate they have particular interest in, and they get paid for it.

Despite the camera we have recording in the room with them, I prefer to stay in the viewing room so I can gauge the participants' reactions in real time and take notes. Sonja welcomes everyone and begins to explain what the subject for tonight's discussion is. The packet in front of her has the list of questions Chadwick wants covered for this session, which allow her to guide and steer the conversation around the relevant talking points.

The oxygen is suddenly sucked out of the viewing room.

Creating a vacuum.

I don't need to turn around to know that Ryder has just entered the room. I feel his presence. Smell his aftershave. My body instantly responds to being snared in his unyielding orbit.

Ever since the wine tasting with my girls, Ryder has been wreaking unbelievable havoc on my self-control. Without me saying a word, he seemed to sense that I decided to pump the brakes. To not pursue this train wreck of a hookup.

He's just been a *tad* resistant to the idea.

Three days ago, he called me into his office…

"I received a summons," is the first thing I droll when I enter Ryder's office and close the door behind me.

What I actually received was a text from him that simply said, "My office. Now."

He's sitting behind his desk, attention focused on the spreadsheets in his hands. "I just got off the phone with the studio. They have to push back the date of the commercial shoot for the Chadwick account."

"What? Why? That date was in the contract."

He doesn't look up. "Something about errors with their new computer system and things got double booked. They only need to push it back by a week."

I anxiously tap the toe of my boot on his carpeted floor, already mentally readjusting the project schedule. "Okay. I'll get in touch with the television network about rescheduling the commercial air date. I'll call Baldwin and tell him."

"I've already spoken to Chadwick," Ryder clips out harshly. "He says the new date will still work for them."

Well, that's a relief. We don't need them pissed off this early into their contract.

"I'll go make those calls, then, if that's all." I turn to leave—

"I want to rip your clothes off and throw your naked ass onto my desk."

I freeze.

My breathing quickens, my palms dampen, but I don't face him.

I can't *face him.*

I hear his chair swivel around, followed by his footsteps that move across the room toward me. "Then I want to throw those legs over my shoulders and put my mouth on your pussy."

It feels like I'm sprinting up a summit, and the air is getting thin at this altitude. I sense him come up behind me and lower his head until his mouth is hovering right over my ear.

"I want to tongue-fuck you, duchess. I want your thighs to squeeze my face when you come so"—his lips brush the shell of my ear—"fucking"—his tongue snakes out—"hard in my mouth." His teeth take a nip of my flesh. I gasp. "All while your co-workers sit on the other side of that door without a clue of what's going on in here."

My eyes slide shut as those images flash through my mind. A bucket of arousal is dumped on my head, like I'm standing under a sex-spiked waterfall. It's so powerful it has me rocking on my feet, like a ship about to capsize.

"If there's one thing I've learned about you," he whispers, "it's that you give as good as you get. And I've been imagining what else that mouth can do besides spit wisecracks at me." His hand slides down my thigh and doesn't stop until he's cupping my mound, groaning in my ear. "Though I prefer it if you swallow."

I bolted out of that room like the fuzz was hot on my tail. *Ma'am, you're under arrest for conspiracy to commit grand sex throttle.*

I hate that he's managing to turn me into a skittish animal. That he's making me forget why I've hired extra bricklayers to build the walls around my defenses up even higher since that night in the conference room. Leave it to Ryder to take a jackhammer to them until they crumble to bits.

My resistance toward him is shit.

Case in point, what happened yesterday when he cornered me in the break room...

I finish spreading cream cheese over my bagel and end up smearing a dab of it on my finger. Before I can lick it off, my wrist is suddenly snatched up, startling the hell out of me.

Ryder wraps his lips around my finger and sucks it into his mouth.

His hot, wet, hungry *mouth.*

The knife in my hand clatters onto the counter.

He licks my finger with the flat of his tongue, swirling it around like he's trying to get to the center of a Tootsie Pop. There's nothing I want more in this moment than to pull that voracious mouth up to mine and let him do literally anything he wants to me on this countertop. Without a morsel of shame. I want to get him naked so bad, rip his suit clean off his shredded body, that my hands twitch with the urge.

My finger slowly slips free of his lips. "We have the same needs, duchess," he breathes against my slickened flesh. "You like it dirty, I like it rough. We're both passionate people. We're quick to heat up and slow to cool down. And we both know how raw *our fucking would be. The kind of rutting you're sore the next day from. The kind that's so unleashed and uninhibited that you tear through every piece of clothing...you leave marks...you break the bed. The kind that leaves you feeling like a junkie because you'd sell your soul for your next hit."*

He's still holding my wrist, so I can't make a run for it.

But I don't want to run...and yet I do.

Because his next move is to guide my hand to his abs and slide it down. Past his belt, past his zipper. His own hand covers mine as he molds my fingers around his rock-hard cock.

Oh, please, God. Give me strength.

I've never been strong-willed against my desires. Never had a concrete sexual constitution. I've always surrendered when temptation has gripped me because what fun is there in resisting? I've never denied my needs, never not slaked my lusts when they pull me under.

But they've never been this...oppressive before.

"This is constant,*" he growls angrily. "You're the only one who can fix this, and you keep telling me no. What's it gonna take, duchess? I don't even have to see you in person to get this hard. I picture your face, your legs in those fucking skirts, your striking silver eyes, and I'm instantly boned up."*

Really? *How long has it been like that for him?*

"You can't tell me you didn't want me sinking it so fucking deep the other night in your building," he rasps. "And in the helicopter. I felt you, I heard you, I saw *you. You* want *this."*

More than I would have ever believed possible. But—

"My career would never recover if it got out," I admit shakily. "I mean, think about it. You're not even being discreet now, Ryder. Anyone could walk in here and see us. And we're barely even touching."

His answering groan is full of pain. "I can't—"

And that's when someone *did* walk in, though Ryder jerked away from me before Polly, one of the administrative assistants, looked up from her phone and saw us.

"Chadwick and Baldwin can't make it," Ryder's deep rumble fills the viewing room, yanking me back to the present. "There's some emergency at one of their warehouses they have to deal with."

"No problem," I croak. "I'll send them the video tomorrow so they can review it themselves."

"Stop deflecting me, Gretchen."

The small room gets very still. "I'm not. You suddenly have a problem with me doing my job?"

He comes up behind me where I'm sitting at the table, his crotch way the hell too close to my face. "Do I need to remind you of the noises you made? How easily my fingers slipped inside you, yet how tight you were when they were knuckle-deep? You don't deny fire like that. You know as well as I do how rare it is. And for you to just dismiss it like it's nothing... It fucking pisses me off."

Damn him, he always knows how to get me. I used to be under the impression that he was clueless. But I'm starting to think he might know me *too* well.

When he brushes my hair off my shoulder, I spring to my feet and launch myself across the room. I need distance. If he starts touching me, it's game over.

"Don't," I tell him weakly. I can already feel myself slipping. "You don't understand what this means for me. 'It's just sex' can't apply to this situation. I'd be putting everything on the line, Ryder."

His muscles flex, no doubt sensing a chink in my armor. "I would protect you. For Christ's sake, I wouldn't put your career in jeopardy like that. Despite what you think, I'm not a complete bastard. I've never wanted anything bad for you, Gretchen."

Now I know how meerkats at the zoo feel. I'm trapped in this tiny room with him and nowhere to go. It's like an escape room with no clues for how to get out.

He stalks me around the room—predatorily—intentionally keeping himself between me and the door. Determination is tattooed clearly on his ruggedly handsome face. With no options, I end up standing in front of the two-way mirror, my back to Ryder.

Just because I'm going down doesn't mean I have to stare into the face of my doom.

Banding his arm across my waist, he hauls me back against his chest, his stiff manhood pressing against my ass. "If you keep rejecting me," he whispers in my ear, "make it about not wanting anything to do with this." He punctuates his words with a thrust of his hips. "Not because you're too scared to go after something you want."

I bristle at the accusation. "I'm not scared. I'm being smart." For once.

It's the first time in my life that sensibility has reigned supreme over sex, which is something I've never been afraid of before. But everything with Ryder is different. It's new. It's—

Okay, yeah, it's scary.

His hands curl around my arms and squeeze. "You're being *safe*. And that's not the Gretchen I know."

But how much do you really *know?*

He eases his grip a bit when I don't respond. "I know why you're resisting, duchess. I get it and I respect you for it." His next words come out shaky. "But I'm fucking *dying* here. Everything was different before last week. It wasn't easy, but it was…manageable. Now, it's not even containable."

When I squeeze my eyes shut, I wish I could squeeze my ears shut, too. Just block him out. Block out the truth of his words, the graveness of his tone. He practically stole the words right out of my mouth and it infuriates me.

The air between us shifts.

The energy swirling around our bodies becomes highly charged as he awaits my acquiescence…or my retreat.

With every second that ticks by, the steel vault protecting everything inside me that I hold dear—like my unwavering resolve when I've made up my mind about something—cracks open a millimeter further. He's burrowing his way beneath my skin, like the gofer digging holes in your backyard that you can't get rid of.

Actually, Ryder is more like the bear trap I'm wittingly stepping into.

What the hell kind of person voluntarily steps into a goddamn bear trap?

"If we do this," I find myself saying without processing the words, "it's a one-off thing. One time to burn through this, and then we go back to the way things were."

Every muscle in his body locks up behind me. His hands begin to tremble, though I can't tell if it's from excitement or...anger. Why would me offering no-strings sex make him angry? You'd think, as a man, he'd be rejoicing.

"What if once doesn't cut it?" he bites out.

"It'll have to."

"Counterproposal. One night. An entire night to do whatever I want."

"And what about what I want?"

He takes a deep inhale of my hair. "Consider this the one occasion where I won't fight you on anything. You said to burn through it? Fine. But we're going to burn through *all* of it."

There are those damn tingles again.

I hate how much I love the sound of that. Resentment courses through my bloodstream that he has the nerve to be so freaking sexy and convincing at the same time. My drawbridge is lowering for the first time ever and it's because of *this* irresistible man.

I *despise* him.

I blow out the breath I've been holding ever since he walked into this room. "Fine. One night. Anything goes. Then that's it."

He doesn't even wait for me to finish the sentence before he has my skirt rucked up over my ass and bunched around my waist.

My head whirls around. "What are you doing?"

His eyes find mine and sharpen. "You just said one night."

"I didn't mean tonight! Here. We're at the office, Ryder."

He scowls and goes back to what he was doing: baring me. "You expect me to wait after you just agreed? Fuck that. I'm not giving you the chance to change your mind, or let you walk away from another hard-on that *you* caused. This is happening tonight, duchess."

Tonight?!

Oh, God… *Tonight.*

His fingers splay over my ass cheeks in a hard grip. "So, strap in…and hang the fuck on."

16

The Viewing Room Vacuum

RYDER'S HANDS ARE ALL OVER ME. Tearing, groping, kneading.
He's feral.

He's out of control.

He's my fucking dream come true.

"Jesus Christ," he pants. "This. *This* is what I've needed for so long. Finally, finally, finally…"

It takes me a second to realize he's talking more to himself than to me.

"We can't do this here," I whisper frantically.

My actions belie my words. I'm leaning back into him, thrusting my ass into his persistent hands, encouraging him with every gasping breath. I'm skating on the thin ice of single-minded desperation, and he's not moving fast enough.

Pinning my skirt in place with his hips, he rubs his suit pants over my bare cheeks, grinding that ever-growing bulge into my crevice. The move frees up his hands so he can start deftly unbuttoning my silk blouse. But because his fingers are too big for the delicate buttons, the action is accompanied by the sound of ripping material.

"The only people in this office besides us are all in that room," he rasps. "No one's coming in here."

He's using that negotiator voice again. The one that fells lesser men and women into signing contracts and agreeing to whatever price Ryder lays on the table. I'm usually immune to that dominant, sensual timbre.

But I'm waving my white flag.

Resisting has become far too exhausting. This is my sweet surrender that might very well turn into a suicide mission.

Still, I try to maintain what little ground I have left. Even as I feel it crumbling beneath my feet. "Those other people are literally on the other side of this wall."

We can *see* them through the two-way mirror. And if I just flip the switch on the wall in front of me, we could hear them, too.

Ryder releases the last button and pulls my blouse apart with a drawn-out sigh of relief. As if his throat was constricting but now, he's finally allowed to breathe. "This room is soundproofed. With a lock on the door. Any other objections?"

I pinch my lips together. I can't believe how easy he's made this for me. "I think I'm good."

His hands cover my breasts. Head falling forward on a groan, his forehead rests against my neck. "No, *that's* good. It's about time I had these in my hands again."

My eyes roll back when he traces circles around my nipples with the lightest of touches. Reaching back, I slide my fingers through his hair, pulling his mouth closer when he starts leaving a trail of open-mouthed kisses across my flesh. The closer his lips get to my jawline, the more frenzied he becomes. In the blink of an eye, he's opened the front clasp of my bra and my breasts are spilling out.

"Fuck, duchess," he breathes, his gaze falling on them over my shoulder. "Look at you. You are the sexiest woman I've ever seen."

My blood turns to lava. I'm so incredibly hot, and not just because of his touch or the delicious stimulation his compliments bring. It's the wickedness of the moment that's sending me over the edge. The dense fog of forbidden sex that's swallowing us whole, closing us off from the rest of the world. The sight of nineteen people sitting in the next room, talking amongst each other, completely oblivious to the debauchery taking place mere feet from them.

They can't hear us. Can't see us.

But in a weird way, it feels like their eyes are still on us. Watching.

I drown in the quicksand of my arousal in seconds.

Lowering my hand, I grip him. Then I grin when he hisses through his teeth and punches his hips forward.

"You want me to fuck you with that?" His hand skates down my torso and traces my belly button, before lowering to the lace trim of my panties. "You want that pounding you into the wall?"

"What the hell do you think?"

I feel his mouth curve into a smile against my skin. "Not good enough, duchess. You've gotta say it."

When I give him a particularly hard tug, he chuckles darkly.

I'm about to make myself the most vulnerable I've ever been with this man by capitulating to his demands. Part of me wonders if he's going to hold it against me for the rest of my days. And the other part of me is telling that first part to shut the hell up because it wants to reap the rewards of giving in.

The prospect of the latter wins me over.

"I want it, Ryder."

He shudders. "You want what, Gretchen?"

I turn my head to the side, bringing our mouths within inches of each other. "You, railing me against the wall with your huge, hard cock."

He takes a nip of my lower lip, holding it between his teeth. "It's all yours. Fair warning, you might regret it."

I don't doubt it.

Two of his fingers find my opening and spread the moisture there. "But is this mine?"

There's weight to the question. Just like there will be weight to my answer.

But I'm choosing to ignore both and think simply in terms of physical gratification. For this one night, we've agreed to belong solely to each other. Give everything to the other for one single, solitary, no-holds-barred, no-limits, sweaty night.

Something forces me to meet his eyes when I answer, though I can't say what. "It's yours."

His expression hardens. His fingers move faster. "More."

My hands free the button on his pants. "My pussy belongs to you, Ryder."

Why I don't tack on *just for tonight* to that proclamation, I have no fracking idea.

His impatient hands fumble against mine as we both work to release his zipper. He shoves his slacks and boxer briefs down, allowing his stiff cock to spring out and greet my fingers. Pre-cum covers the tip, making it slick under the pad of my thumb. His whole shaft is pulsing in my hand, as if he's seconds away from losing his grip on reality and blowing.

"You're about to get it so deep."

With jerky movements, he tears my underwear off my body in one vicious yank. Such a beastly, primitive move. My body flushes from head to toe when his fingers find my throbbing clit.

"*Yes*. Just like that."

"Yeah?" He grunts. "That how you need it, duchess? That how I'm gonna make you come for me?"

My head lolls on my neck in what I think is a nod.

"Well, too fucking bad." He rips his hand away.

"*What?*" I go from delirium to outrage so fast I get pre-orgasm whiplash. "Don't stop! I'm so close."

"You're not coming on my fingers this time," he growls. "Not unless I'm inside you while it happens."

The sound of a crinkling condom wrapper fills the room. This should be the moment where I second guess myself. Where I allow doubt to trickle in until I'm pushing him away out of self-preservation. For any sensible person, it would be. But my survival instincts went out the window the moment he shoved my skirt out of the way and nearly shredded it to pieces. The moment he proved how viscerally I affect him by driving his raging erection against me. Any hope of walking away ceased to exist after that.

Once sheathed, he places himself at my entrance. "This room may be soundproofed, but I know you've got a set of lungs on you. I'll hear the full force of those later. But for now, can you promise me you'll be quiet?"

I brace my palms against the two-way mirror, raising an eyebrow at him over my shoulder. "Can you promise me you'll be rough?"

His eyes drink in every inch of me. "As if I have a choice."

"Then I can push my mute button."

As if to prove me wrong, he slams inside with a bone-jarring, thigh-clenching thrust that basically catapults me into an insta-orgasm. It's so unexpected and so powerful that my mouth automatically opens on reflex. Just before I can release the moan that's slingshotted up my throat, Ryder clamps his hand over my mouth.

He bites down on my earlobe. "*Liar.*"

And I still can't stay silent. I scream against his hand as he pounds me into that mirror. His pumps are so forceful, it's all I can do to move my hips in tandem with his. It's not long before I just give up and let him do all the work.

My attention catches on the participants sitting around the table in the next room. A middle-aged woman is talking with her hands while the rest listen to her. Sonja writes down some notes on her packet, nodding at the woman.

While I'm getting fucked raw by my boss behind the mirror.

Ryder keeps his hand on my neck, holding me steady. The wet slapping of our skin predominates the silence of the room. It's just too good. I didn't know it could be this good, as cliché as that sounds. His grunts mingle with my whimpers, and I know neither of us can hold on much longer.

Then he…slows down.

Frustrated, I'm about to yell that I need it fast and I need it hard when I peek around at him. He's watching himself slide in and out of me, appearing in awe of the sight. Like he's in a trance.

"Feel that, Gretchen. Feel *me* and know who's inside you. Fucking *remember* it."

A shiver travels down my spine at the leashed fury in his voice. Where is that anger coming from? His tone is definitely saying a lot more than his words. But the snug fit of him massaging my inner channel suddenly takes hold of all my faculties, including the ability to think.

"Goddamn, that's sweet," he groans. "Too sweet." His hips pick up speed once again. "Shit, I'm not gonna last. You're too fucking tight. And I've needed this for too fucking *long*."

His fingers dig into my waist so hard they'll probably leave bruises. I'm sure I'll regret seeing that evidence tomorrow. But right now, I need him to grip me harder.

Instead of tightening his hold, though, he lets go. Again.

But only in order to spin me around and lift me up by my ass. My legs coil around his waist as he plunges back inside. The abrupt penetration pulls another scream from me, but this time, he muffles my sounds with his mouth.

I need him closer.

I need him deeper.

In an almost tender gesture, he cups the back of my head as his tongue duels with mine. My circuit is overloaded. My hyper-sensitive nipples are rubbing against his starched dress shirt, his mouth tastes of espresso and chocolate, and he's filling me so *full*. He absolutely has to buy the extra-large rubbers. No question. If I wasn't so wet, he would be having a hard time squeezing in there.

And then it really dawns on me.

How long I've wanted this man. How attracted I've secretly been to him ever since that first day in his office. How fantasies about him have crept into my mind during those lonely nights with my vibrator. Was it all fueled by the remnants of what I thought was the best sex of my life?

Because…I'm pretty sure *this* right here is the best.

Whatever it all means, it isn't Myles inside me right now, kissing me. This is Ryder, my infuriating, too-clever-for-his-own-good, movie star gorgeous boss. As far as I'm concerned, anything that happened in the past between me and his brother has been wiped clean. Ryder's managing to obliterate any drunken memory still lingering from that night.

Now has nothing to do with *then*.

All it takes is the slight adjustment of his angle inside me to pull the pin out of the hand grenade and set off my explosion.

"Holy shit, duchess. Yeah, come for me, baby."

My limbs act on their own as they tighten around him—legs around his waist, arms around his shoulders, hands in his hair. A kaleidoscope of lights flickers behind my eyelids that I don't want to look away from but need to before I lose my sight altogether.

Seconds later, Ryder plummets after me into the abyss. I return the favor and swallow his shouts of pleasure with my mouth. I love the feel of his face stubble as it scratches my chin. The fact that he has a five o'clock shadow by noon every day is another thing I secretly love about him.

Ryder is *all* man.

He slams deep one final time, emptying the last of his release. The thrust is so hard that my ass bumps against the mirror with a *thump* that I have no doubt the participants can hear in the next room.

That's when I know I'm truly fucked.

Because *I don't care.*

Who cares about getting caught now that I know sex like this exists? And that a man who's been right under my nose this whole time can give it to me?

We take several minutes to catch our breath—disturbing moments that I spend petting his hair while his face is buried in my chest. When he eventually raises his head, I expect to see that signature cocky grin. Maybe a smug smirk that I'll be all-too-happy to slap off his face.

But I see neither of those.

He looks just as determined as he did when he first entered this room. Before he ever touched me. Before he made me admit to wanting him. Before he made me come so hard that I lost all semblance of reason.

He looks nowhere close to being done.

In fact, he's barely softened inside me. I'm sensing that we've only scratched the surface of what's to come.

"So," he drawls. "Your place or mine?"

17

The Oral High Club

My loft is no man's land.

Ryder is literally going where no man has gone before.

Which leads me to the inescapable conclusion that I've suffered a brain aneurysm.

He's right behind me in his car as I park outside my building. For some reason that's beyond me in this moment, I thought I'd have more control over our anything-goes night if I was in my territory. My comfort zone. I can better control an environment that has my name stamped on everything in it.

Having sex with my boss at the office is one thing. I can easily write that off as an anomaly or a fracture in the spacetime continuum.

But having sex with my boss in *his* bed?

Pfft.

There's no rebuking that as anything less than a tawdry affair between a woman and her superior, where he holds all the cards and she's got nada. Plus, it will be a pleasure to kick Ryder's beautiful ass out of my place whenever I've had my fill of him.

That ought to teach him a lesson.

Gretchen Castellanos is *always* in control.

Since my torn underwear are nestled at the bottom of Ryder's pocket, my ass nakedly swishes and sways under my pencil skirt as I approach the door to my building. My fingers tremble when I twist the key in the lock. His stomping footsteps closing in at such a clipped pace intensifies the anticipation.

I get the door open the moment I get a whiff of his aftershave. Scurrying up the stairs with him hot on my heels, the tension builds to a fever pitch with every step we climb. By the time we enter my home, my awareness of him is so heightened that my breathing unconsciously synchronizes with his.

Steeling myself, I pivot on my heel—

And find myself in an Old West-style shootout.

Only instead of guns, the weapons holstered at our sides are our sexual powers of persuasion. Whoever draws first could control the pace and course of the evening. And possibly our entire relationship from here on out.

Neither of us move.

He stands just inside my door, chest heaving, hands fisting at his sides. All body language of someone exhibiting massive amounts of restraint. Eyes intent on mine, he shrugs out of his suit jacket and lays it over the nearby armchair. His dexterous fingers efficiently remove his cufflinks, then loosen his tie until it's hanging haphazardly below his collarbone.

"In some kind of hurry?"

His expression remains stony. "You gave me one night and one night only. We have a lot of ground to cover. Why wait?"

"And you think you're going to dictate everything we do and how we do it?"

His eyes spark with intrigue. "Okay, fair point. How about we take turns being in charge? God knows we're both better at giving orders than following them. This way, it's a balanced exchange of power."

I drum my fingers against my hipbone.

And try not to smile triumphantly.

Frankly, Ryder is the first man with a dominant side that not only rivals mine, but even trounces mine at times. I've never trusted anyone to be capable of steering the S.S. Gretchen. Of knowing what I need without me having to say it. Of reading my body's signals so well that I don't have to do any of the work.

You'll never know if you never try.

"Deal. I'm up first."

"I didn't hear you call dibs."

"We're in my place, boss man. You don't like it, feel free to leave."

The look he gives me...

Him's got the devil in his eyes.

"Like you want me to."

His keen perceptiveness is without a doubt his most annoying quality. Sometimes it feels like I can't hide anything from him.

"Hey, I'm not the one who suggested an entire night," I remind him. "I told you, one time and I'd be good."

Canting his head to the side, he takes slow, deliberate steps toward me. "You're saying you don't want me now that I've been inside you?"

Ha! If anything, I want him more. But I fight to keep that from showing on my face.

I brilliantly answer with a shrug.

He studies me for a moment, eyes searching mine, before a grin touches the corners of his mouth. "You're full of shit, duchess."

When I cock out my hip, his eyes track the movement. "You want to test that theory?"

His eyes bounce back up to mine. "Yeah, I do."

Instead of taking me into his arms when he gets within dick's reach, he bypasses me entirely. Wheeling around in curiosity, I watch in frozen wonderment as he prowls down my hallway, unbuttoning his shirt as he goes. When he shrugs out of it and lets it fall onto my hardwood floor, my jaw drops.

Naked from the waist up, Ryder is a fantastical sight.

Flawless tanned skin, lean muscles toned to perfection, and a tapered waist that frames the tightest, most spectacular ass I've ever seen.

When he moves to pull the tie over his head, I call out, "Leave the tie."

He stops at the end of the hall, twisting his torso to glance back at me. Smirking, he leaves the tie on. "Let's see how long you last before you decide you want me again. But FYI, you might want to get over your stubborn pride sooner rather than later. Otherwise, I'm going to get this party started all by myself."

The old hag starts hand-fanning herself. *Either these are hot flashes, or I'm having feelings I haven't had since Nixon was in the White House.*

Okay, everyone needs to cool it. So, he's managed to surprise me.

He peeks his head into my bedroom and is about to step through the doorway when his attention snags on the opposite side of the hall where the bathroom is.

He does a double take.

Then he disappears inside the room. The next thing I hear is, "Oh, this will do just fine."

Okay, now he's managed to reel me in.

My feet can't help but follow him down the hallway and into the spacious bathroom. He's standing in the middle of the room, staring at the mammoth bathtub that I spent my hard-earned first-ever paycheck on.

"Very nice, duchess. This looks new."

I nod even though he's got his back to me. "I renovated it earlier this year."

"Take your comforts seriously, do you?"

"Shouldn't everyone?"

He somehow manages to reach behind him and blindly snatch up my arm without turning around. Shocked, I stumble in my heels when he hauls me around to face him.

"Naked," he grates out. Almost menacingly. "Get there."

The command dropkicks me out of my surprised stupor. Notching up my chin, I settle comfortably back into my saucy sweet spot. "I thought I was in charge first."

Emotions flit across his chiseled face, as if he's deciding whether or not to fight me on that. But the lust in his navy eyes sparkles too brightly for him to risk challenging me.

He releases his grip on my arm, one finger at a time. "Tell me what you want from me, duchess."

God, the *need* in his voice. It's thick and scratchy, like he's munching on a mouthful of broken glass. Familiar confidence rolls over me. *Hello there, old friend.* There are an infinite number of filthy demands I could make on him right now. But one in particular stands out above all the rest.

"Take off my clothes."

His nostrils flare.

The tension between us mounts as I fight the urge to dive on him and slobber all over his egg-carton abs. His smooth, sculpted chest is a damn work of art. The impulse to attack simmers between us, making our desire that much sharper. Our irrepressible need that much more acute.

One tug of his hand and my shirt is untucked from my skirt. Unbuttoned, spread wide. He doesn't bother looking down at his hands as he strips me. Making quick work of the task, he releases the front clasp of my bra.

Then he looks down.

Snaring me in that penetrating gaze. My skin feels singed, it burns so hot.

With more gentleness than I expect, he nudges my shirt and bra off my shoulders and down my arms. My breath hitches when they flutter silently to the floor. Standing under these bright lights, facing him straight-on, I'm baring myself to his lascivious gaze far more than I did in the viewing room. But I'm not self-conscious. Not nervous. In fact, basking in the spotlight of his worshipful gaze is liberating.

After drinking me in for several long pulls, he reaches around and lowers the zipper of my skirt. This brings his mouth to rest just above my ear, so I hear every minute change in his breathing. How ragged it's gotten. And his hands...they're...shaking?

Holy shit, is *he* nervous?

Would never have guessed that.

The material whooshes down my legs in a whisper of fabric and pools around my ankles. I carefully step out of it, my heels quietly clicking on the tiled floor. Ryder takes a step back and lets his hungry gaze drag over every naked inch of me. When it reaches my bare sex, he drags his hand over his mouth.

"*Fuck*." He mutters it in such a low voice, I almost don't hear him. "Keep it together, man."

Heat thrums low in my belly. Between his hoarse words and the sight of his red tie hanging over his naked chest, it feels like someone tossed my body into an incinerator.

"Now what?" He doesn't raise his eyes when he asks the question. I get the sense he's committing everything he's looking at to memory.

This is suddenly feeling too serious for my liking. I want to go all sassy on him and address how undone he looks at the sight of me. Infusing levity into a situation via sarcasm is my defense mechanism—my go-to when I'm uncomfortable. But I just can't grasp onto it.

Because I'm being pulled under by him, too.

"Now..." I take a step back.

Then another.

And another.

When my heels bump into the first step that leads to the tub, I lower myself onto the second one. Propping my elbows onto the highest step, ass resting on the second, I spread my legs wide, putting every waxed bit of my goods on display.

He curses under his breath. "Goddamn, woman. You should be fucking illegal."

"You going to lock me up and throw away the key? I might be a bad girl and resist." I inch my thighs even further apart. "You might have to cuff me."

His body surges forward.

Then, amazingly, he stops.

But the blood has left his fisted hands. His pupils are the size of frisbees. His shoulders oddly appear even broader when he's turned on like this. He looks on the razor's edge of losing his shit. I don't know how long I'll be able to prolong the foreplay before he goes catatonic.

I nod. "Good boy."

He licks his lips, eyes locked on the apex of my thighs. "Is that for me? Do I get to have that?"

The way he phrases that has currents shooting through my body like I just received an electric shock.

"I did tell you it was yours tonight, didn't I?"

I might as well have just told the eight-year-old version of him he could open his Christmas presents early. "All mine."

I ignore the possessiveness in those words. Mostly.

"Now, it's your turn to tell me what you want."

"I want to kiss you there." No hesitation. "Want to finally figure out what you taste like. I think about burying my head between your legs at least five times a day. Most of the time, I fantasize that you're lying across my desk when I do it. Then I have your taste in my mouth all day. When I meet with clients or talk on the phone, all I can smell, all I can taste, is my duchess."

If some part of me was unconsciously testing him with that question, he just passed with flying fucking colors.

"Like I said." My voice comes out thready, breathy. "It belongs to you tonight. I'm giving you the right to touch me, Ryder."

That's all the permission he needs to spring into action. *Spring* being the operative word. His erection is jutting against his slacks so insistently, a sliver of sympathy ripples through me. Though that quickly disappears the moment he drops to his knees and crawls toward me. His jaw is hanging open, like an animal salivating over its next meal. When he gets close enough for my thighs to cradle his head, he stops.

"Never could I have imagined that you'd offer yourself to me like this. I am the luckiest damn bastard on the planet, because you?" He shakes his head. "You're *perfect*, Gretchen Castellanos."

Actually, what I am is...speechless. The level of emotion weighing down his words is staggering.

And a bit alarming.

I pull him in the rest of the way by his tie so he can put his mouth to better use. But there's no denying it. He's getting me higher than my weed does. And that's *before* I feel his mouth on me. I go from sighing dreamily to throwing my head back and moaning the ceiling down after one raunchy drag of his tongue.

"Oh, my *Gooooood*."

I mean, Je-*zus*.

Who needs a Rabbit vibrator when Ryder Colson's mouth is a thing?

My hands clutch the edges of the tub, my hair dangling over the sides, as Ryder's mouth takes me on an upward trajectory toward a heavenly paradise, the likes of which I've never known. I feel like an empress of ancient Rome, sitting atop her throne while one of her faithful servants *services* her. Such depravity. Such hedonism.

I luxuriate in it.

Ryder drags his mouth over my inner thighs, sinking his teeth in with a soft growl. You'd think he was punishing me for something with the way he's assaulting me. Taking no prisoners. His mouth returns to my swollen entrance, the flat of his tongue taking a long swipe along my slit. When it pushes inside, my thighs quiver uncontrollably around his head. He acts like he could do this forever. Like he has all the time in the world. Like he's actually *enjoying* it.

The wetter I get, the deeper he goes.

The more noises I make, the harder he sucks on my clit.

The more eagerly I thrust against his mouth, the faster he licks.

And dammit if that doesn't do something otherworldly to me.

I've always believed in putting as much effort into sex as I do in my job, or anything else that requires skill or finesse. I want to do it well, I want to enjoy it, and I expect the other person to do the same. I should have known Ryder would be an over-achiever. Having worked with him for almost a year now, I should have anticipated his sex ethic to be on the same level as his work ethic.

He might be perfect, too.

He waits until I'm rocking against his mouth, begging for release, before he delivers on the big finale. Over and over and *over*, my hips buck. His tongue works over that bundle of nerves so expertly, it creates a dangerous cocktail of pleasure and pain. I give him all the sounds he demanded earlier. I scream his name, I moan for more. I basically vow my undying devotion to his mouth.

I might have been in charge when we walked into this room.

But he just led a coup into my royal chambers and knocked me off my throne.

His next statement confirms that very fact.

"After I'm finished with you tonight, duchess, you'll never be able to say no to me again. I'm about to make goddamn sure of it."

18

The Kiss of Death

REAL TALK ROMANCE, EPISODE 28

"I'm here today with three newly-engaged couples," Kennedy *says before introducing each guest. "First of all, congratulations all around. Very exciting time with the upcoming weddings. My first question to all couples is one I hear all the time. When did you know without a doubt that you had found The One? Was there a specific moment when you just knew, or was it more of a gradual thing?"*

"For me, it was on our first date. She said she loved my favorite band, and I'd never met a woman who had even heard of them before. I was ready to put a ring on it right there in that parking garage."

Everyone laughs.

"Mine was when I introduced him to my grandmother, who has Alzheimer's, for the first time. He was incredibly patient and sweet with her. I knew I'd never find anyone with a bigger heart."

"Awww," all the women say at once.

"Mine was really innocuous," one of the guys says. *"We were just going on a day trip one day, and I looked over at her sitting in the passenger seat. Something about the way the light was hitting her face in that exact moment made me think, 'God, I want to stare at this woman for the rest of my life.' I proposed a week later. It doesn't always take these grand, romantic gestures for you to realize that you can't live without someone. You just have to pay attention to all those little moments because they're almost always telling you something."*

I'm no monk.

I'll give you a moment to recover from the shock.

But here's the thing, I've been sitting motionless in the same spot for hours with a glazed look on my face. If you didn't know me and didn't know that the closest I've ever come to meditating was when I got higher than Apollo 13 off some stellar weed that my Jamaican former neighbors gave me, then you would think I've converted to Buddhism.

Let me just say, my insides are anything but at peace right now.

Because there's a *man* in my *bed*.

My boss, to be more specific.

Why didn't I kick Ryder out last night? Why didn't I boot him to the curb before I fell asleep? Why in God's name did I let him stay?

Probably because the sex didn't actually stop until four o'clock this morning.

Ryder definitely made every second of our "one night only" count. Literally. The man has stamina for days. He just kept going like a sex-crazed Energizer Bunny, defying all logic by pounding those drums even after the batteries in his little butt went dead. His dick didn't even get soft until after the *third round*. And mind you, there was a lot of foreplay in between those rounds.

The old hag tuts disapprovingly. *We called your kind* loose *back in my day, girlie. Fresh women.*

We covered every square inch of my loft. No surface was left undefiled by the time we dragged ourselves into bed and instantly passed out from exhaustion. Ever since I was startled into consciousness two hours ago by the presence of a warm body next to mine in bed, I've been sitting cross-legged on my living room rug, staring out the window at absolutely nothing. I managed to nakedly stumble into the bathroom and throw on my robe before I collapsed in this heap on the floor. Since then? I've been numb.

That is, until Ryder leaves my bed.

I hear every squeak of the bedsprings as he moves around in the next room, followed by the creaking of the hardwood floor as he leaves it.

"I see the regretting phase has started early," he deadpans after entering the living room.

I don't turn around. "I never said I regret anything."

"I don't think your face got that message."

"You can't even see my face."

He snorts. "Like that bird outside your window is that fascinating."

With a deep breath, I scoot my butt around on the rug, turning my folded-up body to face him.

Oh, and *screw* him.

A Hollywood hair and makeup crew must have visited my place this morning and forgotten about me. Because Ryder is beautifully disheveled with his stupid face stubble and sleep-rumpled hair that looks like it was purposely styled in those askew angles. His wrinkled slacks hang low on his hips with no belt. His white dress shirt is open, exposing his ripped-to-the-bone abs. And he's got the glazed look of a well-fucked man who wouldn't be opposed to some good old-fashioned morning-after shower sex.

While *I* look like a rabid raccoon that's just come off a five-day bender.

"Forgive me if I don't follow protocol here," I say haughtily. "This isn't exactly my schtick."

"What isn't? Letting your boss give you four screaming orgasms and going on a sex crime spree all over your place with him?"

Surrealism is starting to creep in.

"I vote for the name Sex Slaughterhouse."

Ew. Nevermind. Sounded way better in my head.

He spreads his feet, his hands casually slipping inside his pockets. An authoritative pose. "Not used to kicking the guy out during daylight? You prefer that to happen under the cover of night?"

I don't know what to make of the bitterness in his tone. "I wouldn't know. You're the first guy I've ever brought here."

He narrows his eyes. I can't tell if he's pleased by the admission or not. And I don't care either way. "FYI, coffee's a good place to start."

"Noted."

"But I'm guessing you already knew that." He quirks an eyebrow. "Intentionally not making it so I won't stick around longer than you want me to? That move's as old as the playbook itself, duchess."

My mouth forms a thin line. "For the last time, I don't play games."

He *tsk*s. "Ah, but you certainly have the strategy for them down well enough."

That has me shoving to my feet, hands stamped on my hips. "I resent that. You're the one who wanted one night, and you agreed to it. There's no need for strategy when the outcome has already been written."

"Then I guess I better haul ass out of here since it's no longer night, huh?" he snaps. "Carriage turned back into a pumpkin and all that?"

What's his problem? This was the deal from the beginning. Why is he acting like that conversation in the viewing room never happened? We were sober as judges and mostly clear-headed at the time.

I shrug. "I don't do fairytales. You're more like the vampire that has to haul ass out of here before the sun gets too high in the sky and you turn to dust."

His mouth forms a *not bad* expression. "I agree, that's more your speed. Vampire *slayer* is the role you were born to play."

There's more to those words than I want to acknowledge. But I didn't *slay* anything or anyone here. We both knew what this was. Slake our lusts one time, then close the door on them forever. End o' story.

I keep my emotionless mask in place. He confiscated it last night when his dreamboat mouth went down on me on my bathtub stairs. Now, it's firmly back in place and never coming off in his presence again.

I've super glued that bitch *down*.

"I take that as I compliment," I tell him flippantly. "Buffy is an idol of mine. I might even start hoarding stakes in my desk drawer."

He nods in approval. "Smart girl. You're going to need them."

Wait…what the hell does *that* mean?

He better not be strategizing his next tactic. Thanks to his snarky remarks, I have no issues kicking him out my door anymore.

"Don't worry, duchess. I know I've overstayed my welcome. Can I just wash up real quick before you officially give me my walking papers?"

I wince. He's making me sound like such a cold bitch.

Maybe you are.

"Sure."

His feet start moving in my direction.

I frown. "What are you doing?"

Instead of answering, he just keeps walking toward me. Then he bends down and lifts me over his shoulder.

"Hey!" I scream at his upside-down ass as he marches down the hallway. "What the hell are you doing, Ryder?"

"Washing up."

"I didn't say I'd be joining you!"

"I'm aware."

My punches to his kidneys don't deter him in the slightest. He enters my bathroom and deposits me on the vanity like it ain't no thang. Admittedly, I'm too stunned to move as he reaches over and turns on my shower. The nerve this man has is so infuriating, I can literally feel my blood running faster.

It turns me on like *nooo*obody's business.

And he knows it.

I've always been drawn to people who are on my level. It's why I instantly bonded with Sloane, Harper, and Quinn all those years ago. Why Ross and I are so close. Why Ryder and I have always made an efficient, competent team, though not exactly a harmonious one.

It's also why I've never been in a serious, long-term relationship.

I've never met a man who I feel can be my equal in all ways. Who can rise to my various personality challenges. Who can match me quip-for-quip. Who can give me all the nuances and excitement in a relationship that I'll need to keep me happy.

No one has even come close to fitting that mold.

No one except...the man standing in front of me.

Nuh-uh. He's not what you're thinking. He's not that.

Close but no cigar.

Some people look a hell of a lot like the person you're supposed to spend the rest of your life with, but there's not enough likeness. There might be a resemblance to The One, but it's not doppelganger material. It's where a lot of people get tricked in life. They search desperately for love, thinking they've finally—blessedly—found it, and they end up marrying the wrong person.

It's like a Celebrities Who Look Like Their Pets kind of deal. And Ryder is the Miniature Schnauzer to my Sam Elliot.

Being with him in any capacity outside of work beyond last night just isn't possible

Before I even realize his hands are touching me, he has the knot of my robe undone and is pulling the material open.

I smack his hands, trying to wriggle away. "If you think I'm getting in that shower with you, I must have knocked more than one screw loose last night."

His laughter is without mirth. "Oh, you're getting in that shower, duchess." He leans back, eyebrow up. "Unless you'd rather smell like me all day? 'Cuz that works for me. I like the idea of you wearing me on your inner thighs when you go to the grocery store later."

"How do you know I have to go to the grocery store?"

He brings our mouths closer, just enough to graze our lips. "Because you ran out of your last bag of chocolate espresso beans last night. And I know you can't go longer than twenty-four hours without them."

Oh, yeah. That. We gorged ourselves on them between rounds last night.

"I'll get in the shower," I concede softly. "*After* you leave."

His mouth curves into a triumphant grin right before he closes that final distance between our lips. It's not a hungry, greedy kiss like the ones from last night. This one is soft, tender, exploratory. Though I don't know what could possibly be left to explore. Not after all the very thorough expeditions we embarked on last night.

Yet...he's kissing me like he's still learning me.

He's almost worshipful in the way his lips close over my bottom one and tug. The way his hands frame my face, holding me like *I'm* the most precious treasure he unearthed on all those expeditions. There's a sweetness to this kiss I didn't anticipate and am wildly unprepared for. After the fire he scorched me with last night, I didn't expect the maddening slow burn of his technique now.

In fact, I'm so caught up in the dramatic contrasts of this kiss that I don't notice when he effortlessly picks me up and moves us toward the shower. My robe is abandoned on the vanity behind me, baring me completely. As if it's the most natural thing in the world, I sling my arms around his neck and take the kiss deeper. Suddenly, I don't care about how insistent I was on not taking a shower together. Don't care that this is extending the intimacy far beyond what I'm ready for. I'm in a place right now where I will give him a pass to do anything he wants.

Which is, apparently, letting me go.

My eyes shoot open when he pulls out of the kiss and gingerly places me on my feet inside the shower stall. I can't find words as we stare at each other intently. There's too much traffic passing between us on the electrical power lines connecting our bodies. I'm naked, for Christ's sake, and he's acting like he doesn't even notice. Like he's far too preoccupied with maintaining this suffocating eye contact in order to communicate whatever the hell he's transmitting with his eyes.

Then he steps back.

"I'll see you Monday morning, duchess."

And walks out of my bathroom.

I take my own step back and let the full force of the shower spray hit me square in the face.

But even that doesn't wash off that kiss.

19

The Therapy Hour Sloshing

I FEEL LIKE EVERY PERSON IN THE OFFICE knows what we did the second I walk through those doors Monday morning. They're the Salem hanging committee, and I'm the witch they're about to burn at the stake.

But of course, no one's the wiser.

Except me.

I know what Ryder can do between the sheets now. And against a wall. And on top of the kitchen counter. And over a table. I'm prepared for him to remind me of our twelve-hour sex-a-thon at every opportunity. I brace myself for those heated looks, for the innuendo, for the subtle touches he'll sneak in when no one's looking.

I'm ready for anything he tosses my way—except for the one thing he actually does.

Nothing.

Well, not exactly nothing. But like I feared, it's a whole new tactic. He's...nice. Considerate. Doing thoughtful things that punch holes in my defenses.

He walks in on Monday with a bag of chocolate espresso beans and my favorite hazelnut coffee, slaps them both down on my desk, and trudges to his office without a word.

On Tuesday, he gives me an actual heartfelt compliment on my quarterly client report that all account managers are required to turn in to him. Which he's never, *ever* done before. Heartfelt compliments aren't our thing.

Wednesday afternoon, he texts me the link to a song by Keb' Mo', one of my favorite bluesy/jazz musicians, that I've never heard before. After carefully listening to the lyrics, I have to wonder...

What in the great balls of hellfire is he playing at?

I tried to put out the fire, but the flames still burn,
And as she pleases, she comes and goes,
She's got the wind in her hair.
She never ceases to hurt me so.
Where am I goin', what am I gonna do?
I know I'm not crazy, I'm just hooked on you.
So go on and use me, endlessly, could you let me know
When you need me, hold me close and, baby, don't let go.

I'm on a hairpin trigger by the time Thursday rolls around. I spend all morning tip-toeing around the office, just waiting for him to pop out behind every corner with a thoughtful gesture or a kind word.

It's my own personal horror flick.

Things only get worse later that afternoon. After Ross calls to tell me he can't be my date to the annual Aid for Veterans Benefit Dinner that night on the base. The Major invites us every year, and we're happy to go because it's a great cause. And every year, Ross and I always go together. Because if I bring my own date, the Major will feel obligated to grill him, no matter how insistent I am that the relationship isn't serious. Been there, never doing it again. If I don't bring a date, then the Major will use it as an opportunity to throw every swinging dick in a uniform at me in hopes that just one will make good husband material. Ross is an old hand at running interference for me at this thing.

But he decides to bring a date of his own this year.

Leaving me to the wolves.

My accusations of treason are only half-assed because he actually sounds interested in this woman. I know he wouldn't bail on me simply to get laid, so it must be more than that. And who am I to stand in the way of a possible connection in the making? Even if I wanted to go with a date, it's such short notice that I don't bother trying.

Sure enough, the Major pimps me out to every young officer in attendance that night. If I wasn't so eager to hear the keynote speaker talk—a bona fide hero with an incredible story—I would have done an about-face and marched my happy butt right out of that ballroom. My life is not about to become *An Officer and a Gentleman*. But here's the kicker…many of the men he introduced me to were actually quite attractive.

There were just two problems.

One, I could never date a guy who's too intimidated by my father to behave like his normal self around me. Each one of them acted too petrified to look at me anywhere but directly in the eyes. For tough military guys, they seemed like a bunch of sissies.

And two, none of them kept me on my toes…like Ryder does.

That's when I decided to get drunk. Once I started imagining Ryder's face in place of every man's I met. So, I relied on my trusty 'ol vodka gimlets to make all those faces too blurry to even distinguish identity.

And on top of *that* hell fest, my favorite vibrator broke. After stumbling home from the dinner with Ryder still on my mind, I needed release in a bad way. I hadn't been able to stop thinking about our one glorious night together. The expertise with which he dominated our love-making—

No, not making love. You fucked. A few times. Spectacularly and brilliantly, but it was still just fucking. No love involved.

Anyway, I thought I could take care of my little problem with a quick tickle from my eleven-inch pickle. And I blew out the damn motor. Or whatever the hell those things run on. There were fresh batteries in it and everything.

How pathetic is that?

I *broke* my vibrator over my *boss*.

Needless to say, I'm in full hangover-bitch mode by the time I drag myself into work on Friday. Noting the way I'm stomping around and banging my shit all over the place, my co-workers give me a wide berth for fear of losing a limb if they venture too close.

All except for boss man, that is.

"Aw, did the sun rise without Queen Gretchen's permission this morning?" his too-deep voice rumbles. "Or did someone just forget to take her Xanax?"

My eyes dart to Ryder's.

That's the first time all week he's spoken to me like the Ryder of old. Pre-sexplosion Ryder. All week, he's bitten back the snark and general jackassery. Is it possible he's actually picking up on things I don't want him to? Like my thoughts and feelings?

Leaning against my cubicle wall, his gaze is sharp as it takes in my strained features and tense muscles. I know that look. It's the same one he wears when he's reviewing data or assessing our monthly financial report. He's reading me, analyzing me, and applying that knowledge to determine the best strategy moving forward.

Despite his too-focused scrutiny, the familiarity of his attitude relaxes me.

Somehow, he knows I need him to be the version of himself I'm most comfortable with. The a-hole boss with an ego the size of Alaska and a mouth as cutting as a scalpel. The fact that he reverts back to it without blinking an eye is mind-boggling. And a little distressing. He knows that friendly robot Ryder isn't going to work with my mood right now.

Back to old habits.

I return my attention to the line graphs on my computer screen. "That's right, boss. I'm off my meds. Better keep your distance or I might have a schizophrenic episode and come at you with a letter opener."

"How would that be different from any other day?"

I almost smile. "Any other day I would settle for a pen."

"And what, may I ask, has brought out your inner Catherine Tramell today?"

I shoot him an impressed side glance at the *Basic Instinct* reference. "It was last night, actually."

Why did I admit that?

He goes silent for a moment. "Were there not enough vampires out to slay or something?"

I snort. "It was more about being paraded around like the pick of the litter in front of a military smorgasbord."

Why, Gretchen? Why don't I have that *knowing when to shut up* instinct ingrained in my brain?

"Is that supposed to make sense to me?" Ryder snaps, sounding annoyed. "Why would you be treated like the pick of the litter and by whom?"

I flick my wrist, uncharacteristically flustered by my big mouth. "It's nothing. Classic case of failed parental matchmaking, that's all."

"*Matchmaking?*"

I gasp when my chair is yanked away from my desk.

Inertia pins me to the backrest as Ryder spins the chair around, bringing us face-to-face. "Are you telling me that your parents tried to set you up last night?" he whisper-shouts. If we weren't in the middle of the bustling office right now, he'd be flat-out yelling those words. "With *more* than one man?"

"Just my dad," I find myself confessing. "He thinks my biological clock is going to stop ticking any day now and then *poof.*" I snap my fingers. "There's goes any chance I have at love and procreation."

Ryder straightens to his full height, looking furious. "Come with me."

"Uh, I kind of have work to do here, you know."

"Leave it." He adjusts his cufflinks as he turns away. "I know none of what you're working on right now is time-sensitive. Let's go."

I'm still pinned to the chair. "Where are we going?"

He looks down at his watch. "Happy hour's almost over, duchess. Move your ass."

Ryder sets our drinks down on the table, sloshing a little over the rims and soaking the cocktail napkins underneath. He lifts his to his mouth, watching me intently as he drinks. "So, spill. What's the deal with you and your dad?"

"I thought this was happy hour. Not therapy hour."

He barks out a laugh. "Happy hour has *always* been therapy hour. 'Let's go to a bar and bitch about our work troubles while getting tipsy off four-dollar margaritas so we can survive another week' doesn't market as well."

I tip my head in agreement. "True."

"Come on, duchess," he coaxes in a softer voice. "I think you can afford to give me something, since I was so *giving* the other night."

My mouth twists unattractively as I struggle to fight off another smile.

Oh, yes. He was very generous last week.

"My father is lifetime military. He doesn't know how to function without order and regiment. In his mind, marriage and reproducing should fall under that same strict structure of regulation. Black-and-white, no complications. He married my mother right after she graduated high school, and he can't understand why it's not that simple for everyone."

Ryder doesn't react. Just sips on his beer, taking in all this new information with a placid expression. "Well, that certainly explains a lot."

"About what?"

He inclines his glass in my direction. "You. Why you're anything *but* structure and order. I can only imagine what your teenage rebellious streak looked like. Especially since there seems to be no end to the adult rebellious streak."

I smirk. "You wish you knew me when I had pink hair and a tongue ring."

His glass freezes halfway to his mouth. "Tongue ring?"

I stick out my tongue and press my teeth against the not-quite-healed hole in the center.

His lips part as he stares at my open mouth. "You still got the jewelry for it, duchess?"

I stopped wearing my barbell on a daily basis, back when I felt I'd made my point to the Major that he wasn't going to control my life so he needn't keep trying. But I don't want the piercing to close up. I still put it in every few days after work. As silly as it sounds, it gives me a secret thrill. I can't exactly wear it to client meetings, so wearing it when I go out at night allows me to feel like my younger self who never wants to fully grow up.

I've always wondered what the hell Wendy Darling was thinking, leaving Neverland to go back to the real world and all her responsibilities.

Cartoon bitches be crazy.

"Yes, I do," I tell him coyly. "Quite the collection, actually."

"Why haven't I seen one in before?"

"I don't wear it at work."

"The next time I see you *outside* of work, I want you to have it in." His voice leaves no room for argument.

Hot damn, there's that adrenaline he always sparks in me. The implication that he'll see me again outside of work hangs in the air for several moments. And I'm not sure how I feel about it.

We said one night.

We *had* our one night.

There isn't supposed to be more. Though why I don't immediately remind him of this I can't fathom. Perhaps some part of me loves that he not only wants to see the tongue ring, but that the mere idea of it turns him on.

He takes mercy on me by reverting back to the previous subject. "So, your father is pulling a Cinderella in reverse on you? Instead of every eligible maiden attending the ball to meet the prince, it's every eligible bachelor attending to meet the princess?"

I roll my eyes at the comparison. "What is it with you and fairytales?"

He grins. "My nieces are really into Disney princesses right now. I haven't been able to get those damn songs out of my head for the last six months."

I pause. "How do you have nieces? Does Myles have...?" *No way.*

Ryder shakes his head. "Our stepsister has two daughters. She's ten years older than us, so we were never close to her growing up. But Myles and I are suckers for her girls."

Why do I feel a pang in my chest at the idea of him being a doting uncle? A month ago, I never would have been able to picture it. But now...*whew.*

My ovaries have never behaved like this before. Weird.

Maybe I have a cyst.

I prop my elbows on the table, leaning forward. "Do they live around here?"

"Greenville. I usually get to see them one weekend a month, but I Zoom with them all the time. We end up having a Disney sing-a-long about ninety percent of the time."

I smile. "Put me on a three-way call for the next one, would you?"

He chuckles. "Sorry, duchess. The only girls in my life who have that kind of dirt on me are the ones whose only friends are their stuffed animals and a few at school who know me simply as 'Your Cool Uncle Ryder.'"

I burst into laughter. I can't help it. Picturing him belting out *The Little Mermaid's* "Part of Your World" with a couple of cuties playing dress-up finally gets to me and I lose it.

He looks mesmerized.

"I'm hiring you for my next birthday party," I wheeze. "I'm feeling a princess theme."

"You never answered my question," he reminds me gently.

After catching my breath, I give in. "The Major is a stubborn control freak. I haven't found a husband all by myself yet, so he thinks he has to do it for me. Don't ask why. I've been asking myself that for seven years, and all I've come up with is that he must think I'm wasting my life and that marriage would calm me down."

"I'm sorry to hear that."

I wave him off. "Seven years is long enough to get used to it. Doesn't mean I appreciate the chauvinism, but I handle it well enough. I just wasn't in the mood to deal with it last night."

Ryder mimics my position, leaning farther over the table. "No, I mean, I'm sorry to hear that your father doesn't know you very well."

When my throat closes up, I chug down my drink to lubricate it. He takes the hint when I don't respond and drops the topic. Thankfully, we always have work talk to circle back around to.

"Oh, that reminds me. Allen's wife is having knee replacement surgery on the twenty-ninth, so he's not going to be able to come to New York with us."

I drop my glass.

Amazingly, it doesn't shatter and only spills a little onto the table.

Allen is another senior account manager who is supposed to round out the trio going to the two-day Southeast Marketing and Advertising Expo in New York City over New Year's— me, Allen, and Ryder. This event has been scheduled for months, but with all the…distractions…over the last several weeks, I honestly forgot all about it.

"He's not coming to the expo?" I ask Ryder in a panic. "Can't they reschedule the surgery until after the New Year?"

His brow furrows as he takes in my reaction. "The surgeon had something open up that day and doesn't have any availability for another two months."

Which means it's just going to be the two of us for two full days in New York City.

For New Year's Eve.

"Is that going to be a problem for you, Gretchen?" His tone is challenging. Daring me to say yes.

I meet his infallible gaze. "That depends."

"On?"

"On why you brought me here today."

He leans back, tapping his finger on the table. "I saw that you were having a bad day. Figured you needed to take your mind off things."

"I don't see you taking any of your other employees out for happy hour."

His finger stills. "There's a lot of things I don't do with my other employees."

I order another vodka gimlet.

Between that comment and the pregnant pause that follows, the admission about having sing-a-longs with his nieces, and the realization that we'll be alone in NYC for two days together, a good therapy hour sloshing is just what the doctor ordered.

20

The Night Before Christmas Puns

I'VE HEARD THAT THE COLSON GROUP'S CHRISTMAS PARTIES ARE EPIC. Since this is my first Christmas with the company, I decided I would have to judge that for myself. But I will say, The Westin's penthouse ballroom in downtown Charleston looks pretty fucking epic to me.

Overlooking the river, the penthouse bar and rooftop patio are decked out with wall-to-wall twinkling white lights, frosted garland, ginormous floor vases full of glittery sprays, and numerous fully-decorated Christmas trees that are at least twelve feet tall. It's gorgeous. It's breathtaking. It's...

Romantic.

No, it's not. It's hideous and dreary. It's doesn't look anything like a dreamy Hallmark movie.

"Sweet baby in a manger, Gretch," Quinn groans, sipping from her glass. "You've got to try some of this eggnog. The cinnamon on top makes all the difference."

I hold up my glass. "I'll stick with my Santa's Got a Brand New Bag punch, but thanks. You know I don't drink eggnog."

Harper approaches us with Sloane right behind her. "No, this is where it's at," the blonde says, pointing to her drink.

"Peppermint schnapps, Irish cream, and Kahlua. The bartender calls it 'And a Schnappy New Year.'"

"You're all wrong," Sloane cuts in, holding up a glass filled with a white liquid. "I'll be dreaming of this White Christmarita later tonight. Coconut milk, tequila, triple sec, and lime juice. *Feliz Navidad* to me."

"Hold up," I bite out, offended. "Is no one seriously going to try my punch? I worked hard on this recipe, dammit. And I made a shit ton of it."

They all shoot each other uneasy looks.

"Gretch, even the bartender is warning people away from that punch bowl," Sloane says in the same way you would placate a child.

"Yeah, he's saying it should come with a label that has the number for poison control on it," Quinn adds.

I scoff, disgusted. "Some mixologist he is. Like liquid nitrogen ever hurt anyone."

They all stare at me blankly.

I roll my eyes. "I'm *kidding*. People with heart conditions can drink this stuff, I promise. And it won't show up in a piss test."

"You mean like the Pot Punch you made for St. Patty's Day that contained cannabis products?" Harper grumbles. "It was basically liquid weed."

"Oh, that was killer," Quinn says, high-fiving me.

"Thank you, Quinn. At least someone here isn't a complete pansy. Besides, you know you loved that shit, Barbie. You went on and on about how the Midori in it made it all green and *so, so preeeetty*."

Sloane and Quinn smother their laughter behind their glasses.

It's so cute when Harper glares. "Yeah, I was so high that I made out with a cardboard cut-out of a leprechaun."

"And you showed him a night he'll never forget," I retort. "You were his pot of gold, babe."

When she eventually loses her battle with her smile, I blow her a kiss.

"Where are Carter and West?" I ask after glancing around the patio.

It's Charleston, so it's not terribly cold tonight, even in December. But there are heated lamps spread around the patio that provide just enough warmth to make it cozy.

Sloane snorts. "Waiting for drinks at the bar that, and I quote, 'don't have a girly, Christmas pun in the name.'"

"Well, aren't they just little snowballs of fun tonight."

Harper winks at me. "Don't worry, West has got too much on the line to risk being a party pooper. I told him that if he behaves himself, I'll give him what's underneath my tree skirt before Christmas."

Quinn pretends to gag. "We don't need to hear about your unwrapping festivities. I prefer to *not* see Mommy kissing Santa Claus."

Harper bumps her shoulder against her ex-stepsister's, giggling.

"Speaking of Santa Claus," Sloane interjects, "where is the jolly old boss in the suit?"

"Making the rounds," I mutter bitterly as my gaze tracks the man in question across the room. "And heading toward your men, by the looks of it."

Yes, I've been watching Ryder closely all night. Like an idiot. My posture has been aloof and disinterested, but my eyes have been daring him to flirt with even one woman. Which is unfair and hypocritical of me, I know. I'd get redder than Rudolph's nose and kick him in his jingle bells if he warned me against flirting with other men.

Regardless…

I'll go Jackie Frost on his ass and stab him with an icicle if he starts spreading his holiday cheer to any female that isn't me.

It's not like I can blame them, though. What sane, straight woman wouldn't want to sit on that man's lap and take his sleigh for a ride? Even I want to lick him like a candy cane. *More like lick* his *candy cane*. He's wearing a red and black velvet sport coat over a black shirt, black tie, and black slacks.

On anyone else, I'd probably say the velvet jacket would be tacky, but I don't think there's a look that Ryder can't pull off. His hair has that characteristic floppy thing going on up top, looking messy and put together at the same time, and he kept his day-old facial stubble.

Five minutes under the mistletoe with that man is all I need.

He's been watching me, too. We've been circling each other like two opponents in the ring about to come to blows. And *blow* is exactly what I have in mind.

Ryder follows Carter and West as they cross the patio to us, drinks in hand. I zone in on the one Ryder has in his hand because—

It's my punch.

He's drinking my Santa's Got a Brand New Bag and he seems to be enjoying it. In fact, his glass is already halfway empty. The way my skin instantly warms has nothing to do with that, though. I'm just standing too close to one of those heated lamps.

Watching my boss closely as the three of them near, I intentionally cock my hip to the side, widening the slit in my hip-hugging maxi skirt.

Ryder's eyes lower to my exposed skin.

My wine-colored, two-piece velvet outfit is sleek with a slender silhouette. The long-sleeved top is fitted and cropped, with a deep V in the back. The matching skirt would look almost demure if it wasn't for the near-indecently high slit that runs along my left leg, all the way up to the top of my thigh.

Not gonna lie, I feel like a Bond woman in this outfit.

If only I had a tube of lipstick that doubled as a gun.

I rarely wear my hair up. It has a mind of its own, and I gave up trying to tame it a long time ago. The thick strands are heavy and fall into the same wavy look every day without me having to take a hair wand to them. It works for me. But I wanted if off my shoulders tonight in order to showcase the back of my top, so I pinned it up with some silver glittery clips and called it good.

Judging by Ryder's expression, I'd say I made the right call.

"You throw quite the party," Sloane muses to Ryder.

My boss ducks his head sheepishly. "Oh, I can't take credit. All I did was make a phone call and book the place."

"If this is how you do Christmas, I can only imagine what your New Year's Eve looks like," Quinn comments.

"Yeah, I'm jealous," Harper pipes up, leaning into West when he slips his arm around her waist. "Gretchen was just telling us how you two will be at a conference in New York for the New Year. What better city to celebrate the holiday in, right?" Blondie tosses me a discreet wink behind her glass.

"I'm thrilled." I glare at her. "Can't you tell by my face?"

"Trick question," Ryder quips. "You always wear that scowl."

Everyone snickers while Ryder grins at me proudly.

"If you weren't such an overbearing hard-ass, Ebenezer, I wouldn't have to scowl so much," I shoot back.

"If you weren't such a sarcastic insubordinate, I wouldn't have to be a hard-ass."

"And a Merry Christmas to you, Mr. Colson!" Sonja flamboyantly declares as she slaps a Santa hat on Ryder's head. "You know the rules. You cuss, you sing. You screw up, you drink."

I bite my lip to keep from cracking up.

That was one of several party rules tonight, accompanying the many drinking games going on. If someone hears you cuss, you have to sing the Christmas song of that someone's choosing. If you mess up the lyrics before they tell you to stop, you have to take a shot.

The only reason I'm not already hammered at this point is not because I *haven't* been cussing. I've just been using my inside voice. Who knew I even had one, right?

"'Have Yourself a Merry Little Christmas,'" Sonja tells Ryder gleefully, stating the name of the song he's supposed to belt out.

The corner of his mouth twitches confidently as he moves his gaze back to me. Locking eyes, he begins to croon the first verse.

My breath slowly leaves me.

Ryder...can sing.

Like, he's not bad. Almost Frank Sinatra-esque. And he actually knows the words. The melody rolls over me like a lover's caress, giving me chills. The way he's looking at me, the way his voice dips on certain notes, it feels like he's singing to *me*. It's thrilling and unnerving at the same time, considering we're not exactly alone here. Everyone at the party has stopped what they're doing and is now listening to our leader as he stands before me in a sexy Santa hat, singing with a voice that can only be described as pure seduction.

By the time he finishes the chorus, the entire patio has broken out in applause. Whistles and cheers distantly echo in my ears as my gaze remains interlocked with Ryder's. It feels like I'm wearing earmuffs. Like there's a disconnect between the two of us and the rest of the party. The growing lust radiating from his features is overpowering any arrogance from winning the challenge.

What other hidden talents has he been keeping from me?

Sonja holds up the shot she was saving for Ryder. "I guess this will have to wait for the next victim."

"Not so fast there, Sonja," Ryder cuts in before she can walk away. He pulls the Santa hat off his head and plops it onto mine. "I believe someone else here has a potty mouth."

My group of friends laughs while everyone else cheers.

"'Do You Hear What I Hear?' Ms. Castellanos," Ryder says happily. "Other than my victory, of course."

I glower. He winks.

He damn well *knows* I hate that song. Don't know why, just always have. I refuse to listen to it, so I'm sure has hell not going to sing it. I swipe the shot glass out of Sonja's hand and down it.

At least it's not Jägermeister.

Catcalls and a few disappointed *awws* follow the action. With the show now over, the party resumes as everyone gets back to their own conversations and games.

"You gonna be okay?" Ryder asks me sarcastically. "I know admitting defeat is a painful process for you."

I snort. "It's only defeat if both parties have agreed to compete. And I don't play games I think I'll lose."

His eyes bore into me.

I mentally kick myself.

In a way, I've just admitted that he's a game I think I could lose, seeing as how I've so vehemently insisted that I *don't* play mind games at all. In other words, I'm not going to compete with him because I'm not a hundred percent sure that I'd win. I've just unwittingly tipped the scales in his favor, and I need to rectify it immediately.

I feel everyone's eyes flicker back and forth between us while we face off in a heated staring contest. I probably should be annoyed by his attitude in front of my friends, and yet, I'm anything but. In fact, this is the most excited I've been all night.

I blame that excitement for what I do next.

Bringing my glass to my lips, I subtly lick along the rim, my tongue snaking out just enough to reveal a little something extra I slipped on for tonight's festivities.

Ryder's face goes slack.

The diamond barbell in the middle of my tongue winks at him with a tinny clinking noise against the glass. His gaze is glued to it, mouth hanging open, eyes drooping. My head is barely turned away from my friends, so they can't see what's brought on this odd reaction in him.

My mouth quirks. "You say I'm insubordinate, boss, but even you have to admit I follow orders every now and then." *Like when you told me yesterday to wear this baby the next time you see me outside of work.* "I just pick and choose my moments."

His eyes fill with heat.

Static silently crackles and pops in the air between us.

Quinn clears her throat. "What a fun work environment."

Visibly shaking himself, Ryder finally breaks our eye contact to shoot her a wry grin. "As you can see, it's never boring with this one."

I curtsy. "Such is my curse."

I take a huge sip of my punch until my cheeks bulge. Then swallow it all down in one audible gulp.

Patient needs 20 ccs of liquid courage, doc. STAT.

I won't allow Ryder to knock me off kilter. Not tonight. No siree.

"If you'll all excuse me, I have an appointment with the bartender." I place my empty glass onto a passing server's tray. "Try to entertain yourselves while I'm gone."

Carter chuckles over the top of Sloane's head. "Gee, that's asking a lot, Gretchen. However will we survive?"

"How did people entertain themselves back in your day? Kick the can? Maybe you can find some marbles and string around here somewhere." I pat him on the back. "Well, I'm sure you'll figure something out, old man."

Sloane playfully flips me off while Carter just shakes his head and laughs. He's gotten used to my good-natured ribbing about the fact that he's fifteen years older than Sloane. We all know how perfect he is for our homegirl.

As I leave our circle, I shoot Ryder a look. A message that can't possibly be misinterpreted. *Follow me right now or you'll regret it.*

Making my way across the patio, I say my hellos and engage in the appropriate small talk in an effort to not make my exodus appear too hurried. And desperate. It's hard, though. I'm beyond the brink. I've had a plan culminating all night. I've just been waiting for the right opportunity to set it in motion.

But screw waiting.

As I enter the penthouse ballroom, I feel a looming presence behind me, stalking me. *Good to know he can follow orders, too.* I shuffle down the carpeted hallway of the hotel, my footsteps silent. Because his are just as silent, I can't necessarily *hear* Ryder behind me, but I *feel* him. I know he's there because my skin is tingling, the hairs on the back of my neck are prickling, and my heart is racing.

My attention catches on a sign ahead of me, next to the elevator: *Stairs.*

Bingo.

I shove open the heavy door and skirt my way down the first flight of stairs just as "Santa Baby" comes over the hallway speakers. Thankfully, the lighting in this stairwell is soft, rather than harsh. Sporadic sconces on the wall illuminate a path, though there are still intermittent shadows. The landing between flights happens to be shrouded in one of those shadows.

That's where I put on the brakes.

Ryder's steps are quick as they descend the stairs after me. Desire swamps me the closer he gets. My nipples pucker beneath my velvet top, my breathing turns choppy—

He clamps his hand on my shoulder and spins me around.

Backing me up against the wall, he slants his mouth over mine. Our groans of pleasure reverberate through our bodies and off the walls of this hollow space. Our tongues not only seek, they demand. They're impatient. His swipes against my barbell, eliciting a deep rumble from his chest. If I didn't know better, judging from his frustrated growling, I'd say he resents me for forcing him to go without any contact for an entire week. But dammit, it's *his* fault that I've been starved for him. *His* fault that I've been on edge for the past seven days.

I tug on his hair, breaking the kiss. "Would you like your Christmas present early?"

His fingers explore the exposed skin of my stomach. "Depends on what I'm unwrapping."

"Have you been a good boy?"

He licks his lips. "You tell me, Mrs. Claus."

I forgot I still have on that damn Santa hat. I transfer it from my head to his, delighting when his eyes glaze over. "From what I've heard, you've been pretty bad."

"That so?"

"Mm-hmm." Hands gliding down his torso, I yank open his belt and tug down his zipper. "Lucky for you, though, I've decided to give you more than a lump of coal in your stocking."

His head falls back on his shoulders when I reach inside his briefs to palm him. "I thought you said one night only, duchess."

He really wants to discuss this *now?*

"What could once more hurt?" I tighten my grip in hopes that he'll stop talking. "We can blame it on the eggnog."

He places his palms against the wall, caging me in. He looks almost...conflicted. "You don't like eggnog."

"You're telling me you don't want to feel *this*"—I stick out my tongue, displaying the barbell—"on your dick?"

He growls. "You also never ask a question you don't already know the answer to."

"Then for once in your life... Shut. Up."

He snatches my jaw before I can kneel, cupping it firmly. Those navy eyes of his blaze bright with need. "Don't ever pretend that you don't fucking love the way I talk to you. You're not that good of a liar."

"Maybe you just don't know me as well as you think you do."

He pinches my chin between his fingers. "And maybe it's time you accept that I really *do* know you that well, Gretchen."

I squeeze him hard enough to draw a guttural groan from him. "I'll take that as a challenge."

"Why does it have to be such a challenge for anyone to know you? To *really* know you?"

Because opening yourself up to someone means you're opening yourself up to a world of complicated emotions, including pain. Letting someone in gives them the ability to hurt you at some point. The more intimate knowledge about you they have, the more weapons they can use against you. It's no different than war tactics.

Protect your secrets. Guard the stronghold.

Thanks for the life lesson, Major.

Breaking Ryder's hold on my chin, I go to my knees, his fingers slipping free. The wall at my back steadies me in my stilettos. Maintaining our eye contact, I take him between my lips.

This isn't a real talk gab fest.

The only talking I want happening here is of the dirty variety. I will *make* him shut up if he wants to keep running his mouth. I might be on my knees for him, but he's not going to have the upper hand by the end of this exchange.

His expression tells me he knows what I'm doing. But he's either helpless to the feeling of my tongue ring dragging down the length of him, or he's simply ceding control to me.

With one hand massaging his base, I swirl my tongue around his bulbous head before taking him to the back of my throat.

"Jesus *Christ*, duchess. That's it. Blow my fucking mind. Bury my cock in that hungry little mouth."

I know I just told him to shut up, but his words are abducting me and taking me to another planet. In a different universe. His voice alone has the ability to do that, I'm learning. To pull me out of my own head. To open up that trapdoor I so often need. The one with a portal leading to another dimension.

Total escapism.

That's what being with Ryder is.

The only problem with that? Escape is temporary. It's a form of avoidance. Eventually, you have to return to reality and all of its limitations. Ryder might be real, but whatever this is between us can't be. Can *never* be. Hooking up with one's boss doesn't have a happy ending—beyond the orgasms, that is. So, even though I'm extending the pre-determined parameters I set in place last weekend, this will still have to end.

This is just me taking an extra vacation day, that's all.

"I've wanted you to myself all night," he whispers. His forehead scrunches, his eyes squeezing shut. "The way you look in that skirt...and that fucking *thing* in your tongue... Goddamn you, woman. You're wrecking me."

I realize then how high my slit has ridden up in my crouched position, completely baring my black thong.

His hips rock faster. "Can you take me deeper, baby?"

With pleasure.

"Yeah, that's my girl. Swallow me all the way down."

He's long and smooth in my mouth. The lingering scents of his spicy body wash invades my senses, increasing my appetite. His fingers sift through my hair to help guide me until we both find a pace we like. One of the silver pins comes loose and clatters to the floor at my feet. His fingers are there to replace it and keep the freed strands out of my face.

Then we hear muffled voices on the other side of the stairwell door. They get closer, clearer. Until I can tell they're *right* there. Even as I brace for the door to open any second, my lips stay wrapped around Ryder.

"Shit," he spits angrily. "You're going to have to touch yourself, duchess. I had much better plans in mind, but I can't let you leave this stairwell aching. Touch your pussy for me and finish us both off."

My fingers find my slick entrance, swollen, throbbing. I had other plans, too, but he's right. If we're about to be interrupted, this is better than nothing. As I take him deeper and suck him harder, his breathing grows louder. I can feel his release building inside him, can feel my own climbing up that same peak.

The door creaks open.

But no one enters the stairwell. I hear the woman's voice, but she's clearly still talking to someone out in the hallway.

"Hurry," Ryder urges in a whisper. "Come on those fingers for me, duchess."

Is he waiting on me?

Aw, how sweet.

And no, that wasn't sarcasm.

When I rub my clit, I swear I achieve nirvana. My thighs are shaking so violently with my climax that I almost lose my balance. My nails dig into Ryder's thigh to hold myself upright.

He follows closely behind me, his release shooting down my throat and sending my mind reeling all over again. When his fingers tighten in my hair, I know he's exhibiting monumental restraint to stay quiet. After experiencing how vocal he can be in the bedroom last weekend, it's probably painful for him.

The door at the top of the stairs clicks shut. The woman is still talking on the other side of it, giving us a few more moments of seclusion.

I rise to my feet and smooth down my skirt. He doesn't immediately tuck himself back in his pants. Instead, he looks like he wants to strangle me and devour me in the same breath. Then, as if he can't help himself, he collapses against me and claims my mouth with his own.

Something about that surrendering action cuts through me—deep—like a machete in the bush. Even though we're on the verge of being discovered, he can't even be bothered to cover himself because he's too focused on stealing another kiss. Too overwrought by his passion to care about getting caught by that woman.

Nothing will stop me from kissing you right now, duchess.

That's the vibe I'm getting.

So many aspects of Ryder's personality call to me. His rebellious, non-conformist side. His aversion to convention. His unrelenting insistence that he do things his own way and no one is going to tell him otherwise. Ryder is his own person through and through. In all honesty, he's had my admiration ever since my first week at TCG.

But could I give him something more? And would he even want it?

"That was one hell of a Christmas bonus," I say breathlessly as I replace the silver pin in my hair.

He chokes out a laugh, finally shoving himself back inside his briefs. "Duchess, I think you've earned one hell of a raise."

I pat him on the cheek. "I'd like that in writing, please."

With his hand on my lower back, he guides us back up the stairs and out into the hallway. The woman is still talking to her friend, who both seem oblivious to what just took place inside that stairwell. I catch Ryder's eye out of the corner of mine as we enter the ballroom, and we both burst into laughter. I know we need to flip that switch that turns us back into the boss and employee who hate each other.

But laughing with him just feels so good.

We're still smiling like pre-teens who just had their first seven minutes in heaven experience when we step onto the patio. He discreetly gives my waist a quick goodbye squeeze just before he traipses off to once again mingle with the crowd. I scan the area in search of my friends when I sense someone watching me.

Sonja.

From one of the high-top tables, she watches me over the rim of her wine glass. Because I know how intelligent the woman is, my guard is immediately thrown back up as wariness creeps into my bones. Her gaze sidles over to where Ryder is speaking with a group of people. Then it comes right back to me, narrowing in speculation. The sparkle in her eyes is—knowing.

Mother shit.

We were too obvious and now a co-worker suspects something. Sonja and I have always had a good relationship. She's not a gossip or a bitch. She's a hard worker, and everyone around the office loves her.

But would she talk?

I plaster on a cheerful smile and take the glass of champagne a server offers me. I laugh with the co-workers I pass on my way over to Sloane and the rest of the crew. As intended, the act fools everyone. Not a single person on this roof, my girls included, would think anything was amiss with my behavior.

But Sonja...I feel her eyes follow me for the rest of the night.

What the hell was I thinking?!

No more escapes with Ryder. That's it. We're done. The whole thing is too risky. That trapdoor is sealed shut. Cemented over.

Back to reality.

Permanently.
And now I get why Wendy Darling went home.
Neverland was just too good to be true.

21

The Flight From Hell

REAL TALK ROMANCE, EPISODE 31

"Welcome back to another episode of RTR, all you beautiful people," Kennedy begins her show. *"Today, we're talking with three married couples, all who've recently celebrated milestone anniversaries. Deon and Trinity just made it through their first blissful year of marriage together. Harrison and Katie hit their twenty-five-year mile marker and have two teenagers at home. And Archie and June have now made it fifty glorious years together, with five children and nine grandchildren to show for it."*

Everyone applauds the oldest couple.

"We're going to learn all their secrets for how they make marriage work and keep that flame burning bright," Kennedy continues. *"Let's kick it off with one of the questions I hear most often: what do you consider to be the most important aspect of a relationship?"*

"I think having enough of the same interests is critical," Deon answers. *"You have to enjoy doing a lot of the same things together because that's when all the best memories are made."*

"And not just similar interests, but similar goals," Trinity chimes in. *"If you're not both going in the same direction in life, you'll end up growing apart."*

"For us, I think it's mostly been about balancing each other out," Katies pipes up. *"Your personalities have to complement each other, not combat each other."*

"You have to make a good team," Harrison says in agreement. *"Especially when life gets more hectic and stressful. You've got to be able to work well together or else every little thing will turn into a fight."*

"It might be an old adage," June says, *"but communication is key. It does neither person any good if they keep all their thoughts and feelings to themselves. If you never talk, you'll never be completely in tune with each other."*

Archie grunts. *"Eventually, you'll talk so much that you won't need her to say anything to know exactly what she's thinking. Which is both a blessing and a curse."*

Everyone chuckles.

"What's your wife thinking right now, Archie?" Kennedy asks.

"Well, she's tempted to hide my reading glasses from me when we get home for that comment, but...she knows how much I love her."

"And how do you know that?"

"Because she can read my mind, too."

"So, are you going to tell me why you haven't said more than five words to me this week? Or does Twenty Questions start now?"

Ryder's voice snaps me out of the weird daze I've been in. It's like falling asleep with your eyes open. I don't even think I've blinked for the last five minutes while staring out the small window on the plane.

"I was preoccupied with family at Christmas," I answer in a low voice. "That coupled with end of the year deadlines and getting everything ready for this expo, I've been a little busy."

He doesn't look up from the laptop sitting on the tray table in front of him. "Too busy to answer your texts? Or calls, for that matter?"

Yeah, so I might have been ignoring his after-hours messages ever since the Christmas party. And doing so might have felt like waxing your upper lip with hot bacon grease, but it was necessary. Putting distance between us was the right thing to do, even if he can't see that now.

"The fact that you sent those texts and made those calls outside of the office imply that they weren't work-related."

His finger clicks the mouse on the keyboard, his focus remaining on the screen. "So what if they weren't?"

"That's against the rules."

"Giving me a blowjob at the office Christmas party was against the rules, yet you had no problem going to your knees for me then."

When my head swivels around, he mirrors the action, pinning me with his all-too-familiar glare. Jaw clenched, eyes hard, mouth tight.

"Is that what those messages were about?" I fume. "You wanting to get me on my knees again?"

I can't even blame him for being frustrated because I know I've been sending out some crazy mixed signals. It's not like I'm happy about this either. But I've picked a side now, and we both have to find a way of accepting it.

He blows out a heavy breath as he slams the laptop closed. "For Christ's sake, Gretchen. If I was that hard up to get my dick sucked, I would have called a woman who's fluent in more languages than just Smartass and Stubborn Witch."

"And here I wasted my evenings by *not* picking up the phone for you."

He scrubs his hands down his face, muttering indecipherable words behind them. "I swear to God, it's like talking to a child."

I grin sardonically. "Correction. I've matured since last month. You're now dealing with a pre-teen, buddy. Prepare for the ages."

I return my attention to the window when he goes silent.

"I know you do this whenever you're nervous or uncomfortable," he eventually says in a cajoling tone. "And I know why you're doing it now."

I swallow thickly. "Doing what?"

"Making a joke out of everything. Refusing to be serious. Your sarcasm is an overcompensation for avoiding heavy discussions."

"Thanks for the analysis, Sigmund," I mutter dryly. "I'm definitely going to need that raise if you start charging me by the hour."

Ever so carefully, as if fearful of spooking a skittish woodland creature, his fingers close over mine. Gently. Comfortingly. Warmly.

My eyes slide shut.

I want nothing more than to take what he's offering. I want to thread our fingers together, push the armrest separating us out of the way, and snuggle into his inviting chest. I've never had a steady guy in my life to do that with. To *cuddle* with. I never used to put much stock in the act, but I'm finally starting to understand its appeal.

I want to wrap myself up in Ryder.

I want to be held by him.

"Gretchen..." His voice might as well be the warm milk that lulls you to sleep at night.

"Please, don't," I whisper.

"Why not?"

My lower lip quivers, and I mentally punch myself in the ovaries. *You will* not *cry in front of your boss on a goddamn plane.* The urge to cry right now doesn't even make sense. "Because every time I'm with you, I forget myself. It's like I don't even know who I am."

"Is that really such a bad thing?"

My head whips around so fast that he has to lean back or get smacked in the face by my hair. "If I'm not me, then who the hell am I?" I snap. "Who do you turn me into?"

His eyes soften, which only serves to infuriate me. "You don't become another person, duchess. You just allow a side of yourself that you normally hide from everyone to come out. You've got a lot of layers to peel back, and I'll bet that I've gotten further than anyone else ever has."

If I didn't feel my chest moving up and down, I would swear I've stopped breathing. "Pretty confident, aren't you?"

He slowly shakes his head. "Not around you I'm not. Can't you tell? Why do you think we work so well together? We both posture in similar ways, but we do it for different reasons."

"Those reasons being...?"

He shrugs, his hand still covering mine. "You do it because you're uncomfortable or nervous. I usually do it when I'm intimidated."

My lips part.

This successful multi-millionaire couldn't possibly be intimidated by *me*. He implied as much that day in the office when he met Ross. But I thought he was just trying to charm my brother.

Ryder nods as he takes in my shocked expression. "I've dealt with all manner of powerful and wealthy people, duchess. Tycoons, CEOs, heiresses, billionaires. But I have never been as intimidated by anyone as I have been working with you this past year."

My eyes widen. "*Why?*"

His gaze drifts over my face, as if re-familiarizing himself with it. "Because you see so much deeper inside a person than they want you to. You have the ability to read what's underneath the surface. Then you have the unnerving habit of calling attention to what you learn. Most people can't handle facing that."

Those don't sound like compliments to me.

"You're saying I make you uneasy?" *Because I don't like that.*

I know I don't have much of a filter. I could work on that. And I'm probably too opinionated. And sure, I'm a little crass at times. But—

"I'm saying you've made me see everything in a completely different light."

Where the hell is that cart lady with some pretzels? This conversation is getting way the crap too real and I need out.

I slip my hand out from under his and place it safely back on my lap. "What were all the texts about, then?"

He stares at his now lonely hand, propped on the armrest between us. For seconds on end, he just looks at that space where my hand should still be. Eventually, he straightens in his seat, cracking his neck from side-to-side.

"If you wanted to know that, then you should have responded."

I roll my eyes and turn back to the window. "Just promise me one thing."

"Not in the mood to make promises right now."

I frown at the lack of warmth in his voice that was there just seconds ago. "While we're at this conference—while we're in New York—everything remains professional. This is a business trip, and it needs to stay that way."

As I wait for his response, I hear him start clicking the keys on his laptop again. Ignoring me?

"Ryder? Are we agreed?"

"Like I said, I'm not in the mood to make any promises."

He's completely right. I am a child.

Because the first instinct I have after hearing those clipped words is to retaliate just as immaturely. He wants to be that way whenever I'm trying to re-establish some middle ground so we can get through the next two days without any bloodshed? Fine.

If he wants to be unreasonable, I can, too.

I unbuckle my seatbelt and stand up, but I deliberately place my hand on his thigh for support as I do so. My fingers intentionally drift a little too close to his family jewels, and boy, does he notice. His body locks up, nostrils flaring. He stares straight ahead for several beats before his eyes finally tick up to mine.

"Excuse me," I say in a saccharine sweet voice as I loom above him. "I need to visit the lavatory."

With blue eyes sharp enough to carve out a gaping wound in my chest, he places his laptop in my empty seat and pushes to his feet. The small step he takes into the aisle is barely enough for me to squeeze past. Our proximity forces my body to rub against his. Every inch of our fronts make contact, particularly that bulge I nearly fondled a moment ago. He's clearly making sure I feel all of it because—

He's hard.

As. A. *Rock.*

My breath hitches. He still doesn't move. I have nowhere to look but directly into his eyes.

"You keep saying you don't play games, Gretchen," he breathes against my mouth. "Yet you keep trying to win them."

I end up sitting on the lid of that tiny toilet, head in my hands, wishing I'd answered just one of his texts. Because he's right.

I *am* trying to win.

And the reason I'm getting my ass kicked is because for the first time in my life, I am wildly, ridiculously out of my league.

22

The Best Shopping Partner Ever

"HOW COULD THEY LOSE MY BAG?" I screech in a voice that only dogs can hear. "You'd think that with all the advances in technology these days we wouldn't have to worry about lost luggage anymore. We have cars that drive themselves, for God's sake."

"Did you have GPS tracking on your suitcase?" Ryder asks as he types out something on his phone.

I stare at him like he just said that Woody Harrleson *isn't* one of the greatest comedic treasures of our generation. "Of course not."

"Then shit tends to get misplaced. Not the end of the world, duchess."

"How can you say that?" I wave down at my body. "We're going to be here for two and a half days, and these are the only clothes I now have to wear."

Lifting his head, he leans in close like he's about to spill a secret. "Don't tell anyone, but I hear they have clothing stores in New York City. *Actual* clothing stores, can you believe it? Keep that just between us, though, okay?"

"I don't have time to go shopping right now." I shove my phone in his face. "The conference panels start in thirty minutes."

"The first one I really want to sit in on doesn't start for another two hours. We have time." His phone chimes with a text. "Cab's here. Let's go."

I don't move. "You're not serious."

After nonchalantly picking up my messenger bag and draping it over the handle of his suitcase, he not-so-gently nudges me forward. "I'm taking you shopping, Gretchen. Get over it."

"Yeah, no you're not—"

"Time to nut up or shut up."

Damn him. He knows I can't say no to Woody.

He's got my ass in a cab before I have time to scream, "Help! This guy is kidnapping me!" TSA would have tasered his ass so hard, and I would have laughed in the face of his chauvinistic manhandling.

I spend the entire cab ride pouting.

Opportunities like that don't come around every day.

"Are you insane?" I screech *yet again*. I didn't even know I had this kind of vocal range. "You pay me pretty well, boss man, but I can't afford Chanel." As much as I would like to. "Ever hear of a thing called rent?"

He sighs and holds up a gold credit card. "Ever hear of those things called perks?"

I back away from him on the sidewalk outside of Chanel, shaking my head. "You are not about to buy me designer clothes, Ryder. You start treating me like a kept woman and I will kick your balls so far up into your scrotum, they're going to come out of your nose."

He hangs his head, hands on his hips. "You've got to be kidding me right now. If it can't be a perk of your job or a gift, then consider this part of your goddamn raise." He takes a menacing step toward me, resembling an African big cat just before it pounces. "But so help me, Gretchen, you will get your ass in that store and try on some clothes. Clothes that *I'm* paying for. We actually do have work to do while we're in this city, and I'm not wasting any more time talking about this bullshit." Censure twists his mouth. "And don't you ever say the words 'kept woman' to me again."

He holds the door open for me, waiting.

I haven't moved. Why? Because entering that store feels like yet another step in our relationship that I never agreed to take. I'm also scarily turned on.

Cranky Ryder is *sexxxy*.

Yep, three X's.

"How about this?" he bites out, gnashing his teeth. "Get in there right now or you're fired."

I walk through the door not because of his threats I know he'll never act on. But because that vintage suit in the window is calling my name.

Ten minutes later, I'm decked out in Coco's finest. The smartest, classiest skirt suit in the whole store. This will definitely do for tomorrow's day of panels and the presentation we'll be giving. As one of the most profitable marketing and advertising firms in the Southeast of the last year, we were asked to lead our own session on "How to Implement Conversational Marketing Into Your Business and Growing brand." It's something Ryder's pretty passionate about. He strives to maintain personability and a one-on-one connection with all of our clients and credits this approach to much of TCG's meteoric success.

"How long do you think it'll take for them to track down my bag?" I call out from behind the dressing room curtain as I start undressing again.

"No telling," Ryder responds from the other side. "To be safe, I'd get everything you'll need while you're in New York. Business attire, something to wear to dinner, pajamas…if you're opposed to sleeping naked, of course."

I have the skirt halfway unzipped when his head pops around the curtain. "Out, Colson!"

"And let's not forget undies." Grinning, he produces a few hangers of various lingerie sets. Gorgeous ones.

"You are so not buying me underwear."

His grin widens. "I *so* am because I *so* want to. It's nonnegotiable. This is me being nice by letting you have a say instead of just buying everything *I* like."

I cross my arms over my chest. "Why bother? It's not like you'll be seeing me in it."

His head tilts to the side. "You sure about that?"

"I thought we already had this conversation on the plane. Business only from now on."

He snorts. "Yeah, we'll see how long that lasts."

"What's that supposed to mean?"

He steps all the way inside the room, the curtain fluttering closed behind him. "I'm not the one who went down on *you* at the office Christmas party. Seems like someone can't stay off the naughty list."

"Oh, did I forget to mention that I have a twin, too? That must have been her sucking your dick that night."

He belts out a laugh. "I know your mouth by now, duchess. There's no mistaking that."

The air in this fitting room suddenly gets awfully heavy. I'm tempted to prove him right by pushing him back onto the armless chair in the corner and going for a nice, long *ryde*. He looks so fucking edible in his pinstriped suit, I'm salivating. His hair is a little mussed from the wind outside and yet it still looks as perfectly disheveled as ever. I know he's reading the look on my face for what it is because his own clouds with desire.

I spin around so he can't see more.

He *always* sees more. Too much. And he accused me of being able to unnerve people?

Clearing my throat, I say, "So, we haven't talked about New Year's Eve tomorrow night. Did you have something in mind, or are we going to do our own things?"

"*Our own things?*" he spits, sounding incensed. "You really think I'd unleash you on this strange city by yourself on New Year's Eve?"

I shoot him a rueful smile in the full-length mirror. "Don't think I can handle myself, boss man? How well do you actually know me?"

He glowers. "Plenty well. Which is why I meant I would never release Gretchen Castellanos on the people of New York on the biggest party night of the year. You get a little pyromaniac-y after a few drinks. If I left you to your own devices, the entire city would be ash and rubble by morning. Don't you think these people have suffered enough?"

A genuine smile takes over my entire face. "Good answer."

He winks.

Talk about pyromania. He just started a small fire in my panties.

"I've already got your dress handled," he adds.

I frown. "For tomorrow night? I was planning on going to a cheaper store to look for one. No sense in spending ungodly amounts of money on something that might get beer spilled on it…" I trail off when he reveals what he's been hiding behind his back.

One of the most breathtaking dresses I've ever seen.

Mainly because it's *me*. One hundred percent. I don't know how I missed it out in the store when I was browsing because it would have definitely found its way in here if I had. But Ryder spotted it and knew it was totally and completely *me*.

To say I'm impressed doesn't begin to cover it.

I'm weirdly…touched.

"Holy cheese and rice. Now, *that* is a dress."

It's a stunning ice blue color that will make my silver eyes sparkle like diamonds. The top is a corset-style with a sweetheart neckline, and the material covering most of the bodice is sheer. The skirt looks straight and tight, even on the hanger. It'll probably stretch tight across my ass and stop a few inches above my knees. Despite the relatively simple design, there's an insta-love quality about it.

"Fit for a duchess?"

Lust makes his voice come out hoarse. Lust and...hunger.

I reach out to take it. "I suppose it will do."

"You need a hand with that?"

"I think I can manage." Over my shoulder, I catch him ogling my ass. "If I need help, I'll just call for Lanelle." The associate who's been helping me find my sizes.

"I meant with your top," he clarifies.

"Oh, right." I reach back for the high zipper on the sleeveless blouse. Lanelle had to help me zip it up in the first place because it extends from the nape of my neck to halfway down my back. "I'll get her."

He's in my space with his hands on my back before I even know what's happening. I suck in a sharp breath at the electricity that zings between our bodies. It's like he just attached two jumper cables to my nipples and shocked me with 50,000 volts of charged current.

Which is a little absurd when you think about it.

This man has seen every nook and cranny of my body. He's been inside me, had his mouth on nearly every inch of me. Yet he still manages to get a reaction with a slight brush of his fingertips.

His breath kisses the flesh of my neck as he slowly lowers the blouse zipper. The cadence of my heartbeat is being played in triple time. The heat of my growing arousal is on a southbound road, headed straight for the mecca of my centerfolds. By the time the zipper is undone, my knees are knocking together from my overwhelming need. And judging by his heavy panting, Ryder isn't faring much better.

"Duchess, I—"

"How's it going in there?" Lanelle's melodic voice asks.

I dive for the curtain and yank it open. If I'm left alone with Ryder's hands for one more second, I will not be held accountable for my actions. "Going great."

Her smile widens when she sees Ryder in the room. "Your boyfriend has impeccable taste, I must say. With your coloring, that dress will look radiant on you. And I have the perfect jacket to go with it."

Feeling devious, I return her smile. "Oh, he's actually my brother. His boyfriend had to go out of town for business, so he decided to tag along with me. But you're right about him having impeccable taste. Best shopping partner ever."

Ryder emits a low growl behind me.

I bite my tongue to hold back my laughter.

Lanelle's face softens. "How nice. My sister is literally the worst shopping partner ever. She doesn't have a button to turn off her brutal honesty."

"I have no choice but to be brutally honest with this one, I'm afraid," Ryder cuts in. "A long streak of idiot boyfriends has really chipped away at her self-confidence. But as hard as it might be, the best cure is to just tell it like it is. For instance,"— he slaps my ass hard, sending me tumbling forward with a yelp—"you're going to need a different skirt, *sis*. This one makes your ass look fat." To Lanelle, he adds, "Too many Christmas cookies, you know?"

Oh, that smug bastard is *so* going to get murdered.

And this is New York City. No one will even notice him bleeding out on the dirty street.

Lanelle sighs sympathetically. "I hear you. That holiday weight is a bitch."

"I'll go find something else." Ryder shoves me aside and steps around the curtain that Lanelle holds open for him. Then he ducks his head back in. "I'll grab you a pair of Spanxx, too. Until you can work off all that ham and turkey."

I snatch my heel off the floor and launch it at his head. Dodging it at the last second, he struts off laughing.

I decide to let him off the hook for calling me fat.

I mean, the dude *is* buying me Chanel.

23

The Jaded Non-Believer

SEPARATE HOTEL ROOMS.

Directly across the hall from each other, but they're still separate.

And yes, I'm painfully aware that a couple feet of measly hallway are *all* that separates us as we undress and get ready for dinner. Ryder is getting naked twenty feet away from me, if that. Something about him being out there while I'm in here feels wrong. The fact that we're not together feels inherently wrong.

One night of crazy monkey sex with the man and I go bananas.

My entire life, the one thing I could always count on—could always rely on—were my instincts. But apparently, I can't even trust those anymore.

I glance down at my phone when a text comes through. It's him, asking if I'm ready. Instead of replying, I just grab my coat and clutch and head for the door. It was a long day of listening to panels at the expo, and I'm ready to unwind for the rest of the night. We happen to open our doors at exactly the same time—

Gulp.

Jesus C, I want to tackle him right back into that room.

He's already wearing his wool coat over his black sweater and gray slacks. He attempted to comb his hair back, but I know that one floppy section will be hanging over his forehead by the time we reach the lobby.

"Ready?"

He has yet to meet my eyes. "You look…" He rubs his hand over his chest—right over his heart—looking undone. "Unbelievably beautiful."

I come dangerously close to melting into the carpet.

This ivory Chanel jumpsuit fits me like a glove. It dips into a low V in the front and tapers down at the waist, flattering my shape. I paired it with some classic black pumps and my favorite berry lipstick that Harper made especially for my skin tone. A chunky gold bracelet and delicate gold chain around my neck complement the understated cut of the jumpsuit. For the finishing touch, I pulled one side of my hair back with a gold clip so I could show off my new Chanel stud earrings that Ryder bought me.

He's already buying me jewelry. And we're not even dating. Is that irony? Or…bribery?

"I better mark this day on the calendar."

His eyes connect with mine. "Why is that?"

"That's the first genuine compliment you've ever given me."

He acts as if that comment jars him. "Compliments have never really been our thing, have they?"

He's just now figuring that out? "Not really."

A curt nod. "I can change that."

Please don't.

Because if that changes, then I'll be forced to acknowledge all the other ways our relationship has changed. And I'm not sure I'm mentally capable or emotionally mature enough to do that at the present time.

As I slip on my ivory coat, he holds out his arm for me to take.

I don't.

He rolls his eyes. "Stop overanalyzing, nutbag. I'm escorting a woman to dinner. I can pretend to be a gentleman for that amount of time. It doesn't have to mean anything more."

"Did you just call me a nutbag?"

"Affirmative."

"What happened to the compliments?"

"That can start once the new year hits, and gee,"—he glances down at his watch— "I've got at least another twenty-four hours left to fill with all the insults I want."

I grin. I can't help it. He's always spoken my language. "Don't take it easy on me, then."

"Wouldn't dream of it."

With that, I wind my arm around his and allow him to escort me to dinner. Wearing the clothing and jewelry he bought for me. It doesn't hit me until we're halfway to the elevator.

Holy fucksticks.

This is a date.

When I realize the enormity of that I—

Just keep on walking.

"I swear to you, there is a cow prancing around on some little farm in northern Nebraska right now that's named after me."

Ryder places his wine glass on the table, shaking his head. "Well, that figures. Of all the creatures in the animal kingdom, it makes sense that a heifer would have your namesake."

I throw my cloth napkin at his face, making him laugh. "Hey, I brought life into this world when I helped that calf being born. What have you ever done?"

He hums in the back of his throat. "I once helped an eighty-five-year-old woman carry her groceries out to her car."

I lift an eyebrow. "Filling that good deed of the week quota, were you?"

He winces. "Not really. Turns out she'd stolen them. Filled up her cart and walked right out the door with over a hundred dollars' worth of groceries."

I choke on my wine. "And no one stopped her?"

"I think all the employees just assumed she'd paid for them. And everyone felt bad about questioning her because it looked like she would have fallen over if her cart hadn't been holding her up."

I'm trying to decide if it's appropriate to laugh. "Maybe she had Alzheimer's or something."

"That's what I thought at first." He grins. "But nope. She was just the world's oldest living shoplifter. Had a record going back to her teen years."

I slap my hand over my mouth, but the unattractive snort still escapes.

Ryder's smile stretches from ear to ear.

"Shut up," I grumble. "I might snort when I laugh, but at least I'm not an accomplice to a crime."

"Oh, I don't believe that for a second. Just because you've never been caught doesn't mean you've never broken the law."

With a mouthful of cheesecake, I point my fork at him in agreement.

"Besides, it can't truly be shoplifting if I ended up paying for them, can it?"

My chewing stops. "You paid for them?"

He shrugs. "She was too old to get a thrill from stealing. Her clothes were ratty and dirty, her car could barely run, and I saw all the prescriptions in her purse. She may have had a history with petty crime, and I'm not saying it's right to steal at any age, but what good would it really have done to arrest her?"

I feel the wine making my cheeks flush. I assume it's the wine anyway. It's got to be. Certainly has nothing to do with learning that Ryder has a deeply compassionate side. Or with the romantic ambiance of this elegant restaurant on Fifth Avenue.

"I think you're a lot softer in the middle than you want people to believe."

He holds my gaze hostage for several beats. "I think you are, too, duchess."

That gets a laugh out of me. "As if. I'm the sour surprise you don't expect at the center of hard candy."

His silence draws my attention up from my plate. "You really believe that, don't you? You think you're the bad guy of your own story."

I swallow. "People like me aren't the good guys, Ryder."

"And what are people like you?"

I can't believe I'm actually peeling off this layer of skin in front of him. Just like a facial chemical peel, the end result is bound to be hideous. "Jaded. Cynical. Non-believers aren't the stars of fairytales, Ryder. We're the antagonists." Taking a sip of wine, I tip my glass in his direction. "Those are my people."

He looks almost angry. "For such a perceptive person, you surprise me. You would think the one person you'd know better than anyone is yourself."

I snicker as I lean back in my chair. "Honey, I'm the world's leading expert on understanding myself. You know why? Because I'm surrounded by amateurs. And I make sure everyone stays that way."

"Seems like your friends know you pretty well," he points out.

"They've certainly come farther than anyone else." Even farther than Ross—there are just some things you can't tell your own brother. *Yuck.*

Ryder's expression turns intense. "Don't be so sure."

I tuck my tongue in my cheek. "Don't be so confident. We've worked together for nearly a year, and there's still a lot you don't know about me."

"You're familiar with the story of the tortoise and the hare, right? The tortoise won that race with patience and perseverance." His grin turns mysterious, unnerving me. "I'll win this race by using those same tools."

"I'm a race now?" Not sure how I feel about that.

"It's sure felt like it," he murmurs. "And you can damn well bet I'm going to beat out any hare that challenges me."

That sounds far too on the nose for my comfort. Too possessive. Like how he's behaved with the whole Myles situation. How he reacted when he didn't know Ross was my brother. Is he really saying that he won't let another man come near me?

His expression says *hell yeah, I am, duchess. Took you long enough to figure that one out.*

All of a sudden, I'm feeling very…claimed.

24

The Romantic Ice Skating Montage

DINNER WAS AMAZING, DESPITE THE SERIOUS TURN IT TOOK. The restaurant was swanky as hell, and I'm pretty sure I saw Anna Kendrick sitting at a table in the far back corner as we were leaving. My belly is full of wine and cheesecake, and I'm floating on a cloud that I suspect isn't just from the wine and cheesecake. Sure, New York has an energy about it. There's a vibe in this city you can't find anywhere else.

But Ryder...

He's the real reason why it feels like I'm defying gravity right now.

We're walking arm-in-arm down Fifth Avenue with all the other New Yorkers and tourists in town for tomorrow night's festivities. I'm tucked into his side like a girlfriend would be, but I'm leaning into it. It just feels too damn good. I couldn't care less about the implications of labels right now.

Plus, it's balls cold out—*negative* balls cold—and Ryder emits body heat like a furnace.

We turn a corner amidst a bustling throng of other pedestrians. "This isn't the way back to the hotel."

"Good eye."

"And we're going the wrong way because...?"

He tips his head at something across the street. "Because the night's not over yet."

I follow the direction of his gaze—and my stomach sinks. Taking me to Rockefeller Center at night can only mean one thing. "Pass."

His hold on my waist tightens when I try to walk in the opposite direction. "Scared, duchess? That's a new one. You're right, we definitely have to mark this day on the calendar."

I'm a big enough girl to admit that yes, I'm a little scared.

Big girls would admit that out loud.

"Ryder...I've never ice skated before in my life."

Something about the risk of cracking my head wide open on the hard ice has always freaked me out.

He moves in front of me, blocking my view of the street, and frames my face with his hands. "Then let me be your first."

I choke on a laugh, drawing a smile from him.

"Come on," he coaxes softly. "You don't always have to be so tough, you know. It's okay to lean on me every once in a while. It's good for my masculinity."

I duck my chin to hide my smile. He keeps doing that. Making me smile when I don't really want to. "I'm going to look like an idiot."

"Not possible. In fact, I think you're the only person on the planet who will make falling on her ass look sexy as hell."

I shove him. "You'd let me fall?"

"I'll do my best not to. But there's only one way to really ensure your safety."

"What's that?"

"You have to hold my hand the entire time." As he says it, he laces his fingers through mine. "And you can't let go."

My exhale comes out long and heavy.

"Well played, boss man." I go up on my tip-toes, bringing our mouths closer. "But that means if I go down, you're coming with me."

He brushes his lips against mine. "I wouldn't want it any other way."

❖

"Yeah, I'm still not getting the appeal of this," I complain as Ryder and I slowly shuffle around the ice rink.

He squeezes my gloved hand, which no, he has not let go of. Regardless of his impressive balance, I won't let him move us too far away from the safety of the wall.

"Once you figure out how to skate on your feet and not your ankles, it's pretty fun."

I scowl down at my ankles that won't seem to straighten. "I don't foresee myself ever converting."

"That's because you hate not being good at everything."

"Says the over-achieving perfectionist."

His expression takes on a wistful quality I don't know how to interpret. White puffs billow in front of his mouth as he breathes in the frigid night air. "It doesn't really pay to be an under-achiever, does it? Don't worry, there are plenty of things I'm bad at."

"Name one."

"Have you ever seen my cursive handwriting? It's atrocious."

I tip my head back and laugh. The movement sends me wobbling, and I frantically clutch onto his arm like a drowning cat. "Well, thank God for that. The mystery of whether or not Ryder Colson is actually human is finally solved."

"A super breed of human," he corrects. "I'm in my own special category, wouldn't you agree? After all, you've seen me naked."

"You might have a point, considering the size of your di—"

I'm jostled from behind and knocked against Ryder. We both slip off balance as my skates slide out from under me. Luckily, he has enough wherewithal to make a mad grab for the nearby wall and manages to hold us both upright with his vice-like grip on my waist.

"Sorry, my bad!" the passing skater who bumped me yells.

"The Winter Olympics aren't until next year, Apolo!" I shout back. Some of the people skating by laugh.

Ryder hasn't let go of me.

With his arms cinched tightly around me, we look like two lovers embracing. I stare into his dark blue eyes that are looking at me so intimately, I feel myself sinking into their bottomless, dark depths. My cheeks are ice-cold, my nose probably a rosy red. The tips of my fingers went numb a long time ago. But the heat of that look makes it feel like I'm sweating nakedly in a sauna.

Our mouths come together at the same time, as if an invisible string connected them and pulled us in. Somehow, his lips aren't freezing cold from the Antarctic temperatures. They're warm and firm and fit seamlessly against mine. The kiss isn't frantic like so many others have been. It's passionate, yet tender. And *deep*.

And I'm not just talking about the level of tongue involved.

There's a feeling of wild, uninhibited desperation to this kiss.

You'd think we've never done this before. That we've never slept together. Hell, never even touched. Because we're going at each other like nothing that's happened before has been enough. Almost like a reset button was hit, and the night at my place never even happened. We're greedy for more and have reached our limits waiting for it.

I guess my whole "business only" speech was a bunch of bologna. Mixed signals doesn't begin to cover my erratic behavior.

My breathing is shaky by the time we come up for air. It feels like the train we've been riding on is barreling toward something life-altering, something terrifying. Knowing my luck, the track is about to run out and we're careening straight for a canyon where we'll plummet to our deaths.

Translation from Gretchen to English: I'm falling for this guy. Hard.

Please. You're already flattened to a pancake at the bottom of that canyon. Lying deader than a doornail.

"I think you might be turning me into a believer," I whisper.

"A believer of what?"

"Fairytales."

His upper lip curls. "Happily ever afters are possible outside of princesses and castles, duchess. You can have one of your own without believing in dragons and magic."

"You're making it difficult to argue with that."

"Stay in my room tonight," he breathes against my tingling lips.

"No."

His body deflates, frustration tightening his mouth.

I smile. "But you can stay in mine."

25

The Surrendering

MY HOTEL ROOM DOOR CLICKS SHUT BEHIND US. Sealing us inside this space. Just the two of us. With the rest of the world on the other side of these walls. No one to interrupt, interfere, or judge us. We can do absolutely whatever we want.

I've never been more terrified and oddly at ease at the same time.

It's a strange, drugging combination.

Ryder's long strides eat up the distance between us. His hands cup my cheeks. "Give me all of you tonight, Gretchen. Throw everything else out the window and just be *here* with me. Let me have the real you."

"I thought I already did that."

I let him sleep in *my bed*, for crying out loud.

He tucks my hair behind my ear. "You know you didn't. I felt you holding back." He shakes his head. "No more of that."

That's a little complicated because… "I don't know how." It's not that I pretend to be something I'm not around everyone. "I don't always mean to hold back. I'm just used to…" I don't know how to explain it.

So, he does it for me. "You're used to protecting yourself. I understand that. But there's nothing inside this room you have to protect yourself from tonight."

I recall my revelation at the ice rink. "You're wrong about that."

His expression is knowing as his hands lower to my shoulders. "I could say the same thing. So, for tonight, why don't we leave everything *un*said and not think at all. Can you manage that?"

"Acting first and thinking later is usually how I roll."

"Well, we don't have to make it a habit." His hands find the zipper at my side and lower it. "But I'm going to take advantage of that approach tonight."

With that stagnant declaration suspended above our heads, he seals his mouth over mine and backs me up to the king-sized bed. After he swiftly divests me of my jumpsuit with efficient hands, I step out of it and stand before him in nothing but my white strapless bra, matching panties, and heels.

He strips me out of all that, too.

"You have no idea how fucking gorgeous you are," he rasps against my neck, leaving a trail of hot kisses. "No idea what you've done to me every single day for the past year."

"Show me."

"Oh, I'm about to."

He quickly shrugs out of his suit jacket while I go to work on his shirt buttons. When I get too impatient about halfway down, I rip the material apart, sending buttons flying. He groans when I scrape my nails over his abs and tug hard on his belt. I'm tired of all these damn clothes concealing his nakedness.

I swear, I've never seen a more perfectly sculpted man. Not in the movies, not in the magazines, not in the gym. Ryder is the only man who has ever made me feel unapologetically ravenous. To the point that I simply have no control over my body. All I can process in this moment with him is *want, need, take, keep.*

Wait, no. Not keep.

Ryder's not for my keeping. *My boss* can't be.

Once I've gotten him out of his briefs, I scoot back on the bed and lean against the headboard. I throw my hand up when he starts to follow. "You said you're about to show me," I remind him. "So, do it. Show me what you'd do when you'd think about me in your office. Show me how you've had to relieve yourself all these months."

His mouth twists into a wolfish grin as his hand descends. Wrapping his fingers around his jutting cock, he gives it a stroke. My gaze is locked on the way he pumps the shaft, base to tip. The frenetic pace, the firm squeeze, the subtle rocking of his hips.

"This is what I'd do beneath my desk, duchess," he grounds out.

My gaze lifts to his.

"This is what I'd do behind closed doors, in my shower, in my bed, in the fucking car." He ends that last one on an angry growl. "And you never knew I was picturing your mouth or your hand the whole time. Never knew how utterly you were fucking with my head."

I bite my lip when moisture dampens his tip, making it glisten in the moonlight streaming through the curtains. I can't look away. The act of masturbating in front of me is so wicked and erotic. Even better, he didn't hesitate for a moment when I demanded it.

For once, he didn't fight me.

"And if I had known that you would look at me like this while I was doing it," he goes on, "I'd have been calling you into my office every damn day."

"How am I looking at you?"

"Like you're ready for me to fuck you with this."

My nipples become taut peaks as my breathing accelerates. "Confession? I've been ready since the second you walked out my door that morning."

He gnashes his teeth. "*Goddammit.* I knew I shouldn't have left. As much as I've fought with you this year, I've fought with myself ten times over. But only when it comes to you."

My legs fall open.

His gaze drops. His hand stops.

"Well, I'm not fighting you now, Ryder. And I won't kick you out in the morning." *Probably not.*

"You think I would let you?" he snarls. "Just try it and see what happens. I'm not going anywhere."

His body covers mine in the next instant, his hand immediately cupping my mound. When his finger finds my slick folds, his growl echoes off the ceiling. "That's my duchess. So fucking wet just from watching me. How many times have you had to pet this pretty pussy ever since that night at your place?"

My hips arch upward. "More times than I can count. I broke my favorite vibrator."

"*Sexiest fucking woman,*" he mutters against my fevered skin.

"Ryder, please." I grab for him, the urgency for fulfillment uncontrollable. "In me. Now."

His dripping tip briefly touches my clit before he pulls back. "Shit. Condom."

I stop him from reaching for his pants. "It's okay. I don't want it."

His pupils dilate when they lock on mine. "Seriously? Are you sure?"

I nod, my hands skating over his compact torso. "I have an IUD. And I'm clean."

He shifts all of his weight onto his elbows. "Same. Christ, I've been dying to have you bareback. I can't guarantee this one's gonna last long."

I wiggle my hips to get him at the right angle. "As long as we get there together, I don't care how long it lasts. We've got all night. I need to keep you primed."

"Believe me, duchess, that never requires effort on your part."

He thrusts inside in one smooth movement. Our mouths fall open as we both gasp for air. I might have been wet and ready, but it's still a tight fit with Ryder's size. And it feels fucking sublime.

"Oh, God."

He nuzzles his nose against my chin. "Missed this."

I nod in agreement because I can't find words. Especially when he starts to move. He hips piston back and forth, pushing in, pulling out. When I clamp my legs around his waist, he drives harder until he's pounding me into the mattress. My hands mold to his ass, keeping him right where I need him as he pumps...pumps...*pumps.*

We roll from one side of the bed to the other.

We get tangled in the sheets.

We hold each other close as we surrender to bliss.

He just keeps getting better.

I figured after the night of three rounds at my place, such a thing would be impossible. Yet here I am. Stunned speechless at the realization that I can't imagine any man affecting me more deeply—physically and emotionally—than this man does.

"Somehow, I'm going to find a way to make you mine," he whispers.

You know the phrase *stricken blind*?

Well, that statement has me *stricken mute.*

What the hell does *mine* even mean? And how the hell do I know that Ryder is what's good for me? How can anybody be sure that they've found the "right" person? That it's for real?

He doesn't seem bothered by my silence. Instead, he lays a soft kiss on my lips, as if telling me it's okay that I say nothing. I can hear his voice in my head. *I only said that to give you a fair warning, duchess. So that you're not surprised when I do end up making you mine. Forever.*

With nothing to dispose of after he pulls out, Ryder rolls me over and wraps his body around mine like a sexy burrito, kissing me sweetly until we're drifting off to sleep together. But before I succumb to slumber, something niggles at the back of my mind. Something that won't go away.

Something...feels curiously familiar about the sex we just had.

Déjà vu swarms my mind as my eyes grow heavy, but I can't pinpoint its origin. Sure, we've had sex a few times before, but there's something specific about tonight that stands out.

Somehow, I'm going to find a way to make you mine.

I've heard him say that before.

But when? Where?

I fall asleep still sifting through memories but come up with nothing.

26

The Middle-Aged Hooker

THIS TIME, WHEN I WAKE UP AFTER A FULL NIGHT OF SWEATY SEX with Ryder, I'm still in bed with him, watching him sleep. He looks more peaceful than I've ever seen him. The stress lines around his mouth are relaxed, the creases in his forehead caused by tension are smoothed out. I run my finger over the stubble smattering his cheeks, unable to resist the urge any longer.

I'm still working through what I was trying to untangle last night, but I've decided to table it until we're back in Charleston. No serious discussions yet, no major decisions. An ominous sense of foreboding has been settling like a lead weight in my stomach as we approach our flight tomorrow, and I'm not ready to burst this bubble yet.

Like Ryder said last night, everything will remain unsaid while we're in New York.

When his eyes slowly inch open, I smile. "Regrets?"

"Not a fucking one." His voice is adorably groggy with sleep. "I'm here with you, aren't I? What regrets would I have? Besides, I think our history dictates I should be asking *you* that."

My smile widens as I repeat his words. "Not a fucking one. By the way, how long does it take you to do your hair in the morning?"

There's that forehead crease. "Come again?"

I pat his arm. "Maybe later. Right now, we have to haul ass because someone needed his beauty sleep. I was just trying to figure out who needs more time to do their hair because that person needs to shower first."

Before I can giggle like a pubescent schoolgirl, he drags my naked butt out of bed and throws me over his shoulder. Then I can't contain my giggles, which earns me a firm slap on said naked butt.

"I've got an easy solution to our problem." He reaches inside the shower and turns on the water. "We'll wash each other at the same time. Ingenious, right?" After placing me on my feet, he shoves me inside the stall. "Water's nice and warm."

I scream when the ice-cold spray nails me in the boobs like a thousand tiny knives stabbing me right through the nipples. Scrambling back, I almost break my neck when I slip on the wet floor.

"You're such a dick!"

He laughs as he reaches back inside and turns the faucet to hot. "Better get a move on, duchess. We're going to be late."

"You're lucky I don't have time to hide your body before our presentation. Otherwise, you'd be finding yourself on the wrong end of my Swiss."

The Swiss Army Knife slogan should be, "Gets any job done when you're in a pinch."

Or, "The 2021 Criminal Choice Award Winner for Most Convenient Murder Weapon."

"Speaking of our presentation." Ryder steps into the shower behind me. "I have it on good authority that the CEO of Home Supply & Warehouse will be in attendance."

I wipe the water from my eyes. "You're kidding. That's amazing. If we could get their business…"

Home Supply & Warehouse is the fastest-growing home improvement chain in the United States, headquartered in Atlanta. They pride themselves on their vast inventory of designer brands at reasonable prices and have even been featured in several of the home improvement reality shows on HGTV.

"Then I guess I'd actually have to give you that raise," he quips.

My eyebrow goes up as my gaze darts down. "Speaking of raises..." I slide my hand over his already hardening cock. "Let's see what we can do about this."

Well, we would have saved time washing each other in the shower...if he hadn't fucked me against the wall.

Turns out, we didn't have to worry about coordinating our grooming routines. Ryder was his regular sexy self in under ten minutes. By using nothing more than *hotel products*.

Apparently, he's just a natural beauty.

What an asswipe.

We conclude our presentation to the sound of applause. Ballroom C is standing room only, every chair in the room occupied for our session. We answer several questions from the audience before one of the conference officials eventually has to stop the session altogether so they can get the room ready for the next presentation.

"Not bad, duchess," Ryder says in my ear as we're packing up our presentation materials. "Your PowerPoint skills are almost as impressive as your sucking skills."

He grunts when I very discreetly elbow his solar plexus. "Let me offer you some constructive criticism since you're new to the compliments game: you really *suck* at it."

Just as discreetly, he reaches behind me and pinches my ass. "And she's so eloquent, too. Though I admit I'm kind of *blowing* it with the compliments."

I hide my goofy smile as I continue gathering our things. We're so lame, but I'm kind of loving it. He's pulled into conversation by a man and woman I don't recognize and is still speaking to them by the time I'm ready. I stand off to the side to check email on my phone while I wait.

"That was an impressive presentation."

I glance up at the male voice. The middle-aged man standing in front of me is someone I *do* recognize.

He holds out his hand, smiling brightly. "It's a pleasure, Ms. Castellanos. I'm Jonathan Tremblay."

CEO of Home Supply & Warehouse.

I quickly researched him earlier after Ryder mentioned he might be here. He looks even younger in person than he does in his pictures. Probably mid-forties, with only a touch of gray at his temples. According to the information I found online, he comes from humble beginnings and started his company from the ground up, all on his own. I respect him on that basis alone.

I take his hand. "Pleasure's mine, Mr. Tremblay. I hope you enjoyed the presentation."

He rocks back on his heels, nodding. "Very much. Your firm has some pretty innovative ideas."

"They seem to be working for us so far." This is my window of opportunity. If I can reel him in—at the very least, plant a seed—this could be a groundbreaking account. "Are you in the market for some innovative ideas?"

"Looks that way." His expression turns inquisitive as it flicks to Ryder, who's shooting us side-glances while he continues his conversation. Mr. Tremblay turns back to me. "But what I could really use is some innovative personnel."

My brow furrows. "Personnel?"

He hands me his business card. "I'm looking for a new Marketing Director. Someone with a fresh perspective and cutting-edge ideas. I've heard your name mentioned in certain circles, and I've done my research. Your work at The Colson Group certainly doesn't look like that of a rookie. I'd love to speak with you about how I think we can be of help to each other."

Words claw at my throat, desperate to get out, and I end up stammering like a doofus. "O-oh, I, um. Thank you so much for the offer, sir, but I'm pretty comfortable where I'm at now."

He puts his hand up. "And I respect that. All I'm asking is that you consider it. The position comes with a lot of freedom. You'd be in charge of your own team, lead product release strategies, and develop company-wide marketing campaigns."

That sounds...awesome.

A huge step in my career, to be sure.

"Just think about it," he adds when I don't respond. "I promise it'll be worth it. Call me and we'll set up a meeting."

I nod, dumbfounded as I stare down at the business card in my hand. I intended to get his business, and instead, the CEO of a major international company is actually offering me a dream job. A once in a lifetime opportunity.

"I really appreciate it," I murmur. "Thank you again."

"I look forward to hearing from you."

"One question, sir," I blurt out when he starts to walk away.

He turns around expectantly.

"The position... It would be based out of Atlanta, wouldn't it?" The location of their headquarters.

His eyes crinkle in the corners. "Yes, it would be. We would pay for all moving expenses, of course."

Feeling numb, I nod again. "I'll think about it."

"Please do. I can tell you have a very bright future, Ms. Castellanos, and I'd love to have you on my team."

My heart is pounding as he disappears into the throng of conference attendees. I immediately try to discount everything he said, to forget every word, but I can't. It's inside my head now like a tumor.

"That looked promising," Ryder's voice suddenly rumbles from my left, making me jump. "Did we hook him?"

I crush the business card in my hand and shove it in my pocket before he can see it. I don't want to explain what just happened here. Not yet. Not until I get a handle on how I feel about it first.

And what my answer is going to be.

It scares the hell out of me that, in this moment, I don't know.

"Yeah," I answer flatly. "I think we might have."

He gives my waist a quick squeeze. "That's my girl."

Guilt instantly assails me. The feeling that I've already betrayed Ryder is ridiculous and irrational. I shouldn't feel guilty about considering taking an attractive position at another company. I've worked my ass off to get where I'm at. And yes, I might be young, but I feel like I've earned this.

The betrayal is there, nonetheless.

Because the fact of the matter is... *I* might be the one who just got hooked.

27

The Ball Dropping

"Is everything okay?"

I'm staring up at the Godzilla-sized sparkling ball in Times Square as it slowly descends in the final minute of the year. The scene around me is in full pre-pandemonium swing. Thousands of on-lookers staring in the same direction, buzzing with the same hyped-up energy that's possessing the whole city of New York tonight. It's an atmosphere vibrating with new beginnings and togetherness, and yet...

I've never felt more lost.

"Gretchen?"

My heads whips around to Ryder. "Huh?"

His smile is tight. "You okay? You seem distracted."

In the crammed nightclub we hit up earlier, I was hot in my ice blue Chanel dress, filled with adrenaline and a good buzz. Now, out here in the winter elements, I'm too clear-headed and shivering, even though I'm plastered against Ryder's warmth.

"Yeah, I'm fine. End of the year just inspires a lot of reflection, you know?"

"Sharing is caring, duchess."

The street is packed sidewalk-to-sidewalk with people, like sardines. There's jostling, there's bumping, there's loud noises everywhere. There's also not a lot of privacy for a serious conversation, even if I were inclined to have one.

I shrug. "Just the usual. Mentally composing my New Year's resolutions, regretting how many books I didn't read this year, and making a solemn vow that I'll actually stick to a regular workout routine. Isn't that the norm?"

He gives me an admonishing look. "Not for you. You don't believe in New Year's resolutions because you think they're, and I quote, 'just a platform for disappointment and self-hatred and are leading to the decline of western civilization.' You don't waste your money on books because you know you don't have the attention span to actually get through an entire one. And saying you'll stick to a regular workout routine is like me saying I'm going to be starting forward for the Boston Celtics."

"Do you always feel like you have to know everything? A woman can have inner thoughts that she doesn't share out loud. It's part of our mystery and charm."

He takes my chin between his thumb and index finger. "I'll never force you to share anything you don't want to. But if those thoughts somehow impact me, I hope you'd have the courtesy to at least clue me into what's going on."

He might have a point, but this isn't the time or place to bring up a sensitive subject. As well as he knows me, I know him just as well. And I know he'll lose his ever-loving shit in the middle of Times Square if I tell him that I'm considering Tremblay's offer.

So, I do something I never do with Ryder. At least, not when it's about something important.

I lie to him.

"Contrary to what you might think, not all of my thoughts revolve around you. But the ones that do, you'll be the first to hear."

He looks unconvinced. But the thunderous cheers that suddenly ripple through the crowd abruptly end the conversation. The noise is so loud my ears start ringing.

"Happy New Year, duchess."

Reality bomb! Incoming!

This is our last night in New York. Tomorrow, we have to go back to life as usual, back to sneaking around, back to uncomfortable conversations and life-altering decisions. Who knows what will happen next? Even if this job offer hadn't come around, how long did I expect to stay working at TCG? Until today, I've been living in the moment, day-to-day. I love my job, so there's been no reason to look elsewhere, or even *think* about looking elsewhere. But I suppose I have to at some point, right? I never anticipated that TCG would be a forever job. How many people actually work at just one company for their entire career? This was bound to happen eventually.

But I'm not ready for it to happen *tonight*.

Tonight, I want this man.

Tonight, I want to pretend that we really do have tomorrow.

And tonight, I want to forget that Ryder has never been mine to keep.

They say the person you kiss at the stroke of midnight on New Year's Day is the person you'll kiss for the entire year.

So, I kiss Ryder.

In Times Square, under the neon lights of the marquee, in a sea of gold confetti.

Because…here's hoping.

He's already fucked me once against my hotel window that overlooks West 34th street. Now, I've got him pinned beneath me on the bed, my thighs straddling his hips, as I take him deep inside my body. Nails scraping down his chest, leaving red marks. Whimpers escaping my lips because it's so good it's almost painful.

But once I stop, that's when the desolation will kick in. The melancholy. The agony over the impending loss I don't see how I can prevent. So, I'll keep going all night. Right up until the moment we have to board our flight, if necessary.

"Holy shit," Ryder pants, fingers tweaking my stiff nipples. "That view from the window can't hold a fucking candle to this."

"The compliments are getting better."

He grins. "One of my New Year's resolutions."

"You're off to a good start." I take his hand and place it between my legs. He needs no guidance after that. His fingers stroke my clit, rubbing, applying pressure. "Now, how about a good finish?"

"*Good?*" His voice is laced with genuine disgust. "That's your expectation of me? Fucking *good?* Duchess, I'm insulted."

I hadn't meant that as a challenge, but I'm sure as hell not going to complain about the results I get.

The next few minutes are straight-up *animal.*

My hips undulate over him so hard my thigh muscles burn. My skin is slicked with sweat, my hair a tangled mess. He jackknifes off the bed with a ferocious bellow as he spurts inside me. When he pinches my clit between his fingers, it sets off my own orgasm. I throw my head back in pure ecstasy and scream out my pleasure. Tugging on my hair, he surges upward and groans the rest of his release into my mouth.

We stay like that for a long time. Naked chests pressed together, mouths eating from one another, every inch of our bodies connected in the most intimate way. Possibly the most beautiful moment of my life, and it has to be shattered by the remembrance of how things are…and how they're not.

Just like the countdown at Times Square, there is a countdown on my time with Ryder.

Moments like these are numbered.

And it's hard to say when it's all going to time out.

"I don't want to stop," Ryder says later as we're lying in bed.

He's spooning me from behind. I'm running my fingers over the hair on his forearm. He's drawing circles across my stomach. I've been fighting my sleep because I'm too afraid this will all disappear the second I close my eyes. I've just been lying here silently, committing this feeling to memory, and suspending it as long as I can. I've been wracking my brain for an outcome that works in everyone's favor. One everyone will be happy with.

And I'm terrified beyond belief that none exists.

"You don't want to stop what?" I ask obtusely.

"This. When we get back to Charleston, I want it to continue. I want to be with you."

I swallow back tears. Actual *tears*. In case it wasn't already obvious, I never cry. "I'm not sure that's possible."

"Why?" he bites out. "Just because I'm the boss? I own the company, Gretchen. If anyone has anything to say about it, I'll just fire them."

"There's more to it than that. Everything would change between us. We have a great working relationship, as unorthodox as it might be. I don't think it would be good for the company if we altered that."

He grunts in frustration. "And I think you're running out of excuses. You're really going to try to treat this like some bullshit fling over Spring Break?"

I sigh, squeezing my eyes shut. "You knew the score before we started this, Ryder. And I laid it out for you again on the plane."

"Uh, I think that whole 'business only' spiel went out the window a long fucking time ago." His body stiffens. "Unless...you just don't want to be with me, and you don't know how to say that you don't feel the same way."

This is all going to shit. I didn't want the night to end this way. There's supposed to be a few more hours of heaven left before I go plummeting back to hell.

"It's complicated—"

"Why are you so afraid of being in a real relationship?" he cuts me off. "Why do you treat even the possibility of happiness like an infectious disease?"

Because it eventually fades.

People change. Life changes. *Love* changes. Or maybe it's never real in the first place. It's all just a projection of what you *want*, not what actually *is*. People fool themselves every day into thinking they're happy because it's easier to lie to yourself than to be alone. It's like conditioning your brain to believe whatever is in your best interest in the name of self-preservation.

Take my parents.

They're a shining example of what getting married too young with dreamy notions in your head looks like. Because those dreams usually remain just that: dreams. Enough time passes, kids happen, jobs happen, and you console yourself with the faux happiness because frankly, there are no other options at that point.

Unhappiness is the fruit of naïveté.

And I'm not naïve.

In our case, jobs are already interfering with a potential relationship. Not only do I work for the man—right away, a disaster just waaaiiiting to happen—now, I've been offered an extremely attractive position five hours away. To me, that screams of incompatibility. Just one sign of many more surely to come that we're not meant to be.

"Can we talk about this tomorrow?" Now is the time to give in to my exhaustion. "I'm tired, and we have an early flight."

After releasing a long-suffering sigh, he remains silent for several beats. I know he wants to say more. Hell, he probably wants to strangle the truth out of me with his bare hands because he knows I'm holding back. He asked me last night to give him everything. And I did. Apparently, that was an isolated incident.

And I hate myself for it.

"Fine," he eventually concedes. "But promise me we *will* talk about it. Don't shut me out anymore, duchess. We're past that."

Are we?

"I promise."

It's the only promise to him I've ever broken.

28

The Gas Chamber

"Today, we mourn the break-up of Olivia Wilde and Jason Sudeikis," Kennedy says, sighing. "Which means that Jason is back up for grabs, and there's still a chance for me. In honor of their doomed romance, we're doing worst break-ups. Here's what's been posted on the Facebook page so far:

'I paid over $3,000 to fly to Japan to visit her while she was studying abroad. She broke up with me two hours after I landed.'
'I was in the hospital after getting my appendix removed. He said he thought telling me while I was under anesthesia would make it easier.'
'After six years of marriage, it literally ended with her saying the words *you may not be the father.*'
'He was drunk at my friend's graduation party and said that my blowjobs were like getting sucked off by a piranha. His

own best friend beat the shit out of him for that comment, and I started dating him the next day. We've been together for three years, and he begs for my mouth every chance he gets. ;)'

Dang, girl," Kennedy praises, clapping into the mic. "Danica from Jacksonville, Florida, you are now my new hero."

❖

Thankfully, our flight leaves so early the next morning there's no time to pick up the conversation where we left it off in bed. Then we're both too busy catching up on work emails on the plane to discuss anything personal. We hail a cab at the airport that takes us to the office, where my car is parked. Being a holiday, the whole building is empty when the cab drops us off. I'm technically off for the rest of the day. I just have to run upstairs and grab a flash drive I forgot on my desk, and then I'm going home where I can question my life choices in peace and quiet.

Ryder follows me into the building. Knowing him, he'll put in a full day's work even on a holiday. When we make it through the office's double doors without any personal showdowns, I think I'm in the clear.

Guess again.

He waits a full thirty seconds after we walk through those doors before calling me into his office. A thick, icky feeling of dread settles over me as I approach his door like a death row inmate, heading for the gas chamber.

Everything on his desk looks untouched when I walk in. He's sitting in his chair, facing away from me and staring out the window, finger tapping on the armrest. "Back to avoiding me, huh?" His tone is dark and ominous. "Then I can assume that New York changed nothing?"

"Ryder, this isn't the time or place."

He spins around in the chair, eyes flickering blue flames. "That's the thing with you, duchess. There's never a good time or place because you never want to talk about it. You can't even be serious for ten minutes to discuss what the hell's going on between us. Oh, *no*. Gretchen's gotta make jokes and be sarcastic and act like she doesn't feel a fucking thing." He narrows those blues at me. "I've been inside you. I've seen your passion with my own eyes. I've felt it. So, I know you're not this cold deep down."

I flinch.

I've never considered myself a cold person. Hardened, sure. Guarded, absolutely. Hearing him hurl the word *cold* at me hurts way more than I would have expected. But I can't blame him for his word choice. From his perspective, that's exactly what I sound like.

He flicks his wrist dismissively. "Your constant dodging is either an act, for God knows what reason. Maybe you're scared of commitment, I don't know. Or something else is going on that you're not telling me."

I blurt out the words before I realize my mouth is forming them. "Jonathan Tremblay offered me the Marketing Director job at Home Supply."

Ryder's eyes bulge. "At the Atlanta headquarters?"

I swallow and nod.

He stares at me for several long moments before barking out a harsh laugh. "You were just waiting for the opportune moment to spring that on me, weren't you? It gives you a convenient little out. You dump me and your job here for a cushy new position five hours away. Your decision about us would be made for you. Perfect timing, huh?"

"That's not why I told you."

"No? You're obviously considering it," he argues. "It would certainly put an end to any further entanglements with me, wouldn't it? Lucky for you, it's a great excuse to destroy what we have. Allows you to wrap things up all nice and neat with a pretty little bow and leave this city with a clear conscience. Advancing your career and all? It's a golden opportunity for you to bail on me."

"This has all just happened a little fast, okay? One minute I'm your employee, and the next I'm your employee with benefits."

He swipes his arm across the desk, sending all of its contents flying onto the floor. "Quit making it sound so goddamn seedy! We're more than that. We always have been. And *fast?* Are you serious? We've known each other for almost a year. This started long before that day in here with Myles and you know it. You just never wanted to admit it. And maybe I didn't either for a while, but I got the fuck over it because *I'm* not scared."

I throw my arms up. "And what the hell am I so scared of? You tell me, since you know me so well."

His feet pound across the room until he's right in my face. "You're scared of falling for me. You're scared of the risk involved because putting your faith and trust in someone else is *always* risky." He shakes his head. "But you wouldn't really know that, would you? Because you're incapable of believing in someone that much. Here I thought you were the bravest woman I've ever met." He waves between us. "But you don't even have the courage to give this a chance."

To my horror, I feel the sting of tears for the second time in twenty-four hours. But letting them fall would only confirm what he just accused me of. Although, I think we both know he hit the nail right on the head.

His lip curls in anger. "For all my bragging about knowing you so well, I never knew you at all. Because I thought you were stronger than that."

A sob nearly escapes, but I suck it back at the last moment. My voice still comes out barely above a whisper. "I told you."

"Told me what?"

"That I'm not the good guy."

His eyes flare. "No. You don't *let* yourself be the good guy. There's a big difference. It takes more effort to be the antagonist than the protagonist. And you do it on purpose. You sabotage any chance you have at a real relationship *on purpose*. Maybe it's finally time you start asking yourself why."

He's right, you know.

I wrap my arms protectively around my middle and avert my gaze. If I look him in the eyes, he'll see how deeply his words have impacted me. "Are we done here?"

He snorts, shoving his hands through his hair. "Yeah. Yeah, we're done."

Finality. Defeat. Both are in his voice.

I force myself to put one foot in front of the other and turn for the door. If I don't, I might collapse onto the floor in pathetic agony. I look over my shoulder once I have my hand on the doorknob. "That race you said you were in? The tortoise and the hare?"

His head slowly lifts.

My voice is hoarse from holding back those rising tears. "For your own good, you should probably save yourself anymore trouble and forfeit."

His mouth twitches in a sad smile. "Which is exactly what you wanted all along, isn't it? I could have handled any hare I went up against. But against you? I never stood a chance."

He strides toward me in a manner that is so *I don't give a fuck about anything anymore*—utter dejection—it shatters my heart. I stop breathing altogether as he places his hand over mine on the doorknob. When he leans in close, I'm both afraid and hoping that he'll kiss me. That he'll magically conquer all of my own fears for me.

Instead, he twists the knob and opens the door.

Against my parted lips, he whispers, "You win, duchess. Game over."

I run out of that room with tears on my cheeks and sorrow in my heart, knowing I didn't win anything.

In fact, I'm pretty sure I just lost…everything.

29

The Naked Ambush

SLOANE'S CALLED. Harper's called. Quinn's called. Ross has called. Even Myles has freaking called. Everyone but Ryder.

Guess he really did forfeit.

Can you blame him?

Nope. Not even a little. After all, I *told* him to.

I've called in sick to work the past two days. Once I run out of sick days, I've got two weeks of vacation accumulated. My plan is to burn through them in my bathtub, much like I'm doing right now, with a lit joint and a glass of wine. And if two weeks of hot baths and weed can't solve all my problems, then the world as we know it is ending.

My bathroom door suddenly flies open.

I scream.

Bubbles go flying.

My glass gets knocked over.

And I throw the only weapon I have at the intruder: my doobie.

Sloane appears in the doorway, stroking a thick piece of rope like it's her pet kitty. "Oh, good. You're already in the tub. Hogtying you with this thing will be easier than I thought."

She prances inside the room, Harper and Quinn dutifully following behind her. My former roommate pins me with a look. "The timer's up, Gretch. *Ding*."

I groan loudly. "Can we please reschedule the torture session? Put something on the books for next week. I'll have my people call your people."

"Hate to break it to you, hon," Harper says, hopping up onto the vanity, "but we *are* your people. Which is why we're here to give you the Gretchen Castellanos experience."

"Which is?"

"Blunt honesty, unfiltered opinions, and lots of crude innuendo," Quinn supplies with a wink.

"We finally figured out that tough love is the only thing you're going to respond to, so here we are." Harper throws her arms up, smiling much too happily. "Ta-da."

"Respond to what?" I grumble in my best Grumpy impersonation.

"Ryder told West what happened," Sloane offers. "At least, the boilerplate stuff. We're here to collect the rest of it."

I point a bubbly finger at Barbie. "Your Ken doll is a little tattletale." And apparently, so is Ryder.

The green-eyed skankface blows me a kiss.

I slump further down in the tub. "Can I at least have my joint back? Consider it my talisman against ambushes."

"Oh, you mean this joint?" Quinn swipes it off the tiled floor, takes a long drag without looking away from me...

And stubs it out in the sink.

Harper smothers a giggle with her hand.

Sloane nods in approval. "Nice touch."

Quinn smirks at me.

I glower back at her. "I always knew you were possessed by the devil."

Sloane crosses her arms over her ample chest. "Tell us what happened in New York, Gretch."

This is going to sting like French kissing a beehive.

"Ryder and I slept together."

"And?" Sloane asks.

"And we went on a date."

Harper raises an expectant eyebrow. "And?"

"And I...liked it."

"*And?*" Quinn prompts.

"And he admitted that he didn't want to stop once we got home. He hinted at having feelings for me."

Sloane gives me a knowing look. Leave it to her to be the first one to catch on. "But?"

I sigh. "But I screwed it up. Told him it wasn't a good idea. I said that we should go back to the way things were before his brother showed up."

"Because you don't feel the same way?" This from Quinn.

I stare down at the spilled red wine swirling around in my bathwater. The shame I've been trying to escape from is coming on full-force. "No, because I do."

"Yeah, that's where West got lost, too," Harper told the other two, noting their puzzled expressions. "It didn't make sense to him or to Ryder why she would push him away."

The bubbles are slowly dissipating in my wine water. I hope everyone in this room is comfortable with some female nudity among friends because it's all going to be on display soon.

"I got offered a job while I was up there."

Sloane frowns. "I thought you loved your job."

"I do. But this would be a significant promotion, significant pay raise... A huge step up in my career. I mean, this just fell in my lap. I'd be stupid not to take it."

"Maybe it's the weed," Quinn speaks up, "but I haven't quite connected the dots over here."

I lift my feet out of the water and scoff in disgust. It's amazing how everything else in your life can go to shit, yet a pedicure can look no worse for wear.

"The job is in Atlanta."

The three of them release simultaneous "ahh's."

Sloane sits on the edge of the tub, her expression softening. "Why don't you explain to us what you didn't explain to Ryder?"

Well, I'm about to physically bare all—why not emotionally, too?

"If I turn down this job, I need it to be about wanting to stay at The Colson Group because I love my job, I'm happy where I'm at, and I'm excited about my future there. It can't be about not wanting to be that far away from Ryder."

Harper tilts her head. "Why not?"

"Because that would mean I'm sacrificing my career for a man." It would make me my mother.

"Or it just means that you don't want to leave the man you love," Sloane corrects, emphasizing the last word.

"That's a leap," I mutter bitterly. "You think just because he drives me crazy and gives me the best sex of my life that I'm in love with him?"

"Yes," they all say at the same time.

"Cheeky bitches."

"There's nothing wrong with admitting you want to be with him," Quinn says. "You're saying you'd rather sacrifice love by taking that job and moving to Atlanta than actually being happy?"

"So, it has to be one or the other?" I snap, my temper rising. "Love or a career?"

"No," Sloane says slowly. "Who said you can't have both? Not taking that job and staying at TCG isn't going to hinder your future, Gretch. You've told us over and over again you love that job. Don't let the attraction of *more* ruin your happiness *now*."

"Exactly," I bite out. "I am happy now. But what if that changes? What if I decide somewhere down the road that I do want more and I've squandered my opportunity for it by turning this job down?"

"There are always going to be job opportunities," Harper says emphatically. "But how many opportunities do you think you're going to have in life to find love? Men like Ryder don't grow on trees, hon."

I bite my lip, unused to being the one in the hot seat. "But how do I know it's…forever? Love can fade, right?" I've seen it. "What if that happens to us and I've ended up making all these major life decisions based around him? And by the time I realize it, it'll be too late to go back?"

Like my mom. If she's truly happy with my father, you'd never know it. If she's maintained her own individual identity over the course of their marriage, I don't know what it looks like. All I've ever seen is *military wife* and *devoted mother*. Not bad things, but I want to stay *me* even after the bond of marriage and family.

Ryder has already consumed me.

I feel like this job offer is my first test. I don't want to be weak like my mom and follow Ryder around everywhere like she's followed the Major. I already work for the man. If we actually start dating, I'll feel weirdly beholden to him. Like I'll already be in his shadow.

Sloane swipes her hand through the air. "Whoa, slow down. First of all, no one ever knows whether or not something is forever. That's what trusting and believing in the other person is all about. You have faith that you're going to last forever and you try your best to make it happen. That's all any of us can do. But if you truly love that person, you'll keep trying and you'll never give up, no matter what happens."

A few moments of silence follow as I process that.

"Aside from the career aspect," Quinn says from her position against the wall, "why is this freaking you out so much?"

Now, we're getting to the meat of the animal.

The thick thigh. The juicy tenderloin.

"The more you have in your heart, the more you have to lose," I confess in a low voice. "The stronger you feel, the stronger the heartbreak."

What they may not know, because I'm so skilled at hiding my emotions, is that when I lift that gate and allow everything to pour in, I tend to feel too much. I haven't had to be in love before to know that when it's for real, I'm going to do it with my whole heart and soul. And if I do that and it all goes away one day, where does that leave me? A shell of my former self?

It's why I'm almost grateful to the Major for his methods in raising Ross and I. He taught us how to shut it all down. It's so much easier to go through the daily nuances of life when you can block out your feelings. That way, the unpleasant ones won't be so debilitating.

"All right, you asked for it," Sloane says, standing up. "The time has come. Prepare for the hammer."

I look at her quizzically. "What hammer?"

"I'm going to say it."

"Say what?"

"You ready?"

"I don't get what's happening right now."

She takes a deep breath and lets it out. "Gretchen Castellanos, you are being a total and complete dingbat."

All the air is sucked out of the room from the simultaneous gasps.

"She said the "d" word," Harper whispers to Quinn out of the side of her mouth.

I gape at Sloane.

That word is basically my kill switch.

The four of us made a pact back in college—with the help of one or ten tequila shooters—that they would call to my attention the moment I start to self-destruct. Because I knew it was bound to happen sooner or later. And I determined that I was probably going to need some help pulling my head out of my own ass.

So, we made a deal.

And thanks to our friendly neighborhood tequila, "dingbat" was the safe word we decided on. They swore to only use it in the direst of circumstances—when I refused to see reason and was on the verge of ruining my life beyond repair.

None of them have ever used it before.

This is *no bueno*.

"You've got to start letting people in, Gretch, or you're going to push everyone away to the point that they won't come back," Sloane implores. "Until the day the robots rise up and transplant one of their hearts into you, you're going to feel stuff. And yeah, some of that stuff is going to hurt, but a lot of it is going to be the most amazing stuff you've ever felt. That's what makes us better than the robots."

"The moment you become numb to all of it is the moment your love *will* fade away," Harper adds. "And it may not feel like it now, but feeling pain is better than feeling nothing at all."

I swallow around the growing lump in my throat.

"You can't write the ending of a relationship before you even begin it," Quinn tosses out, pushing off the wall. "And anyway, what is all of this scaredy-cat business about? You're fearless fucking Gretchen. You don't run away from anything, especially a man. *You* make this thing with Ryder work because *you* want it to. And you never let anything stand in the way of what you want. Right?"

I nod woodenly. "Right."

"What was that?"

"Right," I answer a little louder.

"I can't hear you!" she yells.

"Are you trying to drill sergeant me?"

Quinn winces. "I took a shot. Thought it might work."

"So, what's it going to be, Gretch?" Sloane asks. "You going to continue acting like an idiot and throw away the best thing in your life? Or are you going to live up to your name and take a butcher knife to all that bullshit in your head?"

I glance down at the pinkish water I'm submerged in. "I think the Countess is getting all pruney."

All three of them sigh with impatience. "I could have done without that image."

"P.S., I'm thinking maybe I should stop referring to my vagina by name."

"Agreed," they all say in unison.

"Nah, just kidding."

With spirits buoyed and plans forming, I grab both sides of the tub and haul myself to my feet. Nothing is left to the imagination when I throw my arms up in victory. "All hail, the honorable Countess of Charleston!"

"Ahh, no, *why?!*"

"Oh, God, my eyes!"

"Holy shit. You're like a baby seal. Do you have *any* hair below your head?"

I give them a little booby shimmy. "And that's what you buttwads get for interrupting my bath."

Mic. Drop.

30

The Secret Poet

"HAPPY BIRTHDAY, MOM." I kiss her on the cheek as I hand her my gift.

She smiles brightly as she rips off the paper covering the air fryer she's been ceaselessly asking for. I purposely didn't give it to her for Christmas because I wanted to trick her and I'm evil like that.

"Thank you, sweetie." She claps enthusiastically. "I can't wait to use it."

It's just our family at my parents' house to celebrate the occasion, with the notable addition of one particular person.

"I use my air fryer all the time," Lydia, Ross's new girlfriend, says. "It's a blessing and a curse because you'll only want to eat fried foods from now on."

This is the first time any of us have met the very pretty commercial real estate broker. Which means, it's The Inquisition in the Castellanos household.

To my relief, she appears to be a super sweet, down-to-earth woman. Very affectionate toward Ross, but not in a clingy, annoying way. And if her Ivy League education and successful business didn't make her too good to be true, she was also an alternate on the 2008 Beijing Olympic swim team. Naturally, the Major approves of her. Mom seems charmed by her. Ross is clearly infatuated. And I fell in love with her first words to me.

"Ross made you seem pretty intimidating with the way he described you. So, if I say something stupid and embarrass myself, I'm just going to roll with the punches, 'kay?"

If she was trying to pass some sort of test with her boyfriend's sister, her unfettered candidness earned her an A+.

We cut the cake after Mom finishes opening her gifts. I can't help but notice that she didn't open anything from the Major, and I'm wholly annoyed by it. I know she got him some new tools for his last birthday. Would it really have been so hard for him to actually put some effort into making her feel special? To let her know that he still loves her?

As per usual, Ross and I find ourselves washing and drying dishes together at the kitchen sink. Lydia insisted she do them herself, but Ross gently shoved her out the door. "This is kind of our thing," he explained.

"I'm going to marry her."

I drop the bowl I'm washing. Soapy water goes shooting up into the air like a geyser.

"What?"

He nods, smiling. As if he expected that reaction. "Yep. I'm not saying it's going to happen tomorrow or next month. But it will. I don't have to look anymore, Gretch. She's it."

I choose my words carefully because I'm not about to rain on my brother's happy parade. "Hasn't it only been, like, three weeks?"

"Almost a month," he confirms as he dries off one of Mom's platters. "Like I said, we're not getting married next week or anything. But not everyone needs a lot of time to know when it's the real deal. I mean, you and I have always been able to tell right away when someone's *not* for us." He shrugs. "How is knowing when they are any different?"

He's lucky, then, because it's taken me an entire year to figure that out.

Or it's just taken you a year to open your stupid eyes.

"Well, I can see why it didn't take you very long with this one. She's perfect for you."

He bumps me with his shoulder. "Now, how about finding someone perfect for you?"

Ryder's naked ass flashes in my mind. That part of him is certainly perfect.

"I may have already found him."

"Yeah?" I feel Ross's intent gaze burning into the side of my face. "Let me guess...boss man."

I'm only marginally surprised he figured it out. "How did you know?"

He laughs. "Because it takes a special kind of man to work my sister into the kind of lather he does. And you wouldn't go for someone you can steamroll right over. I called it a long time ago. Even before I saw the way you two looked at each other that day in your office."

"Yeah, yeah, yeah. Everyone saw it but me." Broken record much?

"As long as you're seeing it now, that's all that matters."

Emotion clogs my throat, effectively ending the conversation.

I dry my hands off after the last dish is washed and head for the bathroom. A noise further down the hallway grabs my attention before I can open the door. Sounds like it's coming from my parents' bedroom. And I haven't seen either of them since we started washing dishes.

As quietly as possible, I tip-toe over the hardwood floor toward the master bedroom. Their door is cracked the tiniest bit, but it's enough for me to peek inside. Mom is sitting on the bed, her back facing me, head lowered. Her shoulders are shaking, the telltale sign of someone crying. Incensed on her behalf, I'm about to storm in there and finally give the Major a piece of my mind. Ask him if he's happy for making his wife cry on her birthday because he's too much of a freaking military robot to ever show her any affection like a loving husband should.

Then he appears at her side. She springs to her feet and leaps into his arms, shocking the hell out of me. He wraps his tree trunk-like arms around her in a tight hug that has me frozen on the spot.

Then I realize they're both smiling. And laughing.

Mom's tears are tears of...joy?

Oh, gross. Now, they're kissing.

Even though I'm equally shocked and perplexed—and definitely squicked out to see my very reserved parents making out in front of me—I have to admit they look ridiculously sweet. For the first time ever, I can actually picture what they looked like when they first met as youngsters.

Once they finally break apart, Mom bends down and grabs a wooden box from underneath the bed. She places a piece of folded-up paper inside the box, closes the lid, and replaces it under the bed. When they start heading in my direction, hand-in-hand, I quietly slip inside the guest bedroom across the hall. Listening closely, I wait until I hear them leave the hallway and enter the living room before I come out of my hiding place.

I need to see what's inside that box.

Honing my best cat burglar skills, I creep back inside their room and reach under the bed for the mysterious box. But nothing on this earth could have prepared me for what I find.

Literally *nothing*.

Poems. Tons of them. Spanning what appears to be years. Written on notebook paper, graph paper, napkins, even tissues. Some definitely look older, with discolored paper and frayed edges. Some of the ones written in pencil have faded, making them difficult to read. All of them are obviously addressed to Mom. And they're all written in the same handwriting.

My father's.

The Major...writes poetry?

Since frigging *when?* How? Why? So many questions bombard my brain as I digest this new, unbelievable information. I pick up the one on top of the pile, the one Mom just put in there a minute ago.

The blossoms bloomed and the grass grew
Like our love, spring began anew.

The heavens opened up and the rains fell
The seeds sprouted with their honeyed smell.

Then the winds turned balmy and the earth dried
Summer came and Mother Earth sighed.

Autumn past, winter at last
Snow and ice fell swift and fast.

And so it is with every morn
Seasons change and we weather the storm.

Like the roots of the oak that live deep and long
Our love remains alive and strong.

With passing time, memories we make
Smiles, laughter with each sunrise awake.

Because as long as there are seasons
There shall be reasons.

Reasons to love and live
Reasons to share and care.

The way I feel can't be measured
But I swear what you give will always be treasured

For our love was always meant to be

For now and always until eternity.

Tears streak down my face.

My hands are clutching the paper in a vice-like grip. I eventually place it very carefully back inside the box so my teardrops don't ruin the ink of those beautiful words. *That actually came from my father.* I still can't believe it.

"Oh, Gretchen," comes my mother's voice from the doorway. "I didn't know you were in here."

I look at her over my shoulder with watery eyes, the box of her treasures still sitting on my lap. Her gaze lowers to the box and softens.

"Why didn't you ever tell me?" I whisper. "Why have you never showed me this?"

She smiles wistfully and comes to sit next to me on the bed. "Because it's something that's always been private between the two of us. And I wasn't sure he would want me to share it with anyone. Even you and your brother."

"Well, why not?" I sputter. "You know how I've felt about him all these years, Mom. The way he is with you sometimes, he acts like he doesn't even care."

She glances out the window, though it looks like she's somewhere else entirely. Another place, another time. "He cares deeply, sweetie. He just doesn't express it the way you'd expect him to. It was probably the biggest problem in our marriage during those early years. We fought about it all the time. I didn't understand it then, the way he locks up his emotions so fiercely." She looks at me out of the corner of her eye. "Remind you of anyone?"

I duck my head sheepishly.

"But then he started telling me how he felt in his own way." She points to the box of poems. "It wasn't easy for him. His father never approved of his writing. Said it wasn't going to get him anywhere in life. Wasn't going to put food on the table. Your grandfather pretty much snuffed out that light in your father. So, he trained himself to shut out sentiment and hide his feelings. When he met me and realized I wasn't going to put up with it, it scared him. He was afraid of opening himself up when he'd been taught all his life to do the exact opposite."

"What did you do?"

"I told him I was going to leave him," she answers without hesitation. "If he didn't talk to me and let me in on what he was really feeling, I was going to walk right out that door and never come back. That's when he started writing his poetry again." She smiles proudly. "And he hasn't stopped since."

It's still tough for me to process that this side of my father actually exists. He's sure never opened up like that to me.

"He does more for me than you know, Gretchen. More than just poems."

She reaches over to grab a folder off the nightstand and hands it to me. Inside I find two first-class tickets to Hawaii. Booked for next month, during their anniversary.

My gaze jerks back up to her.

I've never seen her look so happy in my life. She has *always* wanted to go to Hawaii.

"Every day, he finds his own unique way of making sure I know that he loves me and that his feelings haven't changed since the day he met me," she continues softly. "You and Ross just don't see it because he's still not comfortable doing it openly, around other people. He probably never will be." She places her hand over her heart. "But as long as *I* get to see it, that's enough for me."

"What made you want to marry him?" I find myself asking. "I mean, if he was so closed off with his emotions, how did you know he was The One?"

She purses her lips in thought. "Because I loved the person he was inside. I knew he had issues with how to communicate it on the outside, and I was willing to work with him on it. I loved him enough to want to improve that part of him. I knew it was something he'd struggled with since he was a kid, and no one had ever tried to help him with it before I came along."

Sounds familiar.

Ryder said very similar things to me in his office the other day.

"I see those same characteristics in you," she goes on. "And I'm sorry I haven't been very good at getting you to open up like I got him to." She chuckles mirthlessly. "You're so much like him. So, I'll just say this and I hope you listen."

I scoot forward, my ears perking.

She places her hand over mine. "When you find a man who not only understands how and why you hide your feelings, but is also willing to work through all of that with you, don't let him go. And don't settle for anything less than that."

Ryder.

Ryder knows.

He addressed those exact issues the other day. He understands what I do, though maybe not why because it's my job to tell him. But the fact is, he knows how shut down I am and he still wants to give us a shot. He still wants to try, when most men would run screaming for the hills.

There's just one more question I can't help but ask because it's always nagged at me.

"Why didn't you pursue your music career?"

She looks confused.

"I know how good you were at the violin, Mom. Grandma let it slip once that you were offered a music scholarship, but you got married and moved away with the Major instead. Why?"

There's no regret on her face. No longing in her voice when she answers. "I enjoyed playing the violin, but it was never a passion of mine. My mother had me in lessons from the time I was five years old because she could tell I had a talent for it. It was more her encouraging it than me actually pursuing it. And when I met your father and realized I had to make a choice, it didn't take me long to decide. I loved him far more than I would ever love playing the violin."

My heart sinks a little. "But you still had to make a choice between the two. Him or your career."

"In that particular case, yes, but I've never once regretted it. How I felt when I played the violin couldn't touch the level of happiness he brought me. I knew without a doubt there was one of those I could live without, and one I couldn't."

"But have you been happy with all the desk jobs you've worked over the years? And moving around so much? Do you ever miss playing?"

She smiles. "I get out my instrument and play every now and then. Your father has always liked it. And yes, you may not understand it, but I've really enjoyed all the jobs I've had. I get to meet a lot of different people, have a lot of interesting conversations, and right now at the vet's office, I get to be around animals all day. Whether you're career-oriented or not, you need something outside of that to make you happy." She looks back down at the box. "And I've always had your father."

I feel like my entire understanding of the universe is being re-written. My mind is completely blown. Yet...

Everything is suddenly making more sense than it ever has.

Fearful that I'm seconds away from blubbering like an old bitty, I bring Mom in for a hug. "Thank you for telling me."

"I'm sorry I didn't sooner," she whispers. "Maybe your relationship with him would be a lot better if I had."

I squeeze her tighter. "It's never too late."

I find the Major in the backyard, messing around in one of the flower beds. He doesn't notice me until I've literally got him wrapped up in the grizzliest bear hug I can manage.

He grunts at the impact, stumbling back. "Uh, everything okay?"

"I'm sorry," I mumble against his chest.

His body tenses. "Sorry for what?"

"For my attitude over the years. For the way I've behaved toward you. I just...didn't understand."

Which is ironic, since we're basically the same person. You'd think out of all the people in this world, the two of us would understand each other best.

His body relaxes as his arms hesitantly come around me. "I'm the one who's sorry." His voice comes out all gravelly. "I should have done so many things differently with you and Ross. I just raised you two the only way I knew how."

I nod. "I know that now. And it's okay."

"No, it's not. I never wanted the two of you to turn out like me, especially you. That's my fault. And that's why I've been pushing marriage on you so much."

I lean back to look at him. He's such a big, burly guy, I still have to crane my neck with my five-seven height. "What do you mean?"

He looks angry with himself. "I probably wouldn't be married to your mother today if she hadn't been the one to introduce herself to me. I've always been a very reserved person, and I had no idea how to navigate my way around girls back then. She could tell, so she was the one who asked me out."

A smile slowly spreads over my face. I've always thought of Mom as a little meek, and I'm ashamed of myself now for it.

His grin is slow to form and quick to fade. "You're just like me, Gretchen. And I don't want you to miss out on an opportunity because of how I raised you. The person you want to spend the rest of your life with could be right in front of you, but he might slip away because of the way *I* taught you to be. I don't want that for you."

Which explains why he's been running his own version of The Bachelorette on me for the past few years.

I get it now.

"I needed someone like your mom in my life," he explains. "She had the patience to deal with me and the determination to understand me. All I want is for you to find that someone for yourself. Because I don't think you'll be happy otherwise."

I rub him arms in reassurance. "Don't worry, okay? I'm working on it."

He looks reluctant, but he eventually nods.

"And by the way," I add, "I don't think being like you is such a bad thing."

He sucks in a sharp breath that I know is from emotional overload because that's usually how I react to feeling overwhelmed, too.

I go up onto my toes to kiss his cheek. "I love you, Da—" I stop myself just in time.

I don't know where that came from. The word just started rolling off my tongue. It felt natural, even though I haven't called him by that name since I was six.

"I love you, sir."

His Adam's apple bobs as he swallows. "Say it, please. Call me 'Dad.'" He scoffs, shaking his head. "It should never have been 'Major.' You're my daughter, for Christ's sake, not a soldier under my command."

Those lines around his mouth and eyes suddenly don't look as harsh as they used to. "Okay, Dad."

He kisses my forehead. "I love you, too."

After all these years, it finally feels right with him.

I finally know my parents.

31
The Reckoning

ONE WEEK.

It's been one week since my blowup with Ryder in his office.

Yesterday was my first day back after my "sick" leave, but I didn't tell anyone except Regina, and she's sworn to secrecy. I've been working in the focus group viewing room because I'm still building up the nerve to face Ryder and say what I need to say. He was out of town yesterday anyway, but today I have no excuse. Despite the nausea churning in my stomach, today is the day I lay it all out for him.

I'm sure of my decision. I am. But this is a huge step for me, and I'm not entirely sure how he'll react.

The door to the focus group room suddenly swings open, drawing my attention to the two-way mirror in front of me.

Myles? What's he doing—

"Get in here," he commands in a curt voice. "I need to talk to you."

Ryder follows him into the room and closes the door.

Damn, he looks good. But tired. There are dark circles under his eyes, and it looks like he hasn't shaved in three days.

"What is it?" Ryder grates out. "I have an office we can talk in, you know."

"I prefer neutral territory for this, if you don't mind."

Ryder's laugh is gritty. "I wouldn't call this neutral. I own this entire floor."

Myles props his hands on his hips, his expression serious. "When was the last time you spoke to Gretchen?"

My eyebrows reach my hairline.

Myles dragged him in there to talk about *me?*

Ryder's face darkens. "Why the hell are you asking? It's none of your business."

"Isn't it?" Myles takes a step toward his brother. "I told you what I would do if you screwed things up with her. She hasn't been to work all week, and she's refusing to speak to you. Sounds to me like you blew your shot."

Ryder rises to his full height and meets Myles chest-to-chest. I've never seen that level of fury on his face. "Don't even fucking think about it. Do you hear me? Stay *away* from her."

"Why should I? She's a beautiful, smart, funny woman. I told you that I'd back off and give you time with her. But I also gave you fair warning that if you struck out, I'd pick my bat back up." He shrugs. "Looks like I'm stepping up to the plate."

"The fuck you are," Ryder snarls. "The only reason she even gave you a second of her time is because you look like me."

Myles snorts, shaking his head. "No, bro, that's why she said yes to a date. Trust me, she would have said yes to a lot more if I'd had more time."

Oh, is that so?

My blood boils with anger. These Colson brothers are too damn cocky for their own damn good.

Ryder shoves Myles, hard. "You really think you have a shot with her? After all the lies you told? She thinks it was *you* that night!"

My mouth falls open.

Yeah, I'm going to need him to repeat that. Did I just hear him say—

"You're damn right she does!" Myles shouts back. "Because you didn't have the balls to speak up and tell her it was *you* she screwed a year ago!"

I.

Knew.

It.

Mother*fudging* knew it.

At least, I was pretty sure up until now. I just couldn't work out all the specifics. But it *had* to have been Ryder that night. Frankly, nothing else makes sense. No two men are that similar in bed. Same facial expressions. Same phrases groaned while they're in the throes of passion. It's just not possible, twins or no twins. But it was what Ryder said the first night in New York that really tipped me off.

Somehow, I'm going to find a way to make you mine.

He said the exact same thing the first night we met.

I may have been tipsy that night, but I distinctly recall him whispering those words to me as we were falling asleep. Because the seriousness in his voice jarred me so violently. I remember convincing myself that I heard him wrong, that he couldn't possibly have meant it after only just meeting me. He was surely drunk and didn't realize what he was saying.

But it definitely happened.

I really did sleep with my boss a year ago.

It really was Ryder, not his twin brother. I never had sex with Myles.

And both of these bastards lied to me about it.

"You had ten months to come clean with her before I showed up, but you didn't," Myles spits out. "So, yeah. You're goddamn right I took advantage of you not stepping up with an incredible woman like that. And by not doing so, you told her some lies of your own, brother. How do you think she's going to react when she finds out you've been keeping the truth from her all this time?"

Ryder averts his gaze—*there's the guilt*—and hangs his head. "I'm going to tell her. I just... It hasn't been the right time."

"Ten months, Ryder. Did you really think you'd have all the time in the world? If I hadn't kicked your ass into gear, it would have been someone else getting in your way. Men are going to want her, and one of them is eventually going to snap her up if you don't get your shit together."

Ryder just glares. "Not while I'm in the picture they're not."

Myles lifts an eyebrow. "Looks to me like you're already out of the picture. Why keep trying? If it hasn't happened between you two by now, it probably won't."

"Because I'm in love with her, you asshole!"

The inertia of those words knocks me back in my chair like a crash test dummy.

Ryder spins away from Myles, stabbing his fingers through his hair. "Christ! I *can't* let her go, Myles. I'm incapable of giving up. I love her too damn much. My head hasn't been right from the moment I met her."

I'm staring into that room, shell-shocked, watching Ryder grapple for control. He's slowly unraveling right before my eyes. Then, with Ryder's back turned, Myles shoots a quick glance at the two-way mirror. Right at me. And winks.

He knows I'm in here. He's known the whole time.

That sneaky son of a bitch.

Despite the smile I feel touching the corners of my mouth, I'm still fuming that these two men have been playing me like a fiddle in the Charlie Daniels Band. They've been keeping secrets and manipulating me, and I sure don't appreciate it. In fact, it's a little...infuriating.

Time to go crack some skulls.

I snatch a particular piece of paper that I've been holding on to off the table and stomp out of the viewing room. Leaving a trail of raging woman behind me, I burst into the focus group room without knocking.

"Since I'm the subject of this little squabble," I snap, "I feel like I should be part of it."

Ryder's eyes widen in panic, all color leaching from his face. "Gretchen... Where did you come from?"

I roll my eyes. "The freaking moon."

Myles just smirks.

"I'll deal with you later," I tell him, my voice cracking like a whip. "Don't think for a second that you're off the hook."

He kisses the top of my head on his way out the door. "Looking forward to it, babe."

And then there were two.

"You..." Ryder licks his lips nervously, "you heard all of that?"

"I heard that you've been lying to me for the past year."

He shakes his head adamantly. "I didn't lie to you."

"Right. Because omitting the truth is better than a flat-out lie."

He blows out a frustrated breath. "I didn't know how to bring up that night after you started working here, okay? Of course, I remembered it. Every fucking second. But I thought you *didn't*. That first day in my office, you acted like you'd never seen me before in your life."

Because I'm a master at blocking out the things I'm too cowardly to face.

But no more.

"I thought *you* didn't remember it," I toss back. "You were the one who didn't let on that you knew me. I figured that if I treated it like it was all in the past, then we could have a clean slate. Sleeping with my boss wasn't exactly how I wanted to start this job."

"Yeah, well, after you made it clear that you hated me, I was kind of in a tough spot. I thought we could start fresh, too. But it was obvious you had a problem with me."

I cross my arms over my chest. "Why did you let me believe it was Myles that night? Neither of you denied it in your office that day."

He chuckles sardonically and scrubs his hand down his face, obviously reluctant to spill his guts.

"The truth, Ryder. And nothing but the truth."

He quirks an eyebrow. "So help me God?"

"God won't be able to save you if you lie to me again."

His jaw hardens. "That day with Myles, I realized how deep of a hole I'd dug myself with you."

"What does that mean?"

"I made the mistake in the beginning of not admitting that I remembered everything about that night. That I knew exactly who you were. Myles didn't. He immediately recognized you, so you thought it was him you'd slept with. If I had changed my tune at that point and insisted it was me all along, you wouldn't have believed me."

I start pacing across the room. "But how did Myles even recognize me? It doesn't make sense."

He tips his head up at the ceiling. "This is where it gets fucked up."

I stop on a dime and slowly turn back around. "If you're about to tell me that you two were pulling some type of twin tag-team on me—"

His face blanches. "Are you fucking serious? What kind of man do you think I am? Do you have any idea how insane it drove me that you even *thought* you'd slept with my brother? That you thought those were *his* hands on you that night. That it was him inside you and not me." He gnashes his teeth. "It's been driving me fucking crazy, Gretchen. I wanted to throw his ass through my office window that day."

"Then explain it to me, Ryder, because I'm not getting it. How did both of you know who I was?"

He looks me dead in the eyes, pinning me in place. "Because it was me you met at the bar. It was me who took you back to my place. And it was me who fucked you in my bed." He swallows, gaze shuttering. "But it *wasn't* me you woke up to in that same bed the next morning."

Confusion and anger swirl around in my chest. "How is that possible?"

He white knuckles the back of the chair in front of him. "I swear I'm going to kill him," he mutters under his breath. Then he sighs. "Myles was still living in Raleigh at the time, but he was in town that weekend to finalize the building contracts for the new factory he manages now. He didn't let me know he was staying with me until the very last minute. He has a spare key, and I told him he could stay in my guest room."

Click, click go the puzzle pieces fitting themselves together.

"I had to catch an early flight to Atlanta the next morning," he goes on. "If I could have rescheduled that meeting I would have, because I sure as hell didn't want to leave you. When I walked out my door around five that morning, you were sleeping soundly in my bed. Since I hadn't even gotten your name or number, I left you a note with my information on the table by my front door." He adds in a lower voice, "It didn't take me long to figure out you never got that note."

No, I didn't.

Oh, how different things would have been if I had.

"Myles was out drinking that night with friends and apparently didn't stumble through my door until sometime after I left," Ryder explains. "The idiot was so drunk that he got the rooms mixed up and went into my room instead of the guest room." A dark cloud settles over his features. "He passed out in *my* bed. The bed *you* were sleeping in. Right next to you."

Ah. "So, when he said he didn't remember much of that night with me…"

"That's because he never did spend the night with you," Ryder finishes in a clipped voice. "He probably woke up at some point, saw you in bed with him, and assumed you two had sex, but he was too shitfaced to remember it."

Which also explains why I woke up and saw an identical version of Ryder asleep next to me. I snuck out of there before Myles opened his eyes, and apparently missed that note on the table. So, when I initially freaked out that first day in Ryder's office, realizing that I'd inadvertently slept with my new boss, my reaction was justified.

"It really was you that night," I whisper.

Ryder nods, expression grim. "*Yes*, goddammit. It was. And in his defense, Myles really did think it was him at first. I didn't know he'd even been in my bed until that day in my office. He never mentioned anything about bringing a girl back to my place. When he recognized you, I pieced it all together. Then after you left, I told him what really happened. And I about lost my fucking mind."

"Why?"

"Because he was taking credit for my—" He cuts himself off, wincing.

"Your what?" I push.

His mouth tightens. "You implied it was the best sex of your life. And you thought it was with *him*. I couldn't let you believe that. I had to convince you that anything you felt that night was for me, not him. But you hated me. So, before I could tell you the truth, I had to make you actually *like* me. And in the meantime, I had to keep Myles the hell away from you."

"Then you admit this all has to do with Myles," I conclude, disappointed. "You only made your move once he started coming after me. I assume you never would have told me the truth otherwise?"

His face contorts into disgust. "The only thing Myles has to do with our situation is being a giant pain in my ass. He's been a complication and nothing more. My plan was set in motion long before you met him."

"Your *plan?*" I fume indignantly. "Want to clue me into exactly what your plan was, boss man?"

He takes a step toward me. "You're not the type of woman who likes to feel pushed around or backed into a corner. Right away, I knew I was going to have to take my time with you. That's what this last year has been about."

"If I can just cut through the bouillon here," I stop him. "You're saying that constantly antagonizing me and arguing at every opportunity was taking your time?"

He grins ruefully. "How many other men in your life have challenged you? How many of them think like you do? Get you as worked up as I do?"

"And you're proud of that?" I blurt out, aghast. "You're proud of driving me to my breaking point every day?"

He takes a final lunge forward until our bodies are inches apart. "Hell, yes, I'm fucking proud of that. Because Gretchen Castellanos is a steel vault. No one gets under your skin. No one throws you off your game. No one...but *me*. Tell me I'm wrong."

I can't.

He looks pleased by my silence. "You never let your emotions rule you. Only when you're around me. And that means something. If you didn't care at all, you'd have more control with me."

My lips purse. "I lose my temper when I'm around you. That's it. What makes you think we'd ever work well together outside of this office?"

"The fact that neither of us was able to forget that first night we had," he answers confidently. "That day in my office with Myles was the first time I knew for sure that you remembered it. Even all those months later, you couldn't get it out of your head, same as me." He stiffens, his muscles locking up. "Then you went and suggested that whole 'one time only' bullshit. Jesus, I had to *talk* you into an entire night. You can't begin to imagine how fucking angry that made me."

"Why?"

"Because it felt like I was cursed to only ever have one night with you! And I couldn't accept that. I needed so much more. Constantly being around you and not having you was torture. I'd leave work every day feeling like I'd once again failed with you. You were still resisting me, yet I was drugged for you. *You* were my drug."

I recall his words from the night in the viewing room.

This. This *is what I've needed for so long. Finally, finally, finally...*

Feel that, Gretchen. Feel me and know who's inside you. Fucking remember *it.*

I feel his body heat seeping into my bones, but I stand my ground. "You're saying that the hostile dynamic of our relationship has all been a ploy to make me like you?"

"Not a ploy, duchess. I've never been anything but myself around you. I've just been more persistent about it. You've been stuck in my head ever since we met at that bar. It's only fair that I be stuck in yours."

Mission accomplished, soldier.

I lift my chin. "Tell me why. Why put all this effort into someone you slept with one time? Only to find out later that she was also your employee."

His nostrils flare. "If you were sitting in the viewing room the whole time Myles was in here, then you already know why."

Ah, right. The love part.

"Can't say it again?" I taunt.

"I've already said it more than you."

"Who says that's how I feel?"

"Let's solve that little mystery right now, then." He takes my chin between his thumb and index finger, his grip unyielding. "Is that how you feel, Gretchen?"

I open my mouth, but nothing comes out and I don't know why.

"Simple yes or no question."

I slam the piece of paper I've had clutched in my hand this entire time against his chest. "Here's my answer. That clear enough for you?"

He takes it from me, but I don't wait around for him to read it. I pivot on my heel and whip the door open with a flourish. Several pairs of eyes dart in my direction, but I ignore my co-workers and stride across the office to my cubicle. But before I can reach my desk—

"Gretchen!"

Ryder's booming voice is a thunderous roar that reverberates through the entire office. Everyone is now on their feet, gaping in our direction. My pulse quickens, but I keep my expression blank as I turn to watch our fearless leader storm toward me. The piece of paper is crumpled in his hand, his face mottled with rage. And if I'm not mistaken... Is that panic I see? *So much for fearless.*

He shoves that paper in my face once he reaches me. "What the hell is this? A resignation letter? You're *quitting?*"

Steeling my nerves—chin up, shoulders back—I force my voice to come out steady and even. "It seems like the only course of action left to take."

A vein pops out on his forehead. "Really. You think quitting your job and moving to Atlanta for a bigger, better gig is your only option? You can't think of anything else?"

After not telling me the truth about the whole Myles situation, he deserves to stew a little. So, I say nothing.

Patience snapping, he rips the paper to shreds and lets the pieces float to the floor. Our gazes remain locked as the torn pieces silently flutter in front of our faces and onto our feet.

"As your boss, I refuse to accept your resignation."

The sadistic side of me is getting a real kick out of his outburst. "Actually..." *Pause.* Again, just to torture him. "I'm resigning so that I'm no longer your employee."

His brow furrows. "What?"

One side of my mouth tips up in a grin that's more smartass than anything else. "I'm not accepting Jonathan Tremblay's offer. I'm not moving to Atlanta."

Ryder waves down at the scattered scraps of paper. "Then what was all that about?"

I'm feeling oddly proud that I finally have the courage to admit this out loud. And in public. "I'm resigning so that there's no further complications or ethical dilemmas with our situation. So that we don't have to hide anything. I'm resigning...so that I can be with you."

Hope flashes in his eyes like a beam of light. "But you love this job."

Here it comes.

Gird your loins, Gretchen girl.

"Yeah, I do," I admit. "But I love you more."

A round of feminine sighs fills the room, but I can't take my eyes off of Ryder's expression because it's one of the best things I've ever seen. It's as if I just breathed life back into his lungs. Like the doctor who told him he only had a week to live comes back and says, "Sorry, my bad. You're actually going to live for another sixty years."

"Why didn't you just say that back there?" Ryder asks, sounding slightly annoyed. I almost laugh in spite of myself. "Why did you run off?"

I shrug, feigning innocence. "I was coming to pack up my desk. And you might not realize it, but I have a flare for the dramatic."

With a growl, he hauls me against his chest. "'Dramatic' is putting it too nicely. You just enjoy pissing me off."

I smooth my hands down the lapels of his jacket. "Well, there is that. It's become one of my favorite pastimes actually. Right up there with paper mâché and playing canasta with old people in the park."

His arms slide around my waist as mine wind around his neck. It's natural, it's familiar. It's *right*. "I could so beat your ass at some canasta."

"I'll give you a little longer to keep thinking that." We both grin at my throwing his own words back in his face. Then my voice gets serious. "I owe you an explanation for why I kept fighting this thing between us. It's ingrained in me to automatically close up when emotions hit too deeply. It's instinctual. I usually do it without even thinking. If you can't tell, I don't handle vulnerability well."

"That's stating the obvious," he deadpans, but with a smile.

I nod. "I know I have to get better at this, and I'm really trying. I just need you to understand that it's not going to be an overnight thing."

His hands frame my face. "Duchess, I know it's difficult for you, but we'll work on it together. If you're worried that you're going to drive me away by snapping at me instead of opening up, don't be. I'm looking forward to it. Because I love you so fucking much, there's nothing you can do that *won't* make me want to spend the rest of my life fighting with you."

Laughter bubbles out of me.

"You don't have to quit, though," he says gravely. "Every single person who works for me is watching us right now. And I don't think any of them have a problem with our relationship."

Surprised, I glance around the room to see—

Smiles.

On everyone.

Sonja shoots me a wink when our eyes meet. Sonja, who I feared knew more than I wanted her to and was going to blab. Regina looks near to bursting with joy. Woods nods at me, grinning. Polly is starry-eyed and telling Ryder with her eyes that she wants to have his babies. Myles is even leaning against the doorframe of Ryder's office with a genuine smile aimed in our direction.

"If you haven't figured it out by now, duchess," Ryder says, drawing my attention back to him, "we're a family here." Bringing his head closer to mine, he adds in a quieter voice, "And I think a lot of them have suspected for a while that something's been going on between us."

Out of the corner of my eye, I see several people nod and raise their hands.

I can't fight off my smile. "And here I thought we've been discreet."

Around the room, I hear, "Not even a little", "A dump truck driving through Mardi Gras would have been more discreet", and, "I called it from the beginning." That last one sounded like Regina.

"What do you say, duchess?" Ryder brushes his lips against mine. "Will you stay here and let me be your boss...*and* your man?"

"On one condition."

"Name it."

"You never criticize my PowerPoint skills again."

He gives me a crooked grin. "Done. There's never been anything wrong with them anyway. I just made all those notes to annoy you."

I yank on a piece of his hair, making him laugh.

"Hey, I told you I was going to find a way to make you mine." He searches my eyes. "Did I? Are you finally mine, duchess?"

I take a moment to act like I'm considering it. "I suppose, for now. Because I respect your bold approach. But I'll let you know when to hit the bricks once I get bored."

He pinches my ass. "You are such a little—"

I cut him off with a kiss.

Our mutual groans are drowned out by the deafening burst of applause.

I never thought I'd be the cheesy romantic ending type. Yet here I am. No more sabotaging a good thing when I see it. No more shutting out the people who matter most. No more being the bad guy of my own story.

Just princess sing-a-longs and happily ever afters from here on out.

32

The Tub for Two

REAL TALK ROMANCE, EPISODE 2

"I wholeheartedly believe that true love is the lifeblood of society," Kennedy says at the beginning of her show. *"And the reason that society is in the state that it's in is because we're suffering from a severe true love deficiency. Call them priorities, call them principles, call it the moral compass of mankind—whatever it is, it's become skewed. Too many outside factors are impeding our desire or ability to find true love and make it last.*

"Despite what we tend to think at times, we aren't fully throwing ourselves into the pursuit of happiness because if we were, we wouldn't be placing so much importance on materialism and image and status. Having said all that, modern romance has become pretty tricky to navigate. The advent of online dating has created a slew of minefields for the younger generations to battle. The pressure of social perception in

American culture to marry and settle down has changed somewhat over the years but in many ways, remains the same.

"Because of my practical, realistic approach to love and relationships, I've been called a cynic. And maybe I am. But I'm also very hopeful that I can find my own true love one day. I just know how difficult that can be for many people, which is why I started this podcast. I want to help others like me who struggle in this department because I know how frustrating and lonely it can also be.

"So, today's show is all about hope. I want to hear your success stories with love. Have you and your significant other faced trials in your relationship but come out the other side all the better for it? Have you had your ups and downs and been able to make it work? Tell me about it. I want to share your happiness with everyone out there who are still looking for theirs.

"Because let's get real…that's all any of us really want."

"I'm impressed."

I glance up from the drink menu to shoot Ryder an inquiring eye.

He grins. "I've been playing footsie under the table with you for the past ten minutes and you have yet to freak out."

I set down the menu and interlace my fingers on the table. "Wait and see how long I let you hold my hand when we leave here. It'll blow your mind. I've become quite mature since I became a girlfriend." I punctuate the claim by raising my pinkie finger when I take a sip of wine.

He snorts into his beer glass. "Doubtful, duchess. Immaturity is part of your charm."

"As long as you recognize."

I see Myles appear near the hostess stand and wave him over. "Thank you for this, by the way," I tell Ryder.

"Why would you thank me?" He sounds bewildered. "I should be thanking you for making me see everything the way I should have been seeing it all along."

I give his hand a quick squeeze before standing to greet Myles with a kiss on the cheek. "We appreciate you coming."

He chucks me under the chin, like a big brother would do. Strange how easily we've been able to fall into a comfortable in-law type of relationship, considering the fact that he kissed me a couple of months ago. "Hey, I'm not the kind of guy to turn down a free meal."

"Beautiful, smart, and frugal with his money?" I quip. "Is it too early to propose?"

He grins. "Not if you're comfortable with rejection."

Ryder looks between us. "I'm not even going to ask."

He and Myles shake hands. Their dynamic has certainly changed in the two weeks that Ryder and I have been official. Us getting together seemed to finally close the door on whatever sibling rivalry they had between them. They're more comfortable around each other now, more brotherly. And if they're ever competitive, it's always in good fun.

"But I'm getting the feeling this isn't just about the two of you taking me to dinner," Myles says after we put in our food and drink orders.

Ryder pushes a manila folder across the table. Looking both curious and wary, Myles opens it and skims over the pages inside.

His eyes shoot up to us. "What is this?"

Ryder steeples his fingers in front of his face. "It's a contract for artist representation."

Myles looks stunned. Eventually, he shakes himself, as if clearing the cobwebs in his head. "I don't get it."

I take over for Ryder. "This agency firm is one of our clients. They recently hired us to create a marketing campaign for an educational packet they developed for beginning and aspiring artists. It covers drawing, painting, pottery, sculpting…all different kinds of mediums. But their primary service is representing local artists and featuring their work in galleries throughout the Lowcountry."

Chadwick and Baldwin were all too happy to offer Myles a contract after Ryder and I took the liberty of sending them his portfolio.

"They said you have raw talent and an authentic style," I add. "They want to work with you, Myles. All you have to do is sign the contract."

His expression is the epitome of denial as he flips through more pages. Then his gaze tentatively meets Ryder's. "I didn't think you knew about my art."

Ryder tips his head at me. "Gretchen here spilled the beans. She showed me the pictures you sent her. They're good, Myles. Really good. And I'm sorry you never felt that you could share that part of your life with me. I've been a real asshole."

I throw my hands up. "He said it, not me."

Both men chuckle. Myles's face even turns red with what I assume is embarrassment. *Aw.*

"Look, I seriously appreciate this," he says, "but I don't have a lot of time to work on my pieces. My hours at the factory are pretty demanding."

"I'm sure that if you talk to Dad and tell him about this, he'll have no problem knocking back your hours." Ryder then slides a small piece of paper across the table. A check. "And hopefully soon, you'll be able to make your art a full-time gig."

Myles curses under his breath when he opens the check. He immediately shoves it back across the table, away from him. "I'm not accepting this."

Beating Ryder to the punch, I place my index finger on the check and pointedly slide it back toward Myles.

"I invest in local businesses," Ryder explains. "And a new art gallery with emerging talent is smart business, plain and simple."

I bite back a grin.

He's so full of shit. This has nothing to do with smart business. After I showed him those pictures of Myles's art, he was bound and determined to back his brother any way he could. Nothing was going to change his mind.

Myles rubs his forehead, conflict warring on his face. "I might not be what they're looking for. It's not like I went to school for this. I've learned all of it on my own." He actually sounds nervous, even self-conscious.

"Which is why they love you," I assure him. "Chadwick said your art, particularly your sculptures, isn't pretentious. It's real and emotional. They don't expect you to be something you're not. They already like what they've seen."

"They really said that?" Myles swings his attention over to his brother. "This isn't just you pulling strings with one of your contacts?"

Ryder laughs. "For all the contacts I have, man, I hold no strings in the art world. Which is another reason why this idea appeals to me."

Sneaky, boss man.

He's trying to play this off as a business transaction that will benefit both of them. Ryder, from a financial perspective and Myles, from a career perspective. Truth is, Ryder could give a rat's ass about art. He's told me on many occasions. This is purely about his desire to help his brother achieve his dreams and repair their relationship. He knows Myles would refuse if this was solely a matter of generosity. The enormous pride these men have is something I can relate to.

Myles looks back down at the check. "I'd rather think of this as a loan that I'll pay back to you in full, rather than as an investment."

I know Ryder and I are thinking the same thing.

Gotcha.

"We can negotiate that," Ryder concedes. "For now, just focus on creating new pieces and procuring building space for your gallery. *After* you sign the contract."

Myles's mouth opens and closes a few times before he's able to push words out. "I-I don't know what to say. I'll never be able to repay you both. And I don't mean financially."

I jab my finger at him. "Never pull that twin crap on me again and we'll call it even."

He laughs. "You're ruining all our fun, babe, but fine. Agreed."

When he turns to Ryder, his expression is full of gratitude and...love. He holds out his hand. "I really appreciate this. Seriously. Thank you."

Ryder takes his hand and nods. "Trust me, I know what it's like to chase down the thing you want most in the world." I flush when he gives me a meaningful side glance. "And you never have to thank me."

I take a long drag before passing the joint to Ryder. "I guess it's nice to finally have someone to share this tub with. FYI, there's Thin Mint Girl Scout cookies in the freezer if you get the munchies."

From the opposite end of my bathtub, he takes a puff and blows out a stream of smoke. "I can see why this is your happy place."

I hum in agreement as I lean my head against the bath pillow and close my eyes. "Nothing more relaxing."

"Really? You can't think of anything that relaxes you more than a hot bath?"

It's so cute how he sounds all offended.

I crack open one eye. "Sorry, boss man. Your dick is great and all, but even an orgasm from you can't beat out some weed and wine in the bath."

He lunges across the tub, sending water and bubbles sloshing over the side. I half scream, half laugh as he braces himself against the sides. "I'm about to show you a whole new world, duchess."

I roll my eyes. "You've really got to stop with the whole fairytale thing. Get your nieces into dinosaurs or something."

His cock hardens under the water as it drifts closer and closer to my sex. "Why would I stop when I finally have irrefutable proof that they're real?"

Proof that I need to share with my girl, Kennedy Rhodes. I make a mental note to call into her Real Talk Romance podcast tomorrow to share my very own success story.

The old hag wipes away a tear. *My little Gretchen's all grown up.*

"Are you saying you want to live happily ever after with me?"

"If you'll let me, duchess, yes. Yes, I am."

I reward him with a quick kiss but pull back before he can take it deeper. "What's the fairytale where the guy and the girl have sex the first night they meet and then he eventually wears her down by being a relentless wiseass?"

He nips at my lower lip. "I think that one's called 'The Duchess and the Boss She Pretended Not to Love the Whole Time.'"

"That's a classic for the ages."

His shaft nudges my entrance, sending a spike of arousal shooting up my middle.

"Somehow, I don't think it'll be appropriate to read to the grandkids one day." He pushes inside in one smooth thrust. "For now, how about we get on with the scene where the two main characters fuck in the bathtub?"

I cinch my legs around his waist. "What are you waiting for, then? Get to work, boss man."

Epilogue

The Birth of Baby Boss Man

Five Years Later

"SON OF A *BITCH!* I'm never touching your dick again! As soon as this kid is out, I'm making the doctor cut it off!"

Everyone in the room—nurses, the doctor—look warily at me. Everyone except Ryder, of course. He's heard and seen it all. Nothing I do can shake that man anymore.

Nothing except giving birth.

As rock solid as he's been throughout this torturous labor, he's looking pretty shaky right now. I've been pushing for the past forty-five minutes, and I think it's finally hitting him.

We're about to meet our son.

I practically heard the universe snickering at me when my labor came on strong and with a vengeance. I was under the impression that your first child usually takes a while to come out. But sure enough, my water broke and my contractions were out of control before we even knew what was happening. By the time we arrived at the hospital, the staff told me I was already too dilated for an epidural.

I about massacred every last person inside this effing hospital.

Five minutes later, the doctor holds up a screaming, slimy blob of the most beautiful baby I've ever seen. I nearly rip him out of the doc's hands, but I refrain so they can clear his airway and check his eyes. I don't think I even breathe until the nurse is bringing him back to me and placing him on my chest.

"*Duchess...*" Ryder whispers in my ear, his voice cracking on that one word. "Holy shit. That's our baby. We made that."

My heart feels so full I don't know how it hasn't burst wide open. Masking my emotions is a thing of the past—at least around my husband. I'm openly crying, openly smiling. I coo baby talk in our son's ear, telling him how much I love him, how I'll always take care of him, how he's the best thing that ever happened to his mommy and daddy.

"I think you're supposed to say something like, 'He's so beautiful, he looks just like you.'"

Ryder kisses my forehead. "Well, that's a given. He already takes after his mother."

"I'll happily take all the credit."

It's crazy how tiny a newborn baby is. My hand spans his entire back. His little chest moves rapidly up and down against mine as he acclimates to his new surroundings and my touch.

"I didn't think there was any way I could possibly love you more than I already do," Ryder rasps as he gently strokes our son's soft head. "But then you give me this. You give me a family."

"Well, you had to do some of the work."

"Not nine months' worth of it." He lays his head against mine as we stare in awe at our child. "Thank you, duchess."

I turn to stare into his gorgeous blue eyes that I hope our son inherited. "Thank you. If you hadn't been so determined to show me exactly what I was missing out on all those years ago, we wouldn't be here."

He grins. "Are you finally admitting to how stubborn you are?"

I shrug. "It's the drugs."

"You didn't have any drugs."

"The new mommy high, then. I'll come to my senses in a few hours."

He places a sweet kiss on my lips, then does the same to our son's cheek. "I love you so much, duchess. I've loved you every single day since that very first night at my place. You have no idea how happy you make me. You know that, don't you?"

I nod. "But that doesn't mean you should ever stop reminding me."

"I think I can manage that."

His hand covers mine on our son's back, the pads of his fingers caressing my wedding band. Right here, in this bed, is everything I could possibly need in this world. This man and this baby have my whole heart, my whole life. I can no longer be me without Ryder because he occupies so much of my soul.

Hell, he *owns* it.

"I love you, too," I whisper to him. "And you can keep your dick. I'll probably want another one of these at some point."

An hour later, we're introducing our families and friends to our son, Gabriel Myles Colson.

Dad's eyes water when he hears that his grandson is named after him. Then he has to abruptly leave the room. Myles gets a little sheepish, though I can tell he's both flattered and honored to share his namesake with his nephew. Ross has his arms around Lydia and their son and daughter. Sloane, Harper, and Quinn are here, too, with their husbands and kids. Along with Ryder's stepsister and her two girls.

The overwhelming love in this room is something that has taken me some time to get used to over the years. As much as I love my parents and am grateful for how they raised us, I never want my son to ever feel like he has to guard parts of himself from the world. I'm going to smother him with so much affection, Ryder's going to have to pry me off the kid. Then, knowing my husband for the impatient tyrant that he is, he'll cart me off to our bedroom where he'll remind me of just how bossy he can truly be.

All night long.

Now, *that's* a fairytale I can work with.

Don't worry…

Quinn's book, Southern Hearts Club #4, is coming soon!

Also by Melanie Munton:

Southern Hearts Club:
The Divorce Attorney
The Six Month Lease

Brooklyn Brothers:
Lace & Lies
Scars & Sins
Booze & Bullets

Sultry Nights:
Salsa (Sultry Nights 1)
Tango (Sultry Nights 2)
Rumba (Sultry Nights 3)
Samba (Sultry Nights 4)
Mambo (Sultry Nights 5)

Standalone romance:
King of the Court
The Unforgettable Kind

Slow Seductions series:

Casual Affair (Slow Seductions #1)
Sweet Attraction (Slow Seductions #2)

Cruz Brothers series:
Playing for Kinley (Cruz Brothers #1)
The Art of Sage (Cruz Brothers #2)
Always Mickie (Cruz Brothers #3)

Timid Souls novellas:
Stubborn Hearts
Unexpected Love

Possession and Politics Trilogy:
Part One
Part Two
Part Three

1

The Counselor and the Corset

I SHOW UP TO MY OWN DIVORCE DRESSED LIKE A TAVERN WENCH.

Because looking like a raging moron has apparently become my new thing in life. My new brand.

(Insert pitying snicker here).

And as sad as it is to admit, walking into the Van Gordon & Associates law firm office while wearing an obscenely tight corset that makes my boobs bulge to an almost lewd degree barely even scratches the surface of my firmly established stupidity. I can barely stuff my dignity into this dress, let alone actual body parts.

Just when I think I can sink no lower...

My heavy messenger bag smacks against my leg as I amble up to the front desk in the lobby. The grandmotherly-type woman sitting behind the desk with a pair of half-moon glasses perched on the end of her nose looks up from her computer as

I approach. She spares my outfit one disapproving glance, punctuating it with a haughty sniff.

Yeah, whatever, lady.

She can't be thinking anything worse than what I've already thought myself.

"Hi," I say, suffusing polite cheeriness into my voice, despite her judgmental frown. "I'm Sloane Westbrook. I have an appointment with Tamra Duprey."

The unimpressed woman returns her stoic gaze to her computer screen. "Ms. Duprey is currently out on maternity leave. Your case is being passed on to another attorney."

Whoa, whoa. Hold the phone.

My mind mentally slams on the brakes so hard the airbags deploy.

"Pardon?" The woman looks like she knows what she's doing behind that desk, but this bulldog must have misplaced her bone. "Ms. Duprey told me she wasn't going on maternity leave for another month."

The bulldog swings her attention back to me, sighing impatiently. "Her labor started very unexpectedly. It was a premature birth. But Mr. Van Gordon has spoken with Ms. Duprey about your case. He has all of your files, so he'll be well-versed on the particulars of your proceedings."

"Mr. Van Gordon?" I ask cautiously. "As in, one of the partners?"

As in, the guy whose name is stamped on your letterhead?

The corners of her eyes crinkle almost condescendingly—and there's The Look.

The one I'm so sick of seeing. The one the older generations tend to give to a millennial like me when they think I'm fulfilling some kind of stereotype of being a too-young-for-life, clueless, entitled dingbat.

Maybe she's right in this one case, except for the entitled part. But it makes it no less grating on my pride.

"He's your new divorce attorney, dear. Carter Van Gordon. He's highly respected and very good at what he does."

I bite my lip, worried I'm about to push my luck with this one. "Is that common? Switching attorneys right before the settlement negotiation?"

This time, her expression says *child, please.* I'm sure she's barely restraining the urge to roll her eyes. "It's not unheard of. His office is the third door on the right down the hallway behind you. You may go on back."

Translation: *Get out of my face and let the real adults get back to work.*

Because I honestly can't come up with a good defense for my ignorance, nor for my outfit—and because yes, I'm a little scared of this consternating woman—I follow her directions down the hallway. Stopping at a frosted glass door with the name "Carter Van Gordon, J.D." emblazoned in big, intimidating letters, I knock softly.

"Come in," comes a muffled voice from inside the room.

Steeling myself with a measured breath, I push open the door and take two steps inside the room before I stop.

Hellooo, Counselor.

The distinguished man sitting behind the cluttered desk is focused on his computer screen, eyes narrowed in concentration behind a pair of black-frame glasses. His face is tan with a five o'clock shadow beginning to sprout, making him appear almost rugged. His dark, honey blond hair is pushed back off his forehead, dipping in way that indicates the presence of a cowlick.

But the suspenders… They're what really do it for me.

Because they frame a set of wide, sturdy shoulders that would look more appropriate at a CrossFit competition than in a law office. His shirt sleeves are rolled up to his forearms, which also seem to have impressive definition. His biceps are straining against the shirt's material, the muscles rippling every time he types something on his keyboard.

All of that magnificence is wrapped up in a pretty red bow.

Literally. His red bowtie makes me think of a present dying to be ripped open.

The look almost doesn't seem right on him, yet it somehow works at the same time. Probably because a man like this can wear literally anything and will never make a mistake. There are special rules for his kind of man. The fashion faux pau doesn't exist for him. The laws of nature don't apply to someone who clearly defies them. On someone my age, his style would be termed as hipster chic or something along those lines.

But on this man—who is clearly *not* my age, though I can't tell by how much—I know instantly that his fashion choice is an authentic reflection of Charleston culture. It's not meant to be seen as modern and ironic or even fashionable. It's just an old southern thing.

And I know that *before* I hear his deep southern drawl.

It's not full-on Charleston where he drops his "r's." I'd guess maybe a North Carolina or Virginia accent. Regardless, the sound makes me want to hand-fan myself and flutter my eyelashes like Scarlett O'Hara.

"Sorry to keep you waiting," he finally says, shifting his gaze away from the screen and down to a folder in front of him. "Are you Mrs. Westbrook?"

It takes me a second to find my voice. "Um, yes. I was told that you will now be handling my divorce?"

"That's correct. I'm taking over for Tamra while she's out. But don't worry, she's gotten me caught up on where we're at."

He still hasn't looked at me. His head is down, his attention focused on the documents in front of him as he furiously scribbles notes in the margins of the papers, clearly lost in his thoughts. I'm not sure whether I should feel offended or not. He's either being purposefully rude, or he's too preoccupied by his job to realize that he's actually speaking to another human being.

I clear my throat, hoping he takes the hint. "Okay. Will this cause any delays with the settlement?"

He shakes his head, still without looking up. "No, there shouldn't be any complications. It's a pretty straightforward case. I spoke with your husband's attorney, and she doesn't have any issues with the change."

"He's *not* my husband," I snap without meaning to.

But I don't want the term applied to that cheating bastard ever again.

That comment manages to grab his attention.

My attorney's head shoots up, his sharp eyes immediately colliding with mine.

I swallow, unnerved by the depth in those hazel eyes. The keen awareness I see there.

"I would appreciate it if we could refer to him as Mr. Westbroook," I add in a much gentler tone. "I'm fine with 'the ex,' too. Or even 'the douchebag.'" *Probably didn't need to tack on that last one.* "And I'd like to refrain from using the Mrs. if we could."

The corner of his mouth tugs up in amusement. "Of course. My apologies, Ms. Westbrook."

I shudder every time I hear that name.

The problem is…it *is* my name. At least for another few days, I guess.

Legally, my name won't be changed back to my maiden one until the divorce papers go through the courts. I'll still have to change it on all my IDs and documents, but at least it will be changed back in the legal system. And of course—*to add salt to the wound*—everything is in my married name. Bank accounts, apartment lease, W-2s, all of my bills, and everything in my student file at the Charleston College graduate school. In summation, I don't have any money, a reliable vehicle, a respectable credit score, my own apartment, but at least I'll have my flipping maiden name back.

I am so winning in life right now.

So, until all the documentation is officially filed, I am cursed to legally remain Mrs. Grant Westbrook.

With his gaze finally raised in my direction, my attorney suddenly takes in his new view.

And drops his pen.

His Adam's apple noticeably bobs as his eyes trail down my body. It's not quite languorous, but it's not exactly brief either. It happens almost absently—as if he doesn't even realize how much time his eyes remain glued to my plunging cleavage.

I know I should feel uncomfortable at being the center of his attention. This so-called "uniform" was tailor-made for one purpose: to turn a lady's bazongas into a flashing marquee. That's what customers come to see at The Suckling Pig, a colonial-themed tavern where the female waitresses dress like sultry wenches from the Revolutionary War days. Think Hooters, back when all the men had wooden teeth and drank a pint of ale with breakfast, lunch, and dinner.

Don't judge me.

I need money. Desperately.

And in a touristy town like Charleston that has a lively downtown scene, working at The Suckling Pig is a surefire way for a well-endowed girl like me to rake in some extra dough.

But his intent expression as he looks me over does not at *all* make me uncomfortable. And again, it *should*. Now that I've seen his entire face, I realize this man is probably a good ten years older than me, at least. Not that he looks old, by any means. But the crow's feet around his eyes and laugh—or frown?—lines around his mouth put him in his mid-to-late thirties.

I'm twenty-three.

Yes, yes, and I'm already getting divorced. Make your jokes now, and stow the judgment.

I quickly scan his left hand but don't see a wedding band. Which is something. Checking out his apparently younger client isn't wrong if he's not married. Right?

For me, it's just…different.

I've only ever hung out with guys my age, and I foolishly married one.

And clearly, that's my problem.

Despite the fact that he's my age, Grant is still too young to handle marriage like a responsible adult. Too inconsiderate to speak up and tell me he doesn't love me anymore and that we never should have gotten married in the first place. Too much of a coward to admit that he felt pressured into the whole thing by his overbearing father. And of course, he hadn't been about to share with me how unreliable he is with money. How he tends to piss it all away the second he can get his grimy little hands on it.

So, instead of communicating with me like a decent human being, he went and buried his relationship woes balls-deep in the barista at our favorite coffee shop.

Unfortunately, I didn't learn just how immature Grant really is until well after our marriage license was notarized. Hence, my presence here today.

Since Grant and I met in college, I haven't done much venturing outside of my own dating pool age group. For whatever reason, I never really look twice at older men. Even when they hit on me at my job, I just don't typically give them much thought.

Yet I'm giving my new attorney *plenty* of thought right now.

But it only takes me a second to realize he's a straight-up Maserati.

So insanely beautiful to look at, yet completely unattainable to someone like me.

I mean, why would a successful man like him, who clearly has his life together, ever find a frazzled, scatterbrained, twenty-three-year-old, soon-to-be-divorcee, hot mess of a graduate student attractive?

Although if I'm not mistaken, the gleam in his hazel eyes is one of...interest.

With my thick, layered black hair pulled up into a loose knot that shows off my long neck and aforementioned cleavage, sky-blue eyes that I've been told are a "mystical" color, narrow waist and hips, and pale Irish skin, I guess I'm not terrible to look at.

Your boobs are basically winking at him. He would probably show the same amount of interest to a stripper that motor-boated him during a lap dance.

No one can put things into perspective quite like my bitch of a conscience, that's for sure.

Then I have to go and make things awkward by actually addressing the elephant in the room. "Yeah, sorry about my attire." I pick at my asymmetrical skirt, trying to cover as much of my legs as possible. "I had to practically sprint here as soon as I got off work."

There was a crazy lunch rush today, so I had to stay later to help with the orders. Between that and the fact that my PMS-ing car decided not to start, forcing me to literally run all the way here, I didn't have time to change.

A coughing sound comes from the back of his throat as he averts his eyes, seeming to shake himself out of his daze. "No problem. It's actually not the strangest thing I've ever seen in this office."

My eyebrow goes up, curiosity piqued. "Care to share?"

His eyes dart back to mine.

I shrug. "I could use a laugh right now."

His upper lip twitches. He leans back in his chair, tapping his finger on the desk's surface. "There was this one client who came into the office for her divorce settlement…and brought along a friend for emotional support. One she'd never mentioned before. And one she failed to mention was an animal." He visibly shudders, staring at the wall behind me. "I just wish I'd known about the peacock before I went to use the facilities. One minute I'm alone in the stall, and the next, I'm face-to-face with the bathroom bird from hell."

I stare at him for four straight seconds—

Then burst into laughter.

My ribs are probably going to bruise from slamming against the tight-ass corset with my every guffaw, but it's totally worth it.

"So, you were 'peacocked' in a men's restroom?" I wipe away tears from the corners of my eyes. "You poor man. How traumatizing that must have been for you."

He slowly shakes his head, his eyes wide. "You have no idea. It haunts me. I avoid public restrooms at all costs these days."

"That's understandable. I mean, you never can be too careful with those pervert birds."

He nods. "I won't get cornered again. I carry a rape whistle with me everywhere I go now."

"You know, you should probably look into taking some self-defense classes," I suggest. "I hear that Toucan Sam is teaching some down at the community center."

He waves me off. "Nah, I've already got it covered. Woody Woodpecker is going to give me some private training lessons."

That brings another round of laughter from me.

It's refreshing to laugh at someone other than myself and the mess I've made of my life for a change.

"Thanks," I eventually say after catching my breath.

His gaze remains locked on me for several long, assessing moments, as if I'm an animal at the zoo. I find myself squirming in my chair at his silent scrutiny. When I almost can't take it anymore, he responds with a curt nod.

Funny how I don't even need to explain what I'm thanking him for. He seems to automatically know.

He glances down at his watch. "We've got a few minutes before the proceedings. You want to go over some details and get through any questions you might have?"

My mood sobers.

Back to giving my joke of a marriage the ax.

"Sure."

So, that's the story of how I meet my drop-dead gorgeous divorce attorney dressed like a lusty tavern wench.

And intriguingly…he doesn't seem to mind it.

The Divorce Attorney is now available!

SIGN UP FOR MY NEWSLETTER AT:

www.melaniemunton.com

FOLLOW ME ON BOOKBUB AT:

www.bookbub.com/profile/melanie-munton

Send me an email at:

melaniemuntonauthor@gmail.com

Also follow me on:

Twitter

Pinterest

Instagram

Goodreads

Acknowledgments

THANK YOU so ridiculously much to all of you readers out there who took a chance on *The Divorce Attorney* by an author you'd probably never heard of and for sticking with me and grabbing up Gretchen and Ryder's story. I HOPE you're itching to read Quinn's book as much as I am to write it!!

The Southern Hearts Club has been a completely different undertaking than any of my previous projects. What motivated me to write these stories more than anything was the concept of these four best friends, sticking together and supporting each other no matter what. I wanted to write their journeys solely from a woman's point of view, a diversion from every other book I've ever written. It honestly didn't occur to me until I was plotting *The Divorce Attorney* that I'd never *not* written a book from both the heroine's and hero's perspectives. So, I looked at this series as both a challenge for me, but also as a way of offering a fresh take on some of the ways we read love stories these days.

I wanted these books to have a kind of Chick Lit vibe. I wanted them to feel light and sexy and sweet, with some emotion thrown in but nothing too heavy. I wanted a sense of comradery among friends with plenty of humor...because honestly, what's life without laughter? And most of all, I wanted to leave room for the reader to interpret the stories from her/his own personal perspective. By not reading the hero's every thought, I think (hope!) it leaves room for the reader's own insight to shape the story and the characters themselves. Ultimately, my goal with each of these books is to offer a feel-good read that will leave you smiling at the end of it. Because if I can infuse even a tiny bit of happiness into your day with my words, then I'll be satisfied that I've done my job. And all the hair-pulling, stress-snacking, sleepless nights, and wino-ing will have been worth it. ;)

As always, to my husband Sean, I probably never would have started writing if it wasn't for you. You've supported and encouraged me from day one, and made me believe that I could accomplish great things. YOU are my Ryder. YOU are in every hero I write. YOU make my dreams possible. Thank you for that, and for every other beautiful thing you bring to my life.

To all of my readers, those who have been with me from the beginning and those who are brand new, THANK YOU times infinity. Your feedback over the years has been amazing, and your support has been overwhelming. I know that if *you* guys aren't happy, *I'm* not happy, so I always want to hear from you. Thank you so much for hopping on this rollercoaster with me, and for sticking with me throughout my journey! I so so *soooo* appreciate all of your love!

About the Author

Melanie grew up in a small town in rural Missouri. After marrying her husband, she decided she wanted to try coastal life because why not? A few months later, they moved to North Carolina where she discovered her passion for writing, and they never looked back. They are now enjoying life with their beautiful daughter in Savannah, GA and loving every minute with their little Georgia peach.

Melanie's other passion is traveling and seeing the world. With anthropology degrees under their belts, she and her husband have made it their goal in life to see as many archaeological sites around the world as possible.

She has a horrible food addiction to pasta and candy (not together...ew). And she gets sad when her wine rack is empty.

At the end of the day, she is a true romantic at heart. She loves writing the cheesy and corny of romantic comedies, and the sassy and sexy of suspense. She aims to make her readers swoon, laugh out loud, maybe sweat a little, and above all, fall in love.

Made in the USA
Columbia, SC
15 April 2021